Loyalty Bound Me, Love Freed Me

L L MOMON

Acknowledgments

This is my 6th novel and while the road has not been easy, it's been worth it. There is no long and drawn out speech this time. I simply want to give myself credit and grace for never giving up and pursuing a dream without deferment. I'm all gas and no breaks baby and thank you all for going on this journey with me.

Dedication

To my sweet children. There is absolutely nothing that I won't do for you. Y'all are the highlight of my life and I want to leave a legacy that you can be proud of. In this treacherous world that we live in...you all make life worth living. To my husband, it's simple. I love you.

Be unapologetically you and never dim your light for anyone. If you're too much for them, advise them to wear shades.

— L.L. MOMON

Patois Dictionary

This book has a heavy patois presence- The MMC is from Jamaica -born and raised. To keep it as authentic as possible, he speaks in Patois only and so does most of his crew. I must admit, sometimes it can be a bit confusing so I have provided a dictionary for those who may need a little help. Don't worry, it flows and once you start to read it, it becomes second nature. It did for me and y'all know I'm country as corn. To my Caribbean readers, much respect to you all.

- Mi-Me
- Yuh-You
- Dem-Them
- Dweet-Do it
- Wi-Us/We

- Di-The
- Ting-Thing
- Tuh-To
- Fi-to/for
- Dere-There
- Wud-Would
- Wah-What
- Nuh-No/ Not/Don't
- Shi-She
- Har-Her
- Undastan-Understand
- Tallaweh-Strong-Frearless
- Ave-Have
- Wid-With
- Fir-For
- Tink-Think
- Neva-Never
- Tek-Take
- Pickney-Children/Child
- Cyan-Can
- Cyaan-Can't
- Nah-Not
- Haffi-have to
- Si-See
- Suh-So
- Say-Seh

- Bady-Body
- Stepping Razors-Bad men
- Likkle-Little
- Eff-If
- Tek-Take
- Irie-Better/Good
- Wan-Want
- Mada-Mother
- Fada-Father
- Bredda-Brother
- Sista-Sister
- Irie-Good
- Zeen-I see
- Tap-Stop
- Yaad-House
- Chat-Talk

Trigger Warning

Loyalty Bound me, Love Freed Me contains themes that may be distressing to some readers. Including offensive language, emotional, physical, and sexual abuse, trauma, domestic violence, and homicide.

These topics may be triggering to some. Please prioritize your well-being as you read.

If you find any part of this story difficult, it's okay to take a break. You are not alone.

Loyalty Bound Me, Love Freed Me

L L MOMON

Rolling over in bed with my eyes still closed, I fumbled across the nightstand for my phone. Might as well answer it. It had been ringing since six this morning. Bill collectors were relentless, and there was no way I'd get any rest if I didn't at least try to put a stop to it.

Letting out a deep breath, I snapped into the receiver. "I don't know what you want, but whatever the amount is, I don't have it. I didn't have it last week, I didn't have it last month, and I don't have shit now. So please, stop calling me and leave me the hell alone!!"

A voice smacked her lips and shouted back, "Girl, I didn't even ask your ass for shit."

"Ummm, Cassie? That you?"

"Yes, it's me. And why are you cursing me out? Hell, I

was calling to see if you wanted to go to brunch with me this morning? But you basically just told me you're broke, so I guess it's on me then, huh?"

I sighed. "I'm sorry, Cuz. My phone's been ringing since the ass crack of dawn. I thought you were another bill collector. They've been calling all morning and won't leave me alone."

"Well, you know how to stop that, right? Just pay your bills on time and they won't have a reason to call."

She popped her lips. Sounding so proud of herself. I started to hang up on her ass, but I was hungry and didn't want to miss out on free brunch.

"Shut up, Cassie. You've always got some smart shit to say. Anyway, I'm starving. And yeah, I want to go to brunch, but like you just heard me say...I'm broke. So, if you want a brunch buddy, it's on you."

"Cool. Put on some clothes and meet me downtown at The Tea Leaf at ten. We've gotta talk."

"Okay, I'll be there. Let me get up and get ready. I'll see you soon."

It had been a hell of a week for me. Cassie had no idea, but I had only three days left before I was due to move out of my apartment. Losing my job a couple months back sent everything spiraling downward faster than I ever imagined. My checking account was empty, my savings were gone, and the bills were two months past due. Just a couple days ago, the city of Roseville came and disconnected my electricity. The water was next. At this point, getting up and washing my ass was a luxury I could no longer afford. The showers at Planet Fitness were about to become my saving grace.

Last night, I tore through my apartment looking for things to pawn just to hold me over another month. A few pieces meant the world to me, but if I wanted a chance at sticking around, I needed to put my pride to the side and let them go. There was the solid gold diamond nugget ring my grandmother left me, an acoustic guitar my ex, London, gave me and a sterling silver tea set gifted from my godmother. I was hoping for at least a stack for all three. It wasn't enough to fix all my problems, but it would help.

Of the three, the ring hurt most to part with. Still, having a roof over my head mattered more. I'd already loaded them into the trunk of my car. Getting up the nerve to actually take them to the pawnshop...that was the hard part.

Shaking the thought away, I jumped to my feet and stepped into the closet to find something to wear. Cassie was always dragging me to these bougie-ass spots, when I would've been fine with a simple Denny's breakfast. I didn't own anything fancy, but I was a savvy chick and could easily pull something together. Before I could hop in the cold shower, the phone rang again.

My ex's name lit up the screen. I grimaced.

"What do you want?" I barked.

"Well, damn. That's rude. Why I gotta want something? I ain't heard from you in a while, just wanted to check in on you. Is that a crime?"

"Hell yeah, it's a crime. You don't remember our last conversation? Matter fact, let me remind you, because I know your lying ass gonna say no. You told me you didn't see this... us, going anywhere, that you were moving out. You said, I deepened my voice in a mocking fashion, 'Shai, I love you and all, but this thing we got isn't working for me.' That's what the fuck you said."

"I was tripping, Baby. I didn't mean half that shit, Shai. I was just frustrated, going through some things. I'm better now."

"Oh, you was just going through some things, huh? Well guess what, so am I. So is everybody. Everybody got something they are dealing with. We all miss our grannies. Ain't that the stupid shit men say when they get caught doing something dumb? Regardless of the fact, that doesn't excuse you leaving the way you did. Like we ain't have bills, like we wasn't building nothing together. Because of you, my lights just got cut off and my water is next. So, unless you calling to say my Cash App or Apple

Pay is about to ring, I don't have anything else to say to you. Goodbye, Calloway."

"Don't hang up, Shai, please. I shouldn't have left the way I did. I'm sorry. I can send you a couple hundred if that'll help."

"A couple hundred? What the fuck I'm supposed to do with $200? Don't insult me."

"Okay... I got $1,000 I can send, but that's it." He sighed deeply into the phone.

"If it comes with strings attached, I don't want it. Calloway, you don't ever do shit without expecting something in return, and I don't have the energy for that today. Any day but today."

I paused and waited for the bullshit because I knew it was coming in three, two, one.

"I wouldn't call it strings, but... I would like to see you. Maybe come over, chill a bit. Catch up."

"And that right there is strings. You're so damn predictable. Keep your money. I don't want shit from you, and I definitely don't want to breathe the same air as you. Bye, Calloway." I hung up.

Shaking off my irritation, I showered, got dressed, and stopped by the apartment office before leaving.

The manager, Charlissa, saw me coming through the door and smiled like always. She was the coolest manager this complex had. She looked out for everybody. She'd even come to my apartment a couple times to hang out, have drinks and chill. Unlike the others, she wasn't snooty, and she would code-switch in a heartbeat.

"Shai-Shai! What it do, baby?" she grinned.

"Heyyy, Char. Can't call it, girl. You got a minute to talk?"

"Sure, come on in." She grabbed my hand, pulling me into the office. "Sorry for grabbing on you like that. Sheila's nosy ass is always eavesdropping and running back to tell the owners everything. Her messy ass gets on my nerves. Anyway, what's up with you?"

"A lot. I lost my job a couple months ago and I haven't been able to find employment since. Then my ex-boyfriend up and moved out on the slick, left me with all the bills. I'm fucked up right now. Rent's due in three days and I don't have it. I was wondering if I could get an extension? Just a few extra days and I should have the full amount."

"Shai, I'm not trying to be funny, but where are you going to get that kind of money in that short of a time? You bout to hit a lick or something?" she whispered, leaning closer.

"Girl, hell no. I'm not hitting nothing. But I've got a plan. If I don't have it in eight days, you can start putting my shit out on the curb. I won't even fight you."

Char giggled. "Alright, girl. You know I fucks with

you, so I'll see what I can do. I'll try and stall the higher ups while you figure things out. You've got eight days, not a day more. These people look for any excuse to get the old tenants out just so they can raise rent on the new ones. I'll try to hold them off. But Shai, if that money does come through...you better put me on."

"I got you, boo. Thank you," I said, chirping as I headed out the office.

Chapter Two

I left the office tickled. Char really thought I had something special going on. Truth was, I had no plan besides pawning my things. I was just too ashamed to admit it to her. Some things just wasn't anyone's business but mine.

Checking my watch, I nearly choked. Twenty-five minutes to get to The Tea Leaf... and it was forty-five minutes away. Cassie would for sure be pissed, but she'd get over it. With everything I had going on, she was lucky I was still coming.

As I sped down the highway, I replayed my situation in my head. No job. At least twenty applications sent in the past two months, and not a single callback. No returned emails, no interviews. My boyfriend gone, leaving me to carry all the bills. Three hundred dollars to my name, with twenty-eight hundred in bills waiting. The math wasn't mathing.

Still, I wasn't stressed. Life was gonna life regardless. And I wasn't the type to sit around wallowing. I was a make-it-work, shake-back type of chick. Glancing at myself in the rearview, I winked. *At least I still got my looks. This ass was still fat. Shiddd, I'ma be alright.*

Normally, I kept my business to myself, but a few days ago I'd confided in my best friend, Umi. She'd begged me to come stay with her. I thought about it for a second but quickly shut that idea down. Umi always had some shit going on, and most of it centered around her no-good boyfriend, Lincoln.

He hailed from the islands and was as mean as a rattlesnake. That man beat her ass for breakfast, lunch and dinner, and I wasn't about to get caught up in that. I'd already intervened once, only for her to run back to him the next day like nothing happened. That was the day I learned my lesson...stay out of folks' relationships.

Umi had two extra rooms, but I couldn't bring myself to live in that mess. The way Lincoln talked to her alone would have had me snapping. I loved my bestie, but when it came to Lincoln, it was like her common sense had fled and ran for cover. Like his mama done worked some Obeah on her or something, because nothing else explained why she was so damn stupid when it came to him.

Because of Lincoln, she'd lost almost every friend she had besides me. We all tried to help but every time someone tried to call him out, Umi would defend him to the grave. It pissed me off to no end, but I couldn't lie, I was low-key amused at her loyalty. Either way, her house was a no-go.

I considered moving back in with my parents, but I'd rather drag my coochie across hot concrete than go through that again. We had a huge blowout before I left home, after I finally worked up the nerve to give them my ass to kiss.

Years of mental abuse had worn me down, but leaving opened my eyes. I saw how other people's parents treated them, and it hit me...mine were narcissists. Both of them.

They never should've had kids. Honestly, if they'd swallowed us all, we'd been better for it. My mama had a way of getting under my skin like nobody else, and my daddy was too far up her ass to notice. She'd already driven three of my siblings away. When I left...I made four.

My father wouldn't stand up to her. Now that we were gone, he was free to be the punching bag she needed.

Grandparents? Gone on both sides. Which meant if I couldn't scrape enough money together, the only person left to call was Cassie's mama, my Aunt Chartreuse. Aunt

Trucee loved me like her own, but she lived five hours away in Macon, Georgia. I wanted to stay close, but honestly... for what? I had no man, no kids, no real village. My parents weren't an option and my siblings all lived out of state.

I always talked shit about Roseville, but I'd been here my whole life. I didn't know anything else. Maybe this was exactly what I needed. A new beginning. A clean start.

Taking in a deep breath and swallowing my pride, I dialed Aunt Trucee.

"Hey, Aunt Trucee. What you up to?"

"Nothing much, niece. Sitting on the porch with a glass of wine and a blunt. What's going on with you?"

"Umm... I don't wanna just come out and say it, but I know you hate when people beat around the bush. So I'll ask. Auntie... if I can't cover my bills this month and end up getting evicted... can I stay with you for a while, just till I get back on my feet?"

I nibbled at my fingertips while I waited. Relief washed over me when she answered without hesitation.

"Girl, you ain't said nothing. Course you can stay. I'd love to have you. Does your mean-ass mama know you ain't got nowhere to go, or you keeping it from her?"

"No, she doesn't know. I don't need them in my business or their unsolicited advice."

"I get it. So how soon we talking? You need help

moving? I got a few young fellas on my payroll I can send your way."

"Soon, Auntie. But let me call you back tonight. I wanna try a few things before I throw in the towel. But yes, if it falls through, I'll need the help. Right now, I'm pulling up to brunch with Cassie. I'm late as hell, and I can already see smoke coming out her ears from here. I gotta go."

"Alright, baby. Tell my daughter she could call her mama sometime. She wouldn't know if I was dead or alive if it weren't for you bridging the gap. Enjoy yourself, and we'll talk later."

Hanging up, I grabbed my purse and slid out the car.

Chapter Three

As I sauntered towards Cassie, she rolled her eyes and snapped. "Where the hell have you been? You're almost thirty minutes late."

"I'm sorry, Cassie. I had to handle some business first, and it made me run behind."

"Whatever Shai, you've always got some excuse for being late. That's probably why you lost your job."

My mouth dropped. "How the hell do you know I lost my job?"

"Because I'm not stupid. Your schedule is nine to five. I've called you at least five times these past few weeks...in the morning and you've answered the phone each time. Which means your ass ain't at work. It's not rocket science, Shai."

"Well, since you must know, I was let go because of

cutbacks, not because I was late. We haven't even sat down yet and you're already starting to piss me off."

She snapped her head. "Oh, you mad... but I'm the one sitting here waiting. You mad, but I'm the one treating you to brunch."

"Girl, I know you fucking lying. First off, you called me. I told you upfront I was broke. You volunteered your money. I didn't ask. If you're gonna talk shit about what you had to do, then don't do it. I don't need handouts. Oh, and your mama said you could call her sometime."

"Yeah, whatever. This ain't about my crazy-ass mama. I'll call her later. This is about you and your lack of respect for people's time. You need to get your shit together and grow up." She stormed into the building.

I almost snapped back, but today wasn't the day. I would've dragged her back out and beat her to a pulp in the middle of the street, so I chose the high road. Doing an about-face, I strutted back to my car.

From across the street, I shouted, "You can eat your bougie ass cat food by your damn self! I didn't want that nasty-ass brunch anyway. What the fuck is a tuna tartare with capers? Bitch, we're from the country. Country people don't eat shit like that! You wanna be something you're not so bad. This place doesn't even have shrimp and grits or Conecuh sausage. So fuck them people and fuck you too! Anyway, I love you. I'll call you later."

She flipped me off and stuck out her tongue before disappearing inside.

I hopped in my car and hunted for a pawn shop. The clerk told me all they could offer was $450. Deciding it wasn't worth it, I reloaded my trunk with my shit.

Sliding back into the driver's seat, I called my aunt. "Four days from now, Aunt Trucee. Give me about four days and I'll be ready."

THE NEXT FEW days I tied up loose ends and boxed my things. Out of courtesy, I called Charlissa to let her know I was forfeiting the deal and would drop off my keys.

Umi came over to "help," but she was more of a distraction than anything.

"Umm... what do you want me to do with these glasses? Am I really supposed to wrap them one by one? Who has time for that?"

"Umi, have you never moved before? Yes, you have to wrap them one by one or they'll break."

"Yeah, I've moved, but the place was already furnished. So I don't know what to do. Maybe I should start in your bathroom." She set the glasses down and headed for the hall.

"Yeah!" I yelled. "Bathroom's better for you. Just pack everything under the sink in that box. Throw in my flat irons with the toiletries and take the shower curtain down too."

As I shouted directions, there was a knock at the door.

"Who is it?"

"It's Lincoln. Is Umi in dere? Eff shi is, mi need yuh tuh tell har tuh bring har ass home. Dis damn baby bin crying since shi left, an mi cyaan duh nutten tuh stop it. Him wan him mada!"

I jumped up from the couch where I'd been flipping through photo albums and bolted to the bathroom. "Why the hell would you tell Lincoln you were coming here? You know I can't stand him, and now he's at my door demanding you come home."

She stood, fidgeting with her hands. "Girl, give me a minute. I'll be right back. Hell, I haven't even been gone an hour. He acts like he can't breathe without me."

Umi strolled to the door and swung it open. Lincoln stepped inside without hesitation.

"Hold up, partner. You know I don't fuck with you like that. Whatever y'all need to talk about, do it outside. Don't walk up in my house like you pay bills here."

"Shiiddd, from wah mi hear, nuhbody paying bills. Dats why all yuh shit cut off an yuh moving, right?"

Before I could answer, Umi shoved him out the door and slammed it shut.

Chapter Four

Fuming, I swung the door back open. "You hold on, you no-count, good-for-nothing, woman-beating, bitch-ass, fuck boy. You don't step up in my house and insult me like that. I ain't done nothing to you. Answer me something, Lincoln. Do you even like women? I'm asking because you've always got something negative to say about us. You beat on her like she's beneath you. You talk down on women like we scum of the earth. Do all men from the islands treat women like second-class citizens, or is it just you?"

"Yea, mi like women. It's yuh ass dat mi nuh like, an mi cyaan speak fi all men. Mi cyan only speak fi miself," he said proudly.

"Trust, the feeling's mutual. I despise your ass. Umi's your one and only fan 'cause nobody else who knows you likes you or gives a fuck about you. You act like Billy Badass with women, but when those yn's got after you that time, you were quiet as a church mouse. You didn't have shit to say then." I giggled as his eyes narrowed, and the arrogance disappeared from his face.

Shaking his head, he spat, "Si, Shai, dats it right dere. Dats dat shit mi talking bout. Yuh got tuh much mout, an yuh nuh kno yuh place. Dats probably why dat man leave yuh. Nuh man wan tuh hear dat shit. Bitch, all yuh duh is yap like a dog. Wah mi duh know is dat a real man wud ave beat yuh ass a long time ago. Yuh betta quit running yuh mout before mi cum in dere an show yuh why yuh shud nuh backtalk a man like mi."

"Oh yeah?" I scowled, stepping backwards into my apartment. "If I run my mouth too much, why don't you shut me up? You like to hit women, right? Show them their place?" I reached behind my front door for the axe handle I kept there for protection. "Lincoln, I didn't even know I had a place to learn, so maybe I need a piece of shit like you to teach me. Come on, fuck boy, learn me something!!"

Umi peered at me, her eyes trailing down to my arms. Seeing them behind the door, she knew what was next. With a frantic look in her eyes, she pleaded with him to leave.

"Come on, Lincoln, let's just go. Ummm, Shai, I'll call

you later when I get the baby down. I'm sorry, girl," she nervously quipped, grabbing his arm and pulling him away from the door.

"Sorry?!?!" Lincoln barked. "Mi nuh sorry bout shit, an yuh ain't eitha. Don't apologize tuh dis bitch, especially eff yuh apologizing fi mi. Mi meant everyting dat mi seh."

I looked at Umi and saw the fear in her eyes. That pissed me off even more. She was truly terrified of Lincoln. I needed to put an end to this shit ASAP. Sucking my teeth, I muttered, "I meant everything that I said too, Lincoln. So let me say it louder. I don't know my place, so why don't you come show me since you think you such a badass."

Furrowing his brow, he took three steps inside my apartment. Which is precisely what I wanted him to do. As soon as I had enough clearance for the door to close, I slammed it shut and tried to channel my inner Jackie Robinson. I swung with everything I had. The axe handle made contact with his head. My intention was to crack his ribs, but our heavenly Father makes no mistakes. Suffering a blow to his dome, he fell against the wall before slumping on the floor directly in front of the door.

I aimed solely at his extremities. I needed to render him helpless, not for a moment, but permanently. Starting with his hands, I beat them until they were bloody, along with his arms. I swung until my arms ached. By the time Umi forced her way back in, I had just finished hitting both of his kneecaps, all while asking him, "Who's doing the ass whooping now?" Lincoln flailed around, flapping like a fish out of water.

"Yuh crazy bitch! Mi gunna kill yuh. Mi swear as soon as mi get up, mi gunna end yuh," he screamed.

"Bitch, yuh a dead woman. Mi promise yuh this," he snarled, looking dejected and ruined.

Tearful, Umi looked up at me. "Shai, look at what you done. Please call the ambulance. Please. He's bleeding bad," she whined.

Throwing my hands in the air, I muttered, "That's the muthafuckin' point, Umi. I bet his ass won't beat anyone else. I tried to crush every bone in his fucking hand. Fuck him. And if you gonna sit there and take up for him again, then fuck you too. I'm tired of men like him always walking over us like we beneath them. He can go to hell as far as I'm concerned."

"Shai, I know you're mad and did this for me, but this isn't what I wanted. I love him and just wanted him to do better. He said he wouldn't hit me again, and I believe him."

"Oh yeah? Well, if you believe that, then you are just as crazy as he is. He was always gonna hit you again because you never defend yourself. Well, guess what? I knew you would never leave. At least this way, he can't hurt you without hurting himself. I say that's a win-win. But if you want me to call the police, I will." I picked up my cell phone and dialed 911.

In a frantic voice, wearing a smile, I pleaded, "Ummm yes, please help me. There's a man in my house...my best friend's boyfriend. He came in threatening to hurt me, and I had to defend myself. I was scared... scared for her life and mine. He has a history of abusing women, and I was scared he would kill her or me or both. I didn't know what else to do, so I grabbed the closest thing to me to protect myself and it went left. Please, can you send a police officer and an ambulance? Please hurry. The address is 302 Seymour Place, Apartment 821. We'll be waiting. Please hurry."

Hanging up, I grabbed my axe handle, sat on the couch, and put my feet on the coffee table. I grabbed my photo album and resumed admiring the pictures.

"Shai, I can't believe you just did that. That's a new low even for you."

"Did what? You asked me to call someone to get him help, and I did. I don't see the problem, Umi. He was in the wrong, not me. This man came to my house, threatened me, and stepped foot in my door. Self-defense, like I said, and don't lie for him either. If you do, we are done."

Umi kneeled down and tended to Lincoln. "Baby, don't worry. We gonna get you to the hospital. The ambulance is on the way." She looked up at me, her face the saddest I ever seen. I almost felt bad---but nahhhh. I said almost.

"Mi gunna kill dat bitch, Umi. Mi serious. Shi dead. Mi cyaan move mi legs or mi arms. Mi in suh much agony."

"Exactly. How you gonna kill someone when you can't lift a finger? You don't think much do you, Lincoln?"

"Fuck yuh, Shai. Mi promise yuh, yuh get yuhs."

"Yeah, yeah, yeah. Fuck you too. And they need to hurry up and get you outta my house before I finish what I started. And please keep threatening me. Say it louder so they hear it when they come to arrest your ass."

"Arrest mi?" he bucked. "Nuh, yuh psycho bitch! Dem gunna arrest yuh. Dis is assault. Dis is battery. Dis... dis is sumting." He groaned, accent thickening as the pain hit.

"It's not assault or battery, Lincoln. It's called redemption. You are from the islands, right? I know you've heard of the Redemption Song by Bob Marley. It says something like, 'But my hands were made strong by the hands of the Almighty.' And he ain't never lied. My hands stronger than a muthafucka today. Won't he do it?" I did a praise dance while cackling.

"Mi hate yuh, Shai," he gritted. "Umi, mi told yuh a long time ago nuh tuh hang wid har. Shi crazy, and now yuh si it fi yuhself."

"What goes around comes around, Lincoln. That's how the world works. I didn't give you anything you didn't have coming. Now please shut the fuck up with all that whining, moaning, and groaning. I'm tired, my head hurts, and I need to finish packing. I've got too much to do."

Chapter Five

The ambulance and police came through and shuffled him off to the hospital. The reporting officer told me I needed to come by the station. I was nervous at first because they put me in the back of the police car but didn't handcuff me. They said it was procedure; they needed to do an investigation and would also get a statement from Umi. I was lowkey worried she'd fold on me for Lincoln, but to my surprise, she held me down.

They grilled me about everything, and I spit it all out. Damn near word for word like I told the dispatcher. I deserved an Oscar. Lincoln had a record for domestic violence and battery, so they believed every word. Within hours, I was free. The officer said once Lincoln was treated, he could possibly be detained for trespassing, harassment, and terroristic threats but they couldn't make any promises. That was typical for Roseville P.D. So many cases slipped through the cracks because of their shitty police work.

I called Cassie to come get me. I knew she'd talk shit about me leaving her at brunch, but I'd rather hear her mouth over paying for an Uber.

"Hey heifer, what you doing?"

"Not much. 'Bout to make stir-fry and call my mama back. She hit me earlier, but I was busy."

"Before you do that, can I ask for a favor?"

Sighing, she said, "Shai, I don't have no money."

"Girl, I'm not no begging ass bitch, and you know that. I've never asked you for a dime before. Why would you think I'm starting now?"

"'Cause you don't got a job, duh."

I laughed. "You swear you be on to something, but you are wrong 95% of the time. I don't need your money. I need a ride from the police station."

"The police station?" she repeated. "Why you at the station? You get arrested or something?"

"No, just for questioning. Come get me, and I'll tell you everything."

"Okay, hold tight. Lemme turn off the stove, I'm on my way."

"Thanks, cuz. See you soon."

Whew, I just knew her ass was going to hang up on me. Luckily my cousin loved to sip some good old fashioned southern tea. She had everyone in Roseville thinking she was upper echelon and in a way she was.

College, multiple degrees in psychology, her own practice, gorgeous estate, dating "high value men," designer everything, and a new Mercedes every two years. She was a beautiful woman that looked flawless on paper.

What folks didn't know: her mama had done time, her dad was still locked up, two abortions before 18, loved drama, drank like a fish, cursed like a sailor, smoked weed like a chimney, very active in swinging and she preferred married men over the single ones. By most standards, trifling, but I didn't care. I was proud of her accomplishments. She was family, and her secrets were safe with me. Loyalty above all.

We didn't always see eye to eye, but we always had each other's backs. I loved her like a sister but sometimes had to remind her of her roots. Especially when she got too high and mighty. She would quickly pipe down because she knew I could drag her like a ragdoll if needed.

Her relationship with Aunt Trucee wasn't the best. When aunt Trucee went to jail, Cassie bounced around foster care, got mistreated and blamed her mama for not being there. Once released from prison, Trucee tried to make amends, but Cassie wasn't ready. Trucee remained hopeful that one day her daughter would come around. Until that day, my aunt kept her distance, but she always had me to call when she was lonely. I planned on loving on her as much as possible when I moved in. Trucee was good people. Cassie just refused to see it.

I told Cassie all the time, "Let's trade mamas, and you'd appreciate yours more."

She pulled up at the station, and I hopped in.

"So, spill it, girl. Why in the hell are you being questioned by the police? What did you do?"

"Beat a negro bloody with an axe handle."

"Excuse me? You beat someone with a stick?" She drew in a deep breath.

"That is exactly what I said. My best friend's boyfriend. Got him right on together and before you ask, yes, he deserved it. He likes to beat women. He won't be beating nothing else for a long time. Not even his dick."

"Damn, Shai! What all did you do to him?"

"I bashed his hands, arms, kneecaps. Was about to start on his ankles, but Umi burst in, so I stopped. So, like I said, he won't be beating nothing for a while."

Cassie laughed in disbelief. "Girl, your ass is certifiable. You could probably get a check or something. I could arrange it. You know your ass need it."

"Fuck you, Cassie. Stop tripping. There isn't anything wrong with me. I saw an opportunity to fix a problem, and

I did. There is nothing crazy about that. I pride myself on being a problem solver." I leaned back, relaxed and tried to enjoy my passenger princess moment.

Cassie shook her head, turned the radio down and sighed deeply. I knew something was on her mind, but after today...I wasn't up for more bullshit.

Chapter Six

"I've got something that I wanted to talk to you about, Shai. I was going to bring it up at brunch the other day, but you dipped before I could."

"Don't do that, Cassie. You know why I left, but just in case you don't, I'll enlighten you. I left because you were talking smack. I was having a shitty day, and you added to it. But go ahead, talk."

"Ok, Shai, but do you promise you won't get mad?"

"Hell no. Why would I promise that before I know what we're talking about? If I get mad, I get mad. But it's not like I'm a goblin or something. I won't attack you like some kind of savage. We're still family."

"I know but I don't need you spazzing out in my car. I just got my baby two months ago." She rubbed the dashboard and beamed with pride.

"Cassie, quit stalling and spit it out."

"Ummm, I know that you and Calloway were togeth—."

"Child, you can stop right there," I said, cutting her off mid-sentence. "If you want to be with him, be with him. I won't be mad, angry, or pissed because I really don't give a damn. Just know that fuck-boy don't like to pay bills for real, and his ass is the reason I'm moving in with your mom in a few days. His dick game goes crazy though, so have fun, cousin, just don't get invested."

She swallowed hard. "Wow, Shai, you handled that better than I expected. Just so you know, it's nothing like that."

"Don't you mean it's nothing like that...yet? You're clearly entertaining the thought; otherwise, you wouldn't have brought it up. Please, Cassie. Don't insult my intelligence. I may play dumb, but I'm far from it."

She gripped the wheel tighter. I could tell she was nervous. "I never thought you were dumb, Shai. I just didn't want you to think I was going behind your back. At first, I didn't know who he was. He approached me at the country club I attend, and he looked nothing like the Calloway I remember you dating."

"Country club? How did he get in? He must know somebody who knows somebody because the only way I see him there is in a domestic capacity. Like somebody's caddy. He's not smart enough to do anything else," I smirked.

"Honestly, I can't answer that. Anyway, he cut those dreads off and had a low Caesar fade. Even though you two were together almost a year, I rarely saw him, so I really didn't know what he looked like. He introduced himself as Randall. He was kind, and we went out on our first date a few days ago. While eating dinner, he told me about the work he does at the Roseville community center. I remembered you telling me your ex worked there. When I asked him if he knew a Calloway, all the blood drained from his face. He had no choice but to tell me *he* was Calloway and admitted that Randall was his middle name. I wanted to leave right then, but he begged me to stay. I have to admit, I enjoyed myself, but I wasn't sure how you'd react, so I had to ask."

"Well, cousin, thank you for that nice lil rundown. But like I told you, I don't care. Just be careful with him, and whatever you do, don't let him drive your car. He'll have your ass waiting like Jody did Yvette." We both chuckled.

"You don't have to worry about that. Nobody is driving my baby but me. Shai, thank you for being so understanding and looking out for me. I have another question though. Why didn't you tell me you were moving in with my mother? First, why are you moving? Is it because of your job situation?"

"Yes, I can't find anything around here. I only have a couple hundred dollars left, and I wasn't trying to be on the streets. I called Aunt Trucee, and she told me to come on. So, that's what I'm going to do."

"You know you could have come to me. I've got a home, a place for you to stay. I could have given you money. Why didn't you ask me?"

My eyes narrowed involuntarily before responding, "Because you talk too much shit, and I'd hate to have to fuck you up. Besides, didn't you just tell me a little while ago that you didn't have any money? That was you, right?"

"Yes, but I... I..." Cassie stuttered.

"No need to explain. It's cool. Trust me, it's better this way. Plus, I get to love on my auntie and spend time with her since her only child refuses."

"Shai, we are not about to have this conversation again," she snapped as we entered my apartment complex.

"We don't have to. I have to finish packing, so we'll revisit this another time. Thanks for the ride, cousin. Be careful with that negro, okay? Love you, and I'll call you later this week."

I entered the house, lit my candles, and became super aware of my surroundings. The place was dim, and the events from the day had me on edge. But I still needed to continue packing because once Aunt Trucee sent the cavalry, I'd be out of here. I wished I could take a shower, but since I couldn't, I changed my clothes and started transferring things into boxes. It was late, around a quarter till 11, when someone lightly tapped on my door.

Grabbing the axe handle, I shouted, "Who is it?" through the door before peeking out the blinds.

"It's Man Man. Hey, I don't mean to bother you, but I just wanted to let you know that there were a couple of men hanging around your spot after you left."

Chapter Seven

Opening the door, I stepped outside, and he continued.

"Yeah man, they were out here for a long time. You know I live two doors down, and I saw them standing around looking crazy. I walked up to them and ask who they were looking for, and they told me to mind my own business."

"Damn, for real? How long was I away before they came by?"

"About two hours. They pulled up in a black Cadillac Escalade. Those men hopped out like they meant business. Now, I ain't no snitch, but I figured you needed to know," he offered.

"Thanks, Man Man. It had to be someone connected

to my best friend's old man. I whooped his ass today. I'm not really tripping; I'll be gone soon."

"Oh yeah? Where to? I see you've got boxes all over the place. Need any help?"

"Not tonight, but maybe first thing in the morning. I plan to get an early start on things. I'm moving to Georgia."

"Listen, Shai," he said, while moving in closer. "You're a nice girl and you've always been kind to me. I'm not a creep or nothing, but I can tell from the candles that your lights are off."

I softly sighed out of shame.

"I don't mean to embarrass you. All I'm trying to say is if you need to come down to my place to take a shower or grab a bite to eat, just give me a holler. I'm home most of the time."

"Don't you work, Man Man?"

"I'm on disability. I'm a vet, and I got fucked up pretty bad out there in the desert. My body's fine, but my mental state... not so much."

I side-eyed him, trying not to look alarmed. He noticed.

"I'm not crazy or anything like that, Shai. I just have flashbacks of what I've been through. You've heard of PTSD, right? That's what I was diagnosed with."

"I understand. I wasn't trying to imply you were crazy.

You just said it messes with your mental state, and that made me a little nervous," I chuckled. "The last thing I need is another somebody mad at me for something."

"Well, like I said, if you need anything, just holla at me. I heard and saw what happened earlier today. We all did but I know that he had to do something to leave your place all fucked up like that. That man was hollering and screaming the whole time they were trying to get him into the ambulance."

"Of course he was. He's bitch-made, that's why. And you're right. He deserved it for threatening to beat me and show me my place. I got the drop on him and gave him a taste of his own medicine."

Laughing, he muttered, "I saw that. That joker was laid out on that stretcher. I see you ain't to be fucked with, lil mama."

"I don't bother anyone unless they bother me. Anyway, thank you, Man Man. If it's okay with you, I'd like to come over in the morning and take a shower. For now, that's all I need. Thanks again for looking out."

Saluting me, he said, "You're welcome," and headed back to his apartment. I closed and locked the door, then continued boxing up my things. By 1:00 A.M., I could barely keep my eyes open and decided to turn in for the night.

The minute my head hit the pillow, my phone rang. It was Umi.

"Shai, Shai, are you asleep?"

"Almost. What's up?"

"I'm still at the hospital with Lincoln, and I know you don't care, but Shai, you fucked him up pretty bad. He's going to be in here for a while. They're talking about amputating one of his hands and he has severe swelling in his arms and knees. The good thing is, his knee caps were barely in tact but he won't have to have total knee replacement surgery like we thought. They are bruised badly but at least he won't be in a wheelchair. Like I said, you fucked him up bad."

"And?" I chirped.

"And I think you should apologize to him. It's his right hand too, Shai. He's going to be handicapped."

"Hahahahaha, Umi. You're bullshitting, right? Are you smoking rock? I'm not apologizing to him. I'd chew my own fingers off before I did that. I said it once, and I'll say it as many times as I need to: Lincoln deserved every lick he got. You should be happy he can't hurt you anymore. He can't slap you with all his might. He can't stomp on you while you're on the ground begging for your life."

"I know, Shai, but I ju—"

Cutting her off mid-sentence, I asked, "Umi, what's

wrong with you? Can't you see that man doesn't really love you? He just wants to control you. That's not love. I promise you it isn't."

I heard her sobbing through the phone. "Listen, I'm sorry, Umi. I'm sorry you haven't realized you deserve better. That you'd rather be with someone who mistreats you than be alone. I'm sorry you've let this man ruin your self-esteem and make you think he's your savior. He isn't."

"Shai, I know you think I'm weak, but I'm just trying to survive. My parents moved back to Ghana two years ago, so I'm here by myself. Much like you, but at least your parents are nearby. I know you don't deal with them like that, but you could if you wanted. I can't. I have no one but Lincoln and Jr. and I don't know how to live without him."

Without thinking, I asked, "Why don't you come with me? We can figure this out together. Just pack your things, and we can roll. The moving truck comes tomorrow evening around three."

"I can't leave him like this. He's all fucked up, Shai."

"Girl, please. That man came over and damn near brought his whole family. He has people to see about him. We have to see about ourselves. Do you know anyone in his family who drives a black Cadillac Escalade? A dude from a couple doors down said a few guys were hanging around my apartment after I left for the police station."

"Ohhh shit. Yes, he has an uncle named Montague."

"Wait, bitch, did you just say Montague, like the Shakespeare character?"

"Shai, the fuck if I know. I don't even know who Shakespeare is. All I know is his name is Montague. Anyway, he doesn't drive the truck himself, but his men drive him around."

"Hmmm, you've been around Lincoln all day. Did you hear him make any phone calls about me? And don't lie to me, Umi."

"Yes, but he didn't tell them it was you. He would never tell his family that a woman beat his ass. He told them a group of thugs attacked him and that he was recovering in the hospital."

"Did you hear him give them an address?"

"Not that I recall. I went to the restroom while he was talking, so he could have."

"What does this Montague look like? I need to know in case he rolls up on me."

"Girl, Montague is fine as hell. I mean fine-fine. Aldis Hodge, Morris Chestnut, young Idris Elba fine. He's about 6'3", dark-skinned, he had long dreads, but he cut them off when he came to the states. He's in his mid-forties and in excellent shape. I always see him sporting huge diamonds in both ears and an iced-out Jesus piece.

That man just exudes power. Whenever he walks into a room, he steals it. He really is *him*."

"Well damn, Umi. You sound like *you* want to fuck him. Is he *that* fine?"

"I'm telling you, he is. But he goes for bad. He's not someone to take lightly. Lincoln does things for him from time to time when we're low on funds. The man doesn't play. As long as I've been around, I've never seen him smile. I tell you what, I'm going to go through Lincoln's phone while he sleeps and find a picture. I'll send it to you, so you know exactly who to look for."

"Thank you, Umi. Will you at least think about leaving with me? My aunt won't mind. She will treat you like her own. That's how she is, especially when I tell her you're getting away from your abusive boyfriend."

"How do you know she won't mind, Shai?" she asked.

"Because my aunt spent a dime in prison defending herself against an abusive man. She stabbed him in the neck, fucked up his spine. He lived, but he can't do anything for himself anymore. I was told that she tried to render him helpless so he couldn't do it again, to her or anyone else. That's what I was trying to do to Lincoln. I wasn't trying to kill him, Umi. I just wanted to protect you and Jr. from his wrath."

"I know you meant well, Shai, and yes, I will think about leaving," she mumbled softly.

"Ok sis, I love you."

"I love you too, Shai."

I ended the call and drifted off. Two hours later, my phone dinged with a text and a picture of one of the finest men I'd ever seen in my life.

Umi: Here he is

Damn, Umi was right. He was definitely fine as fuck. But as fine as he was, he needed to stay far the fuck away from me if his intentions weren't good.

Chapter Eight

W aking up, I grabbed my caddy, a change of clothes, and sauntered down to Man Man's house. Before I could knock, the door swung open. The smell of cinnamon and bacon hit me like a slap.

"Hey Shai, come on in. I knew you'd get an early start, so I made breakfast...French toast, a southwestern omelet, bacon, and sausage. Hope you're hungry," he said, moving about in the kitchen.

"Man Man, it smells amazing, but you didn't have to do all this. I just need to use your shower. I was going to grab a biscuit at the gas station down the street."

Wearing a smile, he pointed to the food. "And now you're not. Have a seat, eat, and when you're done, the bathroom's down the hall to the left. I figured, being that you're leaving the complex, this is the least I could do. Shai, I may never see you again, so let me feed you a good meal to remember me by."

I pulled out a chair at the dining table and sat down, adjusting in my seat before taking in my surroundings. The place was neat and minimalistic. An old box TV sat on a wooden stand, and a curio cabinet held small trinkets. His shoes were perfectly lined up against the wall. Everything had its place. I made a mental note to leave it exactly as I found it once I was done in the bathroom. I didn't want any trouble with the war vet.

A framed picture of a beautiful woman holding two babies caught my eye. I wanted to ask who they were but decided it was better to mind my business. Man Man had lived here much longer than I had. He was quiet, reserved, and kept to himself. I rarely saw him outside of taking out his trash or smoking on the balcony. He was kind and shy, but he made sure to wave or speak whenever we crossed paths. Neighbors whispered about him being "off," but I didn't see "off." I saw someone trying to make light from the darkness in their mind.

"Eat up, girl. I hope you like it," he said, pulling me from my thoughts.

Man Man's food was delicious, far better than the

dried-out, stale sausage biscuit I would have ended up with otherwise. I took a sip of juice and pointed toward the hallway. Before I could move, my phone rang.

"Shit," I groaned. "I can't ever do anything without being interrupted." I ran back to my phone. Umi's picture glowed in the backlight.

"What's up, Umi?"

"I'm going," she whispered.

"You're coming with me? Are you serious?"

"As a heart attack, bitch. I went through his phone last night. This man had four other women he was talking to... three here, one back in Jamaica. He's been cheating on me our entire relationship. Those drugs had him out cold, and I had practically all night to plunder."

"I'm sorry you had to find out like that, but at least you know now."

"You're right, Shai, but it still hurts. He's been mean and hateful to me but treats these other girls like queens. He talks to them so sweet. I'm so mad, so hurt. He fucked up my life, Shai. I didn't even want kids, but I had one for him, and this is how he treats me. I'm done. I'm leaving the hospital, grabbing a few things and my baby from his aunt Toni, and I'm gone."

"Please be careful, Umi. If anyone sees you with a bag or luggage, just say you're packing clothes for Lincoln and yourself to stay at the hospital. Do not tell them you're leaving him. Tell nobody...not his mama, aunts, brothers, sisters, cousins. Nobody. Hear me?"

Crying softly, she sniffled, "Yes, I hear you."

"Sorry again, sis. I'll see you when you get here. I'm hopping in the shower, I'll be back soon."

"Where are you now?" She asked.

"I'll tell you later. Bye, love."

I hung up and shot Man Man an awkward look before returning to the bathroom. I turned the water on full blast. Ten minutes in, a knock came at the door.

"Ummm, yes? Almost done," I called.

"Shai, hate to bother you, but those men are back at your place. Peeking in your window. Thank God you're down here. Want me to go handle it?"

"No," I muttered, quickly stepping out of the shower and drying off. "I can't have you involved. Just stay here and don't open the door."

"Okay, but if they come to my door, I'm answering it."

"Hopefully they won't. Maybe they'll get tired of standing there looking stupid." I hurriedly got dressed and exited the bathroom. Man Man was by the front door.

"What if they don't leave, Shai?" he questioned.

Shrugging my shoulders, I answered. "Then I'll call the damn police. Nothing's going to stop me from leaving today. It took me a while to get used to the idea, but now my mind's made up. I need to call Umi and tell her to hold off coming over. I don't want her showing up while they're here. They might turn on her."

As I picked up the phone, Man Man moved from the door, mouthing for me to be quiet. He whispered, "They're walking down this way." My eyes widened as we stood in silence. A few seconds later, there was a knock on his door.

Without hesitation, he swung it open. Thankfully, I'd stepped back into the hallway to make my call. A man stood there, speaking fast patois.

"How can I help you?" Man Man muttered, voice strong and with authority.

"Mi nuh wan trouble. Mi boss is looking fi a few thugs dat jumped him nefyu. Wi were told it happen at dis apartment building. Di second floor, left side. Him was seeing one of him ladies wen har boyfriend came home wid him buddies and caught him. Do yuh kno anyting bout dat, sir?"

"No. I didn't see anything and haven't seen thugs running around here. This is a decent neighborhood; we are pretty mellow around these parts. Just so you know, there's a heavy police presence in this complex. A sheriff's deputy lives three doors down. You may want to watch out for him."

The man glanced around, muttering, "Tank yuh, sir. Eff yuh si anyone, here mi card. Please give mi a call." He handed Man Man the card and walked away. Man Man closed the door behind him and turned to me.

"I told you, those men are really trying to get to you. It may be a good thing that you are leaving today. Hopefully, you will be long gone by the time they return.

Chapter Nine

I t took an hour for Lincoln's people to leave. During that time, I got to know the man who lived two doors down from me. Before that day, we'd never had a conversation lasting more than a few minutes. Today, I learned that his real name was Rylas and that he had lived in his apartment for eleven years, nine more than me. Rylas was born and raised in a small town in Arkansas. He was a divorced father of twins named Choice and Chance...the same children I'd seen in the picture on his wall. They were now sixteen, and he hadn't seen them or his ex-wife in over seven years. He was deeply spiritual, incredibly intelligent, and held several degrees. Rylas was even an ordained minister.

Before I returned to my apartment to finish boxing up my things and wait for Umi, Rylas spoke life into me and prayed over me. I thanked him, gave him a long hug, and trekked back to my apartment. Luckily, I'd completed most of the work the night before and only had a few things left to deal with. Within thirty minutes of my arrival, Umi showed up with baby Lincoln in tow.

"Girl, we've got to hurry and get out of here. I can't lie to you, Shai. I am so scared. Does anyone know where we are going?" Umi nervously looked around before taking a seat on the couch.

"First, do not be scared. I will make sure nothing happens to us. Second, no one knows but my cousin Cassie, and she won't say a word." I tried to ease the tension and calm her nerves. "So, are you excited about our new beginning? You're going to love my Aunt Trucee. Girl, she's a trip and don't even get me started on how she can cook. She can throw down in the kitchen."

"Yes, I'm excited to get away from that monster of a boyfriend, but I know he's going to find me. I just know it, Shai. I can feel it. There's no way he's going to let Jr. and me go peacefully."

I could tell from the way she shook and trembled that she was scared. I wanted to reassure her that her issues with Lincoln was a thing of the past.

"That's your problem, Umi. You think a man has to let you do something. He's not your father; he's not even your husband. He's your boyfriend and baby daddy. You don't need anyone to think for you. You can think for yourself. Umi, you're twenty-eight. Hell, a year older than me. But Lincoln has convinced you that you need him and you don't. You need to remember who the fuck you were before Lincoln came into your life."

She pursed her lips and muttered, "That's been so long ago that I can't even remember."

"Shiddd, I do. I remember the Umi that would roll up in her Nissan Altima with box braids and a fifth of Hennessy in her hand. The Umi who wouldn't let anybody...man or woman...play on her top. The Umi who hit a lick and paid for us to go to Atlanta to get custom gold grills. The fine-ass Umi that had men inviting us to the V.I.P. section as soon as we walked through the door. That's the Umi I remember."

"I should have kept myself away from the V.I.P. That's where I met Lincoln, and my life has been going downhill ever since," she said as she lowered her head.

"No more Lincoln talk, Umi and I'm serious. Just calm down. The moving truck should be here in a little bit. Then all this drama and strife will be in the rearview. Please, at least try to embrace it."

"I will. I promise. I'm going to make Jr. a bottle and put him to sleep. I may try to take a nap myself. I didn't get any sleep last night. I'm so tired, friend."

"Okay, good. You get some rest, and I'm going to go back here and call Aunt Trucee."

Walking back to my bedroom, I dialed my aunt's number. I prayed she was in a good mood because telling her I was bringing two more mouths to feed might have made her want to tell me to stay where I was. I was willing to take that chance. Lincoln would eventually find a way to hurt her if she didn't get away from him, especially after what I'd done to him.

"Heyyyy, Auntie! What are you doing?"

"Nothing much, Baby. I'm sitting here excited, ready to see my favorite niece walk through the door. The fellas left a few hours ago, so it shouldn't be long before they're pulling up on you."

"About that, Aunt Trucee... I've got something to tell you and ask you. Now, before you say anything, please hear me out. It's serious."

"Go ahead, I'm listening."

"Okay, let me start by thanking you again for doing this for me. You really are the best auntie a girl could ask for."

"You're welcome. Now get to the meat and quit with all the pleasantries."

"Okay, okay, Auntie. My best friend and her four-month-old will be tagging along. Her boyfriend is an abuser, and I beat him bloody yesterday because of it. I went to jail, but I only had to make a statement. I told them it was self-defense."

"Girl, I swear you are just like me...always trying to save somebody. Now go on because I have a feeling that's not all you have to tell me."

"Umm, it's just that her boyfriend's uncle, Montague, has been to my home a couple times looking for the men who beat his nephew up and supposedly, he's somebody I should be afraid of."

Confused, she muttered, "Men? What men?"

"Exactly. There are no men. Just me. He told his uncle that a few men jumped on him...probably because he was ashamed that a woman whooped his ass. They've been to my place twice since it happened. I wasn't there either time, but my neighbor talked to one of the guys, and that's how I found out about these so-called men.'"

"Well, ain't that some shit," Trucee laughed. "Niece, don't worry about any of that and you don't have to be scared of no one. The men coming to pick you up are straight shooters. They are registered to correct a nigga, and I'll be calling them when we hang up to give them a rundown. Don't worry, baby. You'll be protected. This house is huge. It's big enough for five more friends, so I'm not worried. Plus, I have security all around, and ain't shit getting through that gate without me and my team knowing."

"Wait, Auntie, why do you need all that?"

"That's my business, Shai. You'll see when you arrive. I don't live where I used to live. I'm on a whole nother level now, Babygirl. Anyhow, I love you, and I'll see you later tonight. We'll talk when you get here. Until then, stay in that apartment until my boys get there. Kenzo and Rocky are their names. Be nice to them, and they'll be nice to you. Bye, Shug."

"Bye, Auntie."

I exited my bedroom and returned to the common area, where Umi and Jr. were fast asleep. Slumping down in the chair, I patiently waited for them to arrive and whisk us off to our new life.

Chapter Ten

Five minutes till three, Kenzo and Rocky arrived right on schedule. I introduced myself, and we wasted no time loading the truck. Rylas came down to help, and it only took an hour and a half to load everything I owned--leaving only the bed that Calloway had purchased months before he decided to move out. Being the nice guy that he was, Rylas trekked back to his apartment to grab Gatorade for all of us just as the Black Cadillac pulled up behind the moving truck.

A gorgeous, tall, slender, chocolate-skinned man draped in Versace, big rocks in his ears, and that Jesus piece Umi had spoken of slid out of the back seat looking like he meant business. He spotted Umi and gestured for her to come over. With fear in her eyes, she swiped her hair from her face and trotted to him.

"Niece, wah in di fuck are yuh doing here? Mi came ova here trying tuh tek care of di men dat left yuh man lying in di hospital, an here yuh are, congregating wid di damn opps. Weh are dem batty boys? Are dem two men di ones dat jumped on mi nephew?"

"Who, Kenzo and Rocky? No, Uncle Montague. I just met them. They are here to help Shai move. If I can be honest with you, there were no men to jump on Lincoln. He lied to you. He threatened to do harm to my best friend, and she beat him with an axe handle. The police came and everything. It was self-defense."

Narrowing his eyes, he smirked and said, "Zeen, likkle girl, please tell mi yuh are kidding. Are yuh really telling mi dat Lincoln was beat by a uhman?"

"Yes, that's exactly what I'm telling you. God's honest truth," she chimed.

Running his fingers through his beard, he looked around and said, "Let mi meet har. Mi got tuh meet dis uhman. Weh is shi?"

"I'm right here," I quipped, walking up to stand directly in front of Montague.

Shocked, he fixed his eyes on my body, taking in every inch. I looked away, but I could still feel him staring. He called his boys over to where we were.

"Cum here an tek a look. Dis uhman here is di one responsible fi putting in dat work pon Lincoln. Mi always told him dat him mout wud write a check him ass cud nuh cash. Mi neva tink it wud be a uhman, though. Mi dead wid laugh. Likkle miss...umm, wah yuh name?"

"My name is Shai," I said matter-of-factly.

"Miss Shai...Tallawah ehh. Yuh put a hurting on mi nefyu. Normally, dere wud be dire consequences fi doing wah yuh did, but mi nuh lie...dis shit ave mi perplexed. Mi cyaan believe dat a likkle lady like yuh did him bad like dat. Baby, yuh dangerous wid a stick, an mi intrigued. Yuh are much too beautiful tuh be fighting big grown men. Who si bout yuh? Who protects yuh? Ehh?"

"Me. I protect me," I said proudly. Out of the corner of my eye, I saw Rocky and Kenzo watching everything. I could tell they were ready to pounce, but they kept cool and kept loading things in the truck.

"Mi si, Mi si. Suh, yuh are moving, ayy?" he questioned.

"Yes, I'm getting out of this town. There's nothing left for me here, and with all due respect, we need to be on the road before it gets dark. We need to leave now."

"Who is wi'?" Montague asked.

I saw Umi in my peripheral vision, apprehension covering her face. I played it cool. "Just me. Umi came over to help me pack, but I'm guessing she's going to head back to the hospital when we're done. Isn't that right, Umi?"

"Yes, Unk. Yes. I just came to see my friend off. I'll be

heading back to the hospital when we're done here. Since you all know the truth now, you can be on your way."

"Wi will be on our way wen mi seh," he spat. "Yuh kno, if mi nuh kno any betta, Mi tink yuh bout tuh run off wid yuh friend, Umi. Please tell mi dats nuh yuh intention. Yuh nuh bout tuh tek mi great nefyu away from him fada, are yuh? Leave him high an dry afta yuh friend beat him nearly tuh death an leave him wid one hand? Mi kno betta den dat. Right, niece?"

"Nooo, Uncle Montague," she quickly answered.

"Good. Now get di fuck in di truck suh wi cyan leave an let yuh friend be on har way."

My stomach began to churn. "Wait, wait! Umi drove her own car. Are you going to leave her car here? Where are you taking her? Come on, Montague. You don't have to do this. Please, you know he beats her like a damn slave. Let her go, please," I pleaded, feeling the tension and angst building in my body.

His eyes widened. "Dis is nuh longer any of yuh concern, Miss Shai. Mi duh hope dat yuh ave a safe trip an dat yuh new life is filled wid blessings. Bless up."

Grabbing Umi by the arm, he pushed her into the back of the S.U.V. One of his handlers grabbed Jr. from her before hopping in the car, backing up, and speeding away.

Rylas ran down from the stairs, and Kenzo and Rocky

stood there motionless. I quickly tried to regroup and mask my feelings before collapsing to my knees.

"Why did y'all let them take her? Why?" I cried.

"I'm sorry, Shai. Chartreuse told us to protect you at all costs. She said nothing about your friend. That has nothing to do with us." Rocky said nonchalantly.

"She's my best friend," I yelled. "He's probably going to kill her. There's no telling what he may do to her." My stomach churned as the words left my mouth.

"Look, like I said, we were given orders to care for you. She said nothing about her. We've got to get going. It's getting late, and from what I see, that's about everything. Rocky will hitch your car to the back so you can go ahead and hop in. You are riding with us in the front, so grab whatever you are keeping with you, and let's go," Kenzo ordered.

Feeling helpless and like a failure, I hugged and said goodbye to Rylas before handing him the keys to turn into the front office. I then grabbed my purse and hopped in the truck.

Angry, hurt and sobbing the whole way to Aunt Trucee's house. I didn't know Kenzo from a can of paint, but that didn't stop me from using his big arms and shoulder for comfort and his shirt for a snot rag. I was inconsolable. I couldn't think of anything but what Umi must have been going through.

I kept telling her that I wouldn't let anyone get to her, but I couldn't protect her when she needed me the most. Thoughts of Montague crept in. True, he was gorgeous and seeing him hop out of that truck had sent shockwaves through my pelvis. A sensation I hadn't felt in a long time, but I couldn't think of that now.

My lust for him vanished the minute he put my friend in that truck. His looks, swag, and charm meant nothing compared to my worry for Umi. I hurt for her. I knew that if Lincoln had anything to do with it, she would pay for her betrayal. That thought alone brought me to my knees. I called her back-to-back for hours, but her phone went to voicemail every time. I finally fell asleep with my phone in my hand, Umi's picture glowing in the backlight.

After five hours on the road, we finally arrived at Aunt Trucee's house and she was right. This was certainly not where she had lived before.

"Shai, here we are," Rocky announced. "Chateau Chartreuse. Your aunt's house is bad as fuck, isn't it?" He bragged as we approached the huge gates attached to a twelve-foot wall surrounding the estate.

"Yes, it is. I almost can't believe my eyes. This looks like some shit from the movies. What in the fuck is Aunt Trucee into to afford a place like this?"

"That's not our business to tell. She'll advise you of everything you need to know once you enter. Your auntie runs a tight ship. You either get on board or get thrown off."

Chapter Eleven

"Thrown off? What the fuck does that mean?"

Ignoring my question, Rocky punched in a code, and the gates unlatched. He slowly drove the truck into the horseshoe-shaped driveway and stopped in front of the house.

"Go ahead and get out, lil mama. Your aunt rented a storage unit, and we've been instructed to place your things there. Of course, we'll leave your clothing and personal items at your request, but you need to show us what you'd like to take into the house with you."

I hopped out of the truck and ran to the back. There were six boxes I definitely needed. I placed a big X on all of them and instructed them to bring my clothes when they returned. Giving me the okay, they pulled off, and I ran to the front door.

Before I could ring the doorbell, it unlatched and swung open. My aunt stood there with open arms, and I ran straight into them. I didn't realize how much I needed a hug until I received one. I melted into her. Taking in all the love I could. It was something I'd never gotten from my own mother.

"Heeyyyy, Shug! It feels like I've been waiting forever. That was a long ride, huh? Bet you're tired...oh, where's your friend?"

"They took her, Aunt Trucee...her and the baby. Lincoln's uncle arrived just as we were leaving and made her get into the car. I didn't know what to do. In fact, I couldn't do anything. I thought Rocky and Kenzo would stop them, but they did nothing. They told me they had orders to protect me, not Umi," I whined.

"I'm sorry, baby, I really am but those are some of my best guys. I couldn't risk them getting into some shit on account of someone I don't know. Now you? Yes. I told them to burn that muthafucka down if they had to. Your friend, though...well, she's going to have to figure things out for herself."

"But Aunt Trucee, they're going to hurt her. I know they are."

"Didn't you tell me that you beat her man bloody? Do you really think he's going to do something to her?"

"He may not because he can't, but that doesn't mean his uncle won't. I don't know him, and I don't know what he's capable of." I admitted.

"And he doesn't know me or what I'm capable of either, Shug. I had my fellas look into this Montague character. He lays pretty low. Not too much on him. His operation seems small and tight. He doesn't make much noise, so I honestly think your friend will be fine. Enough of that...come on, let me show you to your wing."

"My wing? What do you mean my wing? Are you telling me I have a whole side to myself, Auntie? How many bedrooms are in this place?"

"Yes, you'll have your own wing. There are eleven bedrooms total," she said as we sashayed to the elevator. Ascending to the top, a handsome man greeted us and helped us step off the elevator.

"Shai, meet Teezy. He's my house manager and will assign you a concierge shortly. Now, follow me. Let me show you where you'll be staying."

My lashes fluttered as I looked around at the cathedral ceilings and the stunning chandelier before me. Tall statues were strategically placed at the beginning and end of the hallway. A Picasso painting behind a shadow box adorned the wall, and slick marble stretched beneath my feet. I felt as if I were standing in and on money.

"Aunt Trucee...how in the hell?"

"How in the hell what, baby?" She smiled.

"Come on now, don't be funny. You know what I'm asking. I remember you being at a halfway house. This is a long way from that. Please, I have to know because whatever you're doing, I want in."

"Unfortunately for you, my baby, I don't discuss how I gained my fortune. Even the people that work from me have no idea and I intend on keeping it that way. Just know, you won't have shit to worry about while you're here. I'll supply all your needs while you reside with me, but I will not, under any circumstances, share the inner workings of my business with you, nor will I allow you to work for me. I'm not hiring," she chuckled.

"But Aunt Trucee, I need a job. I like to pay my own way. You're doing enough by letting me crash here. I don't need you taking care of me like a child."

"Shai, stop. Let me do me. It's my pleasure to finally take care of you. Listen, I don't fuck with any of my family, and they don't fuck with me...not even my daughter. Your love for me has always been unconditional. Let me show you I can return that tenfold. Besides, Shai, you're the only one that calls to check on me, and you can't imagine what that does for my heart."

"I know, Auntie, but—"

Her voice filled with a combination of grief and sadness as she interrupted me. "There is no *but*. You are a good child, and you always have been. My sister and that piece-of-shit husband of hers forced you to grow up wayyy too fast...especially having to deal with their bullshit. So please, let me show you what it's like to live free. Without worries. Without fear."

I followed Aunt Trucee down the hall, my steps echoing against the marble floors. Every corner I turned revealed something more extravagant than the last. A gilded mirror here, a towering bookshelf there, overflowing with leather-bound volumes I couldn't begin to read. My eyes kept darting around, trying to take it all in. I felt like a child in a palace, and the magnitude of this place made me dizzy.

"Shug...you're going to have everything you need. Nothing is too small, nothing is too big. I want you comfortable," she said, her eyes twinkling with pride.

"I...Aunt Trucee...this is insane," I whispered, stepping inside. I ran my fingers over the smooth marble, marveling at the luxury I'd never imagined for myself.

"This is just the start, Baby girl," she said, leading me back out. "Now let me show you the rest of your wing."

We passed several more rooms. Each more beautiful than the last. A personal library with floor-to-ceiling shelves, a sunroom that overlooked the gardens, a private study with a desk that could have been plucked straight from a magazine. The attention to detail was overwhelming.

"And here," she said, stopping at the final door, "is your bedroom. Your sanctuary. Everything here is yours. Make it what you want. Feel free to move things, decorate, whatever you need to feel at home."

I opened the door slowly. The room was enormous, with cathedral ceilings and windows stretching from floor to ceiling. Natural light poured in, illuminating a plush king-size bed, a sitting area with velvet armchairs, and a balcony that overlooked the grounds. I stepped inside, feeling like I had stumbled into a dream.

She pointed to the right, "And this is your bathroom," Aunt Trucee said, opening a massive double door. The room was more like a spa than a personal bath. A free-standing tub the size of a small pool, double vanities with marble countertops, and a shower that could have fit a football team. Gold fixtures gleamed under recessed lighting. I could hardly breathe from the shock and awe.

"Shug, I know this is a lot," Aunt Trucee said softly. "But it's yours. You've earned some peace, some safety. You don't have to worry about a damn thing while you're here. Just live."

I sank onto the bed, letting the softness engulf me. I

wanted to believe her, to let go of the tension that had been clawing at my chest, but the image of Umi and baby Lincoln lingered in my mind. The house was beautiful, yes, but safety felt relative when someone I loved was in danger.

Chapter Twelve

A unt Trucee's voice broke through my thoughts. "Shug, your concierge will make sure your wing is stocked with anything you might need. I want you to feel at home, but I also want you to understand...you're under my protection now. Nothing gets past my gates without me knowing. Consider this a new chapter."

I nodded, trying to absorb it all. The opulence, the security, the promise of safety. It was overwhelming, but underneath it all, one thing gnawed at me: Umi. No matter how stunning this place was, I couldn't let myself relax fully until I knew my best friend was safe.

Aunt Trucee must have read my mind because she rested a reassuring hand on my shoulder. "Shug, I'll worry about everything else. You just focus on being you. You've already survived more than most people could imagine." A small smile crept across my face. The weight of the past few days was heavy but I felt like I could catch my wave here.

Aunt Trucee started in. "Shai, we are starting out with a monthly stipend of ten thousand dollars. It will be more than enough for you to do whatever you wish. If you want to save, save. If you want to spend, spend. The choice is yours. I've also purchased a new wardrobe for you. Everything is in your room: clothing, purses, undergarments. There's a full salon downstairs, with an in-house hairstylist and makeup artist. Just call for them, and they'll be there whenever you need."

"Auntie, I can't thank you enough, but you do know I don't plan to stay forever. I just want to build a new life here, find a job, and then I'm out of your hair."

"Shai, you've always been independent, and I'm proud of you. But while you're here, anything you wish for, just ask, and I'll make sure you get it. Your concierge will give you a full tour of the compound once you settle in. I know you're starving and tired, so someone can bring your dinner up here, or you can go down to the kitchen. The chef is on duty 24/7. Just use the phone on your nightstand, give them an hour's notice, and tell them what you want. You can eat in your room or in the kitchen. Your choice."

"I can't lie auntie, I'm hungry as hell. I want something light, like a sandwich, maybe. Can I just go down and fix something myself?"

"Sure, baby. You can do what you want. Chef Morocco doesn't like anyone in his kitchen, but there's also a fully stocked kitchen on the third level. You can cook there if you like."

"That works for me. I don't want to bother them this late, so I'll just make a sandwich myself."

"Suit yourself, Shug." As Aunt Trucee turned to leave,,. my phone rang. Umi's face glowed in the backlight.

"Wait, auntie. Umi's calling. I'm putting her on speaker so we can figure out what's going on."

I answered, "Hey girl, please tell me you're okay?"

"Shai, Wah gwaan? Dis is Montague. Mi wud like tuh speak wid yuh fi a likkle moment if mi may."

"I don't need to speak to you. All I need to know is whether my friend is safe."

"Dat answer depends on yuh, mi luv."

"I'm not your love! And what the fuck do you mean by that?"

"Listen, mi get straight tuh di point since yuh seem inna rush. Mi saw yuh, mi like yuh, and mi wan tuh get tuh kno yuh."

"Are you serious right now? You won't even tell me if my friend is okay, but you're trying to hook up with me? I swear, you island men are something else. What makes you think I'd give someone like you the time of day?"

Aunt Trucee moved away from the door and sat on the bed, listening closely.

"Eff yuh truly give a fuck bout yuh friend, di way dat yuh seh yuh duh, yuh will consider mi proposition."

"What exactly are you asking of me?" I spat.

"Mi asking dat in exchange fi har gud health, mi wud like fi yuh tuh spend two weeks in Jamaica wid mi. Umi will be safe an comfortable di entire time dat wi are away, an mi will mek sure of it, but efff yuh duh nuh agree, den dere is nuh telling wah will happen to har. Maybe shi will lose har hand, finger by finger jus' as Lincoln did. Or maybe har kneecaps will be shattered to pieces. Like mi seh, it is all up tuh yuh, mi luv. Eff a dirt, a dirt. Ya nuh test mi," he muttered in a strong patois accent.

Scoffing, I offered, "Two weeks in Jamaica with a known menace? I don't think so. There has to be another option or something else I can do."

"Nuh, dere is nuh. Dem mi terms an its final. Mi kno dat yuh may nuh kno mi or anyting bout mi, but di first ting dat yuh should kno is dat mi nuh negotiate. Mi will repeat miself one more time. Are yuh willing tuh save yuh friend's life?"

I looked at Aunt Trucee for guidance. She stood up, walked over, and grabbed the phone.

"Montague, is it?" she asked.

"Ya mon, it is. An who might yuh be?"

"My name is Chartreuse. You and I know some of the same people...you may want to ask around. There's only one Chartreuse. Anyhow, that's neither here nor there. My niece will accompany you, but I have terms as well."

"Gwaan," he chirped.

"You must allow me to send two of my men along," she said in a firm, serious tone.

"Auntie, what are you doing?" I whispered. "I don't want to go anywhere with that man."

Shushing me, she continued," I can assure you that they will stay out of your way but will be around if anything goes array. Also, you will not hurt a single hair on her head, or you will have me and mine to deal with. I have more money than God and I can make your whole little operation disappear in seconds with one phone call. I do not play about my family and if your only wish is to get to know her better, then there is no reason for you not to allow my men to accompany her. You must make provisions for them as well and make sure that they are welcomed without hostility. Their only purpose will be to protect her."

"Well, Miss Chartreuse. Mi cyan duh dat. Wi ave a deal. Mi cum tuh yuh wid pure intentions. Mi will nuh harm har in any way. Mi quite smitten by har. Shi beautiful, strong an intriguing. Mi nuh met many American women like dat, an mi wud simply like tuh share time an space wid har. On mi own turf is all."

"Like I said, ask about me." She voiced as she handed the phone back to me and sat back on the bed.

"Montague, may I please speak to Umi?" I pleaded.

"Yah mon, but unfortunately har an mi are nuh in di same place. Shi has bin dropped off, but mi will send word back tuh allow har tuh contact yuh. Now, Miss Shai, mi aware dat yuh jus' traveled, an yuh need yuh rest. Please sleep well cuz wi leave first ting inna di morrows."

"Wait, tomorrow morning? That's too soon. I just got here, now you are telling me that I have to drive back to Roseville."

"Nuh, luv. Dat will nuh be necessary. Mi ave dat all covered. Mi will send a car service tuh retrieve yuh an yuh handlers at 8:00 A.M. Dem will charter yuh tuh mi, an den wi will travel by private jet."

"Can you please hold on for one second?" Putting the phone on mute, I consulted Trucee again. "Should I give him your address now?"

"Absolutely not, I will have my driver take you to meet him. I don't need him knowing our whereabouts."

"Ok. Montague, please send me a location to meet you. My aunt is arranging a driver for us as well."

"Mi nuh need har tuh duh dat. Yuh weh abouts are

known. Did yuh forget? Yuh an Umi share locations, an mi called yuh from har phone. Mi cyan si dat yuh are at 3717 Indian Trail, Macon Georgia. Once again, be ready at eight."

He hung up and my stomach begin to churn. Panic had officially set in.

"Who in the fuck does he think he is to just roll up in my shit?" Trucee ranted. "How fucking dare he."

"Aunt Trucee, how dare *you*?!?! Why would you agree to send me off with that man. I don't know him. He's crazy from what Umi told me."

Letting out a big sigh, she offers, "Shai baby, you can't play with people like that. He would for sure have killed your friend. No questions asked. Women are often disposable to men like him. Now you seem to love this girl like a sister. Sometimes we must sacrifice and take one for the team. Consider this doing just that. Please don't worry though, I'm sending Rocky and Kenzo. You will have nothing to worry about. Like I told you earlier, they are two of my best guys and they will make sure he doesn't hurt a hair on your head. You have my word.

Chapter Thirteen

A unt Trucee exited the room, leaving me to my thoughts. When I first arrived, I was hungry as a hostage. Not anymore. My nerves were shot, and with each passing second, the tighter my chest felt. It was as if all the wind had been knocked out of me. Umi was my girl, and she meant the world to me. I was going to have to suck it up and do whatever it took to bring her back home safely to her son. I wasn't looking forward to this venture at all, but knowing I had handlers helped put my mind at ease.

Even though I wasn't hungry, I knew I needed to put something on my stomach. Woozy and shaking, I trekked to the kitchen on the third level to fix myself a bite to eat. After rambling around in the humongous pantry, I settled on an old faithful....a peanut butter and jelly sandwich and a banana.

Sitting at the huge dining room table, apprehension gnawed at me. I thought about the next two weeks of my life. I had gone from trying to figure out how to keep a roof over my head to being solely responsible for the safe return of my best friend. This was a fucking mess.

As I drifted off into lala land, I exhaled loudly, and the door leading to the kitchen swung open.

"There you are. Hello, my name is Bakari, and I have been assigned to you for the duration of your stay. I am your concierge, and it is a pleasure to meet you. Chartreuse speaks so highly of you, and she was right. You are stunningly gorgeous."

Pursing my lips, I forced a smiled. "Thank you so much. It's nice to know that I still look good, because I sure as hell don't feel like it."

Bakari was strikingly handsome, with dark skin, broad shoulders, and bold features. His face was as smooth as silk, and one could easily get lost in those grey eyes of his. Eve gene was in full effect. He wasn't dressed in a tuxedo or anything like the butlers seen on the big screen. He had on a simple Polo shirt and slacks that fit him like they were tailored specifically for his body, accentuating every inch of his muscular frame.

"Miss Shai, I know we just met, but would you like to

talk about it? As I said, I am at your beck and call for the duration of your stay. I am here to serve you in any capacity you require...that includes emotionally. We want to make sure you are as comfortable as possible. Your approval is vital. I want to impress you."

"Is that so? So, you mean that you will do anything I ask you to do?"

"Yes. Anything. Nothing is off limits." He lowered his eyes and stood there, waiting for a response. I didn't know what to say, but it was clear he wanted me to ask something. I obliged.

"Well, in that case, could you come up to my room and give me a massage? I'm nervous about tomorrow, and I could really use some strong hands. Also, could you get me some bud, strong bud? Please don't come back up here with any reggie. I don't smoke a lot but when I do, I only fuck with straight gas."

"Yes, to both. Give me about twenty minutes, and I will deliver it to your room. I'll let you partake first, then I'll come back and administer your massage. How does that sound?"

"That sounds nice, Bakari. Thank you. I'm going to head back to my room, bathe, and I'll be waiting for you."

"See you soon," he muttered as he exited the kitchen.

I trekked back to my bedroom, undressed, and made my way to the bathroom. While drawing my bath, my phone rang, displaying an unknown number. I answered, "Umi, is that you?"

In a low voice, she whispered, "Yes, Boo, it's me."

"Oh my God. Are you okay? Did that man hurt you?"

"No. Well, not yet anyway. I'm okay physically, but mentally? I'm fucked up. I don't know where I am, Shai. Nor do I know where my baby is. He told me I would remain here for a while but promised not to harm me as long as you held up your end of the bargain. What did you two work out, Shai? What does he want from you?"

"He wants me to spend two weeks with him in Jamaica. He says he wants to get to know me better. I don't know why, but I'll do whatever it takes to get you back home safely to Jr."

"So he did all of this just to get you alone with him? This seems pretty extreme. Even for his ass."

"I agree. I'm scared as hell. I've never been out of the country, let alone with a complete stranger. What else can you tell me about Montague?"

"Truthfully, not much. Lincoln doesn't talk about his business like that with me. I only know what I've heard and a little of what I've seen. He always has a couple of bad bitches around him. He seems levelheaded as long as he isn't crossed. Shai, just please don't be yourself with him."

"What the fuck does that mean, Umi? Don't be me?"

"No. Just don't be sassy like you are. You know how

you like to talk shit and get the last word. I don't know how well that will work out for us. Basically, just be on your best behavior."

"Umi, I'm not a child. I know what's on the line. I'll do my best to be kind to him, but I don't know how he expects me to respect him when he basically blackmailed me into going away with him. He threatened to harm you if I didn't. I can't respect that. In my opinion, he's a piece of shit, but I promise not to let him know that."

"Thank you for looking out for me. I know this is a big ask from anyone, and the fact that you agreed to do this says a lot. I feel like this is all my fault."

"Why, Umi? I'm the one who got us into this. I let my temper get the best of me. If I'd stayed calm, you wouldn't be there," I admitted.

"No, it's my fault. I should have left Lincoln a long time ago. If I had, we wouldn't be in this situation. You've been telling me forever to get away from his no-good ass, and I kept running back like a damn fool. Seriously, I'm sorry. I've got to go now, Shai. I love you, and I hope to see you soon."

"Keep your head up, Umi. I love you too."

The phone disconnected. Placing it on the counter, I slid into the bathtub. Shortly after, there was a light tapping at my door.

"Miss Shai, may I enter?" Bakari asked. "I have your goodies."

"Yes, come in. I'm still in the tub, but you can just put them on the nightstand. If you come back in about thirty minutes, I should be done bathing and ready for you."

"No problem, Miss Shai. I've put your massage oil, lotions, and towels in their warmers. Once I arrive, we can get started. You should be good and high by then."

"I sure as fuck hope so. See you in thirty."

I hopped out of the tub, dried off, and entered the closet to find something to wear after my massage. I was looking forward to this. "Wound up" didn't even begin to describe how tight my body was. Hopefully, Bakari could help ease some of this tension in my shoulders. Now that I thought about it, smoking might be a bad idea. I became super horny when I smoked, and I was sure I'd be tempted to fuck on this man I'd just met if I got too buzzed. Maybe I should make him taste this pussy for me. Hell, he was the one who said he would do whatever I asked. I should put that to the test.

Chapter Fourteen

Sitting outside on the balcony, I fired up my blunt, took a deep drag, and exhaled, watching the smoke curl and twist into the night air. I'd never been a heavy smoker. Three or four puffs was usually enough for me, but tonight, I needed it to steady my nerves. Jamaica. A strange man. Two weeks. Alone. The thought should have terrified me entirely but instead, a flicker of curiosity sat deep inside.

Montague wanting me didn't shock me. On a different day, under different circumstances, I would have wanted him too. I could still feel the heat of his stare when he was at my apartment but that was neither the time nor the place to explore those feelings. Especially with what was going on. I really hoped he wasn't on any dumb shit because I wasn't an easy win. I wouldn't let anything be taken from me that I didn't want to give.

The sensation of my fingertips burning pulled me back. I'd smoked the blunt down to the end without realizing it. My body was buzzing, almost vibrating, and my face was numb. A hand on my shoulder made me jump out of my skin.

"I'm so sorry to startle you, Miss Shai. I've been calling your name for five minutes. I thought you had earbuds in," Bakari said, his voice low and smooth.

"Bakari, there is no need to apologize... I was zoned out and didn't hear shit. Not because of headphones, because I'm higher than a full cart of groceries at Publix," I said, laughing. "My lips are tingling, my face is numb... what in the fuck kind of weed is this?"

"The best of the best. Straight from your aunt's stash," he replied, a small smirk in his tone.

"Aunt Trucee is a G if she's smoking this shit on the regular and still able to function. Bakari, don't laugh but I'm scared to stand. My legs feel like Jello. I think I smoked way too much," I admitted. My nerves were making my chest tight.

"No worries. I'll carry you to the table."

"Wait," I said, glancing at the massage table. "You set this up without me knowing? Oh hell no. I don't ever want any more of this shit...numb, deaf, and buzzing...this is crazy."

"Not just the table. Look around. I've lit candles, set up the diffuser, water on ice and the music is ready. Relax. I've got you Miss Shai."

"Drop the formalities," I chirped, swinging my arms around his neck. "You're about to see me damn near naked."

He laughed softly and carried me to the table, setting me down with surprising gentleness.

"Undress to your comfort and slide under the sheet," he instructed. "I'll return in a few minutes, then we'll begin."

Alone, I hurriedly stripped to my panties and slid beneath the sheet. My body tingled with anticipation, each nerve alive. It had been so long since someone like Bakari had touched me, and just thinking about it sent shivers across my skin.

A soft knock at the door pulled me from my thoughts. He was back. My heart thumped as every inch of me tightened in expectation. I was facedown with my head resting on the cushion. The warmed sheet he'd left for me was draped over my body. I waited patiently...every sense aware of his presence.

"Okay, Shai. Before we get started, I need you to advise me on your pressure preference."

"That's easy. I prefer Swedish, and I'll let you know when you can go a little deeper," I giggled, as the word *deeper* rolled off my tongue.

"Alright, Swedish it is. Do you prefer lotion or oil?"

"Bakari, shit, I don't know. You can mix them if you want. I really don't give a damn. Just get over here and start rubbing. I need this," I said, almost pleading.

Seconds later, he slid the covers back. Immediately, I felt the slick warmth of oil and lotion against my skin. His strong hands pressed into my shoulders. Lord, it felt amazing. Each stroke was deliberate, long and even, melting away the tension in my muscles. His hands were strong, yet gentle enough not to hurt...just perfect.

"Am I doing okay, Shai? You'll tell me if I hurt you, won't you?"

"You're doing fine. And yes, I'll tell you if it gets uncomfortable. Right now, don't stop. It feels incredible," I mumbled.

With every glide of his hands across my back, my body relaxed and a rush of warmth spread through me. The tension I'd been carrying for hours began to dissolve, replaced with a fluttering, almost electric sensation. I could feel my heart beating faster, my muscles unwinding, and a tingling warmth spreading from my shoulders, down my spine and to my pussy. I buried my face in the headrest, trying to hide the intensity of the sensations that were washing over me.

The horniness was hitting a code red level and nothing was going to stop it. As his fingertips danced across my skin, my pussy began to thump. It developed its own heartbeat. I wanted him so badly to slip a finger or two inside my snatch. Good thing I was turned away from him. Otherwise, I wouldn't have been able to hide the glimmers of pleasure etched across my face.

"Shai, I'm about to remove the cover so I can reach your thighs and legs. I've turned on the heat to make sure you're comfortable before I begin."

"Bakari... you don't have to tell me. Just do it, shit." I replied, my voice low and breathy.

He pulled back the covers, a slight stutter in his tone. "Umm...umm."

I reached beneath me and realize that the sheet below me was completely soaked, and I wanted to melt into the table.

"Oh my goodness, Bakari. I am so sorry and ashamed," I giggled. "Wait. Let me not lie because I'm really not sorry, but it sounded like the right thing to say. If I'm being totally honest with you. Weed makes me extremely horny and there isn't shit I can do about it."

"Please don't get it mistaken, Shai, it doesn't bother me at all. I'm just a little surprised. I heard you moaning but I wasn't expecting a full puddle beneath you. If you got this hot and bothered from me rubbing your back and shoulders, what are you going to do when I get down to the lower region of your body?"

"I don't know Bakari. I guess we are just going to have to see."

I heard him squeezing more liquid into his hands. He started with pressure on the top of my ass and worked his way down to my thighs. As he stroked my thigh, his thumb grazed my pussy lips, sending shivers down my spine. Body still vibrating, my pussy began to leak even more.

Fuck this...

"Bakari? I purred.

"Yes, Shai."

"Are you aware that your thumb just grazed my pussy?"

"No, I wasn't aware. I am so sorry. Would you like me to stop?"

"No need to apologize and no, I would not like you to stop. I want you to do it again."

"I beg your pardon."

"You heard me, I didn't stutter. I want you to do it again. I want you to slide my panties to the side and slide your finger in my pussy and finger fuck me until I tell you to stop."

"Are you sure that is what you want?"

"I am positive. You said whatever I ask, you will do. Well get to doing."

"Okay, well if you insist. His hands trailed up my thighs again. He reached my panties and slid them to the side. I felt a slight breeze on my pussy lips. Instead of sliding his fingers in my pussy, his fingers found my clit. He circled it with just the right amount of pressure, and I moaned from the sensation.

"Mmmmhmmm, yes, Bakari. That's it. Now that's what the fuck I'm talking about. Please me. Make me cum."

"You like that Shai?"

"Yes, I love it. My pussy is jealous. Fingers please!"

"Oh, they are coming. Be patient, Sweetness. I'm going to take really good care of you, I promise. By the time I'm finished, you will think that you've taken a sedative. You're going to sleep good tonight."

He increased the pressure and started to circle faster. I could feel the warmth of his body and smell the aroma of his cologne as he stood next to the table. Suddenly, he slid one finger into my honey pot, then two, all while using his thumb to circle my clit. My hips begin to grind to meet his fingers. "My God it feels so good," I cried out.

He used his other hand to massage my other thigh, and he had all my senses wide open. I felt myself getting closer. I didn't want to cum, so I clamped my thighs shut, trapping his hand.

"Wait, let me turn over." I flipped my body over to face him. My big supple breast spread across my chest, and I pointed to them. He understood the assignment. He knelt down, slowly taking my pebbled nipples into his mouth. First kissing one before sliding his mouth over to the next. His tongue was warm and thick. He looked up at me intensely with those grey eyes and for a split second, I envisioned having children with those same beautiful eyes. He felt so good. His fingers felt phenomenal stroking the walls of my pussy and my hips were once again grinding to fuck them.

"Yes, Bakari. Please don't stop. I need more."

"Do you? Because I have more to give."

"Oh, you do? Well, don't talk about it be about it. Get to giving."

"Say less," he mumbled with a mouth full of titties. He reached beneath the table, pulled out a condom and slid out of his clothes. Simultaneously, I pulled off my panties and tossed them to the floor.

"May I taste you first?"

"Bakari, don't ask me no stupid shit like that. Of course you can." I said, basically drooling at the sight of his long, thick, chocolate dick that was now standing at full attention.

Spreading my legs, he buried his face into my pussy and licked me like his life depended on it. As horny as I was, it did. He slow fucked me with his tongue and I whimpered with every lick.

"Fuck, Bakari. Your mouth is everything. Ooooh yes. That's it. Suck that pussy."

"Your pussy taste so good Shai. So good." He moaned as he slurped and circled my clit with his tongue before sliding his fingers deep inside. I was seconds away from cumming and I desperately attempted to hold back but I failed. Edging was my shit, however, he had a mean tongue game, and I couldn't stop my body from betraying me.

While sucking my pussy, his eyes crept to meet mine. He was beautiful. It was such a beautiful sight to see a man who wanted to do nothing more than please me. He genuinely looked happy to have my pussy in his mouth. Grabbing his head, I fucked his face until I creamed so hard that the evidence of my pleasure was smeared all across his nose. He continued to lick as my body shuddered and bucked.

Lifting his head up by his chin, I looked into his eyes.

"Bakari, I think it's time for some dick. I don't want to wait another second. I need that big ass dick deep into my pussy. This weed has me gone and I want to feel every single inch of it. Every centimeter."

He ripped the package open with his teeth. I watched as he rolled the Magnum down on his ten-inch dick and my eyes widened. Suddenly I became super aware that this thick, chocolate veiny monster of a tool was about to be deep into my pussy, and I asked for it. I should have been scared because he was huge, but the Sagittarius in me and the weed wouldn't let me give a fuck.

Climbing onto the table, he nestled between my thighs and circled his dick around the opening of my pussy. Teasing me and taunting me with his swollen head. I don't play that teasing shit. I am the only one that's allowed to tease me. Impatiently, I reached down, grabbed it and guided it into my snatch.

"Hey, I'm just a tool, use me in whatever way that you like." he groaned in a deep sexy voice. He knew that he was huge, and I appreciated him for relinquishing all control. Grabbing him by the waist, I pulled him towards me and slowly rocked and fucked him until my tight pussy was able to take all of him.

He started to stroke my pussy. Our bodies slapping harder than a head on collision. He moaned in my ear while grabbing the bottom of my ass. Lifting me in the air while bringing my pussy to meet his dick. His big hands were in full control and his stroke game was on point. Sweat beaded on us both as he dug deeper into my pussy. Over and over, he ravished me. I couldn't believe I was giving my body up so freely to a perfect stranger, but I couldn't find a fuck to give.

He was giving me everything that I needed and wanted in that moment, and I had no regrets. Bakari and I fucked well into the night. Moving from that little ass massage table to my bed. We fucked in every position manageable. Nothing was off limits but my ass. I had to save something for my future husband.

It was 4:00 A.M. before he escaped my room. Bakari had given me enough dick and feels to last me another month. He wore me out. With only a few hours before I was set to leave for Jamaica with Montague, I climbed back into my bed, grabbed my pillow and put myself in a self-induced coma for the next couple of hours.

Chapter Sixteen

A t 6:00 A.M., my alarm blared, scaring the bejesus out of me. I was still high as Georgia pine and nowhere near in my right mind. Five minutes passed before I realized it wasn't a song playing in my dreams but my phone alerting me that it was go time.

I was exhausted, but I knew I needed to get up and get my shit together. Dragging myself out of bed, I stumbled toward the closet to pack my things and get ready to play super save-a-hoe for the next two weeks. With only two hours of sleep, I was running on fumes. I needed something to wake me up, and fast. I wanted to be as alert as possible.

A line of cocaine probably would've been best, but since I don't partake, coffee would have to do. I placed a call to Bakari to bring me a cup of joe. That was the least he could do, being that he fucked the lining out of my cock last night. I asked for it, but that wasn't the point.

I called the butler's quarters. Bakari answered.

"Hello, Bakari, and good morning to you."

"Good morning, Shai. What can I do for you?"

"A couple of things, actually. I need a pot...not a cup, but a pot...of coffee. And would you mind coming to my room to help me pack? I don't have much time, and I need some assistance."

"Sure thing, I'll be right up. Is there anything else that you need?"

"Yes, find a way to get me out of this shit I've gotten myself into."

"I'm sorry, Sweetness, but unfortunately, I can't do anything about that. However, coffee and packing I can do." I could hear the smile in his voice. "Shai, I'll be up there in a minute."

As I made my way back to the closet to start packing my luggage, Aunt Trucee sauntered into my room and sat on the bed.

"Sweet Dove, are you ready to do this?"

"Not at all, Aunt Trucee, but I don't have a choice. I wouldn't be able to sleep at night if I let something happen to Umi."

"I have to tell you, you've got a big set of balls on you, girl. I'm proud to call you my family, because I know plenty of bitches that would've said hell no to him."

"I don't do my friends or family like that. I will always have their best interest at heart, Auntie."

"You must have gotten that from me, because you sure as hell didn't get it from my sister."

"You sure know what to say, Auntie. My mama don't give a shit about anyone but herself. Anyway, I don't want to talk about her. I want to know where the hell you got that weed from. Bakari brought me some last night, and it put me on my ass. I was on cloud 9,742."

Chuckling, she muttered, "Girl, I only smoke that premium shit. What I smoke isn't for rookies. I take it you are a rookie, niece?"

"And is...and I'm not ashamed. But I plan on being high for the next two weeks. I want to be in the clouds as much as possible."

"I understand that baby girl. Listen, I've got something for you."

She double-clapped her hands, and the door opened. A man walked in with a small duffel bag.

"Now, here is ten thousand dollars in cash and a credit card for you to use at your discretion. This should be enough to last you these two weeks. Keep this money to your damn self."

"Oh, Auntie, I plan on it."

"You better, because he's the one that wanted you, so all your expenses should be provided for by him. This is for emergencies only. There's also an international cell phone in the bottom of that bag along with a tracking device. I'll know where you are every second of the day.

"If shit starts to go left, or if you start to get a bad feeling about anything, you'll have Kenzo and Rocky to call. I'm doing this because they won't be able to be in every room you're in, but they'll be close. Their numbers are already stored as well as mine. If you have any problems and I do mean any, they will handle it. That's what they do. Handle shit."

"Auntie, I still don't know what you do to be able to pull all of this off. Are you going to tell me, or are you going to keep me in the dark forever?"

"No, not forever, just until you get back. I don't want you distracted by anything. There are lots of things I have to share with you, and once I do, it'll all make sense. What I will tell you is that I don't get fucked with. And if Montague knows what's good for him, he won't make me pull his hoe card and prove why I don't get touched. Nothing will stop me from getting to him and his family if anything happens to you." Tightening her lips, she gritted, "I will mow all those bitches down. Mama, daddy, aunts, uncles, grandparents, and kids. I don't give a fuck when it comes to mine."

"Damn, Auntie, fuck them kids, huh," I chuckled. Your ass sound like Scarface or somebody."

"I'm not far from it, but the difference between him and me is I will never get caught like that. Never."

Bakari entered the room with my pot of coffee. Aunt Trucee cracked a smile at him and sashayed to the door. Turning around, she muttered, "Come see me before you walk out that door. I need my hugs and kisses."

"Will do, Auntie."

Bakari set the pot and cup of coffee on the nightstand. I ran over to it like a crackhead. I needed a quick pick-me-up.

"Bakari, let's get to it."

"I tell you what, Shai. I know you've got to be tired." His eyes met mine, and we both cracked a smile.

"Yes, I'm tired. Exhausted...and you know this."

"Yes, I know. So, I want you to grab a chair while I go through the closet. You point, and I'll pack."

Chapter Seventeen

"Ooohhh, I hate this shit. I really do not want to go. Fuuuck!" I screamed.

"Everything is going to be okay, Shai. You've got two of the coldest muthafuckas on this side of the Mississippi going with you. Nothing is going to happen. Trust me." Bakari offered.

Whispering, I asked, "Bakari, can you tell me what my aunt is into? Is it drugs? Is she a pimp or madam or something?"

"Ummmm, did you ask her?" he shot back.

"I did, and she said she'll tell me when I get back. But I'm nosey as hell, and I don't want to wait. Why won't anyone tell me anything around here?"

"Because we all have loyalty to her, and it's not our business to tell. We just work here. We don't ask many questions. Besides, what Chartreuse wants you to know, Chartreuse will tell you."

"Whatever. See, now I'm pissed. I gave you some of this good pussy. As a matter of fact, I gave you all the pussy I had. That should mean something."

"It does, but I've only known you for a day. I've known her for years. Besides, you asked for the dick. I didn't offer," he said with a smirk.

"Touche," I mumbled. "Now, let's go ahead and get this over with."

Bakari seemed to be a master at everything. My clothes were packed and ready to go in less than ten minutes. Next, he grabbed my beauty case, carefully tucking away my toiletries and tools. I let him handle it all and slipped into the shower, hoping the hot water, along with the coffee, would give me a much-needed burst of energy. I thought about doing my makeup but quickly decided against it. I was not trying to impress anyone. He would get the all-natural me.

When I stepped back into my room, a full spread of breakfast was waiting.

I'd never been treated like this before. I could get used to it, but because of this Jamaican menace, I knew I wouldn't have the chance.

I ate slowly, savoring every bite. I had no idea how I'd be treated once I left this mansion, so at least I'd be able to say I had one last great meal before I went. My time was running short, and my stomach began to twist with nerves. I asked Bakari if there were any nausea pills in the house...and maybe a sedative. Flying always rattled me, and normally my doctor prescribed something before takeoff. With this trip happening so suddenly, I hadn't had the chance to ask my doctor for anything.

Bakari disappeared, then returned with everything I'd asked for.

I swallowed both pills and sat waiting for the driver. In the meantime, I joined Aunt Trucee in her courtyard, admiring the lush flowers and careful landscaping. The place sparkled, and so did she. She seemed happier than the last time I saw her. She was lighter. She was freer. She had people to take care of her every need now.

I wanted to stay, to be one of those people for her. But my actions landed me in this situation, and it was on me to fix it. If all went well, I'd return and give her the love Cassie never would. She deserved that and so much more.

"Shai, your ride just arrived at the gate. I think it's time for you to go," Bakari called from inside.

Aunt Trucee and I stood at the same time, exchanging a heavy look.

"Go on, baby. I'll walk you and the fellas out to the car. I'll also get the tag number," she said.

"Okay," I muttered, heading back inside. Bakari and

Teezy stood by the door holding my bags. As I approached, Aunt Trucee pulled me into a tight hug, her hand cupping the back of my neck. She whispered, "Take care of yourself, and watch your back. I need you to come back to me. We've got too much catching up to do, Lovebug."

"Okay, Auntie. I love you. And thank you...for everything."

She smiled warmly as Bakari opened the door, gesturing for me to step out first. Kenzo and Rocky followed close behind. A sleek black Escalade rolled to the front, and a man in a tailored black suit stepped from the driver's side, circling around to open the passenger door.

"Good morning, Miss Shai. I'm Tabby, one of Montague's drivers. I've been sent to retrieve you and take you, along with your handlers, to him."

"They're not my handlers. They're my cousins," I shot back, turning to wink at Aunt Trucee.

Tabby continued, unfazed. "Miss Chartreuse, Montague wanted me to deliver you a message before your niece departs. He asked me to assure you there is no need to worry. She will return safe and sound."

He handed her a slip of paper. "Here are the numbers where she may be reached in case her phone doesn't get service on the island. His personal number is on top, and the other belongs to a secondary phone."

Aunt Trucee snatched the paper with a small nod.

"Well, that was very kind of him. Please tell him I said thank you."

"Will do, ma'am."

"Auntie, I'll call you once I arrive. I'm sure Kenzo and Rocky will too. I love you and I'll see you in two weeks."

Tabby took my bags from Bakari and loaded them into the trunk. Bakari gave me one last look and a sly wink before heading back into the house. Kenzo and Rocky tossed in their own bags as I slid into the back seat. I waved to Aunt Trucee, then let out a long breath. Grabbing Kenzo's arm, I used it as a personal pillow.

Still exhausted, I was asleep before we even cleared the driveway.

Chapter Eighteen

I was jolted out of my sleep when the vehicle stopped in front of a small private airport. Tabby turned to us and said this was our stop.

"There isn't any clearance you need to go through. Just walk straight in, and Montague will meet you and give you all instructions from there."

We hopped out of the car, and the boys went straight to the back for the luggage. I stretched and looked around before asking Tabby how long we'd been traveling.

"Only about an hour. You're here now, and he's inside waiting for you. Please, ma'am. Go ahead and walk inside. We'll take care of your luggage."

As I sauntered toward the building; a heaviness sat in my chest and knots rippled through my stomach. As I approached the door, Montague snatched it open. I was startled by his strong presence.

"Shai, wah gwaan?" Montague asked as he raised a beautiful bouquet of red roses with baby's breath and greenery sprinkled throughout. "Dem fi yuh."

"Hello, Montague and thank you so much. These are beautiful. How are you?"

"Irie. Betta now dat yuh are here."

"Umm... I don't want to insult you, but I don't speak Jamaican."

"Mi neitha. Mi speak English jus' like yuh."

"The hell you say. That's not any English I've heard."

"It's called Patois. Jus' English with Jamaican slang. Yuh nuh undastan?"

"I can understand some of what you say, but your accent is much thicker than Lincoln's."

"Ya mon. Lincoln's been in di States longer den mi, suh him more Americanized. Mi will duh mi best tuh mek sure yuh undastan."

"Okay, I appreciate that. Now, what part of Jamaica are we going to? Is it rough?"

"Ya mon, but yuh need nuh worry bout dat. Yuh are wid me. Mi nuh fucks wid."

"Ummm, I don't quite—"

"Mi sorry, Shai. Dat means as long as yuh are wid me, nuhbody will fuck wid yuh. Truss."

"Ohhh, okay. I get it now."

"Besides, yuh ave yuh bodyguards an mi ave mine. Shai, relax. Yuh look suh nervous. As mi seh, mi nuh trying tuh harm yuh in any way. Jus' be calm. Yuh are gud. Mi swear."

"Trust me, I'm trying. But it's hard. I've got a lot working against me, and my mind is all over the place. I hate planes, I'm on my way to an island with a complete stranger I know nothing about, and on top of that, I don't know where my best friend is or how she's doing. That's what has me worried."

He shot me a peculiar look as I walked over to the coffee stand, trying to wake myself up with another hit of caffeine.

"As mi seh, Shai, mi nuh a guh tuh duh anything tuh harm yuh. Nuh need tuh worry...yuh will be fine. Di plane will be flown by Neeko. Him bin mi pilot fi years, an we've neva had a mishap. Him one of di safest people mi kno. Him mek sure dis plane in pristine condition before every takeoff. An last but not least, Umi is fine. Shi will remain fine as long as yuh are fine. Yuh undastan mi?"

"I do," I replied as we slowly walked toward the plane.

"Good. Now it's time tuh guh. Yuh bodyguards are already settled inside, suh now it's yuh turn." He grabbed my hand and helped me up the stairs.

Inside, my eyes landed on Kenzo and Rocky, who were

already making themselves right at home. They were kicked back, drinking mimosas, laughing, talking, and eating Porterhouse steak and eggs like they were already on vacation. They were supposed to be here for me, but it looked like they were more focused on filling their stomachs. They barely glanced up to wave before going back to their plates. I rolled my eyes. How dare they act like shit was sweet?

"Mi si yuh men are getting comfortable," Montague said. "Look at dere faces. Luk how relaxed dem are. Dat how mi need yuh tuh be. Yuh nuh seem dis uptight back at yuh apartments."

"I wasn't uptight then. Low key, I was happy because I thought my life was changing for the better. But this isn't the better I'd imagined. This is a whole different ballgame. Anyway, where are our seats?"

"Right dis way, Shai."

We weaved through a narrow walkway, and then my breath caught in my throat. This wasn't just a plane. It was a damn palace in the sky.

The cabin stretched long and wide, gleaming like something out of a billionaire's magazine. Cream-colored leather seats lined the walls, so soft they looked like they'd swallow you whole. A crystal chandelier, yes, a chandelier hung low in the center.

A full kitchen sat tucked off to the side, not the kind

with a microwave and hot plate, but with shiny stainless-steel appliances, gold-trimmed cabinets, and bottles of top-shelf liquor displayed like artwork. Beyond that, a bedroom door stood open just enough for me to glimpse a king-sized bed dressed in silk sheets, pillows stacked high, and a fur throw tossed across like it was nothing.

The bathroom? Montague casually mentioned it had both a shower and a garden tub. On a plane!! My broke ass had barely flown coach before, and here I was staring at a damn flying penthouse.

A buttery leather sectional wrapped around the lounge area, with throw pillows that probably cost more than my entire wardrobe. A glass-topped coffee table held a vase of fresh roses that looked like they'd just been plucked from the bush. Every detail screamed money...clean, sharp, untouchable money.

Montague moved through it like it was everyday life. Me? I was trying hard not to let my jaw hit the imported carpet.

"Shai, cum sit next tuh mi. Mi cyan tell yuh a likkle stressed. Wud yuh like sumting tuh eat? Maybe a drink tuh tek di edge off?"

"Don't you think it's a little early for alcohol?"

"Nuh at all, luv. Especially if yuh dis nervous and wi haven't even taken off."

"I took a couple Valium before I left the house, but

they aren't as strong as I'd hoped. I feel like I'm about to have a full-blown panic attack."

"Mi sorry, Shai. Mi ave ganja. Mi will ave one of mi men roll up. Yuh cyan step off di plane, hit it a few times, an feel better."

He snapped his fingers, and within minutes a blunt was being handed to me and I was being escorted off the plane by a man he introduced as Kirk.

I took three deep pulls before climbing back on board. Montague was lounging on the leather couch when I returned.

"Ahhh, dat was quick. Yuh gud now?"

"Yes, I'm good. Let's get this show on the road. The quicker we start, the quicker I can get back to my new life."

I noticed he was eating fruit and sipping coconut water while everyone else enjoyed steak and eggs. "I see your men and mine are enjoying a hearty breakfast. Why aren't you eating what they're eating? Those steaks look good as hell."

"Well, dats simple. Mi nuh eat meat or dairy, nor duh mi put poison in mi bady. Nuh bad stuff.. Mi vegan. But mi had di chef prepare steak and eggs fi yuh as well. Please...sit."

Within seconds, the flight attendant appeared with a covered tray. She lifted the cloche to reveal a perfectly cooked steak, eggs, fresh fruit, and a glass of fresh orange juice.

"Montague, thank you, but I ate before we came. I'm not hungry."

"It's fine, luv. Nuh big deal. Mi will ave dem tek it back. But truss mi...yuh jus' smoked some of di best ganja mi have. In twenty minutes, yuh will be starving." He chuckled, as he brushed a strand of hair from my face. "Now buckle yuh seatbelt. Wi bout tuh tek off. Once wi in di air, yuh cyan loosen up. It's a short flight an will be ova in nuh time. In di meantime, tell mi a likkle bout yuhself. Mi attempted tuh probe Umi bout yuh, but as yuh cyan guess, shi nuh in di talking mood. Betta tuh hear it from di horse's mout anyhow."

"There isn't much to tell. I'm just a normal chick, trying to make it like everybody else. No kids, no job, no place to call my own. Not yet anyway. Just a bunch of unpaid bills and mental issues." I smirked at my own words.

"Violent temper, eh? Is dat wah yuh mean by mental issues, or sumting else?"

"That's exactly what I mean," I shot back.

"Mi knew full well wah yuh meant. Di hurting yuh put on mi nefyu was di wuk of a mad man. Or in yuh case, a mad uhman. Truth is, eff dat mek yuh mental, den mi must be mental too. Mi nuh monster, though. Mi only touch dem dat need tuh be touched."

"Well, while you were busy touching people, Montague, maybe you should've touched Lincoln. Taught him to be a better man. If that's even possible. You may not be a monster, but he sure the fuck is."

"And yuh had tuh duh sumting bout dat, right?" he challenged.

"I was tired of watching him beat her for nothing. I saw it with my own eyes. He's an evil man," I said as the plane began to lift off. "I have a question for you. How do you think Lincoln is going to feel about you dealing with me? Isn't he going to be pissed? After all, Umi said I fucked him up pretty bad."

"Whateva mi duh is mi business. Lincoln is family yea, but mi will neva allow any oddah man on dis earth run mi. Mi duh wah mi wan an mi nuh care who nuh like it. Wah him gunna duh? Besides, him probably had dat coming. Him has a way of pissing people off. Dat's why him mama sent him tuh di states in di first place."

Chapter Nineteen

I looked over at Rocky and Kenzo, needing a familiar shoulder to lean on, but thought better of it. I wasn't sure how Montague would react to me leaning on another man for comfort. True, he wasn't my man, but Umi warned me he wasn't one to be fucked with. I took heed and stayed in my seat, quiet, and praying. I closed my eyes, leaned back, and took deep breaths. The weed was definitely helping.

Once we were airborne, Montague reached over, unbuckled my seatbelt, and slid his hand around mine with an ease that felt far too natural.

"Follow mi," he said smoothly, his voice deep and calm, leaving no room for argument.

He guided me to the rear of the plane and opened a door, revealing the bedroom.

"Listen," I said quickly, my nerves jumping, "I'm not trying to get thrown off this plane or no shit like that, but if you think I'm about to fuck you, then you've got life fucked up."

He tilted his head and studied me with amused eyes before letting out a rich, hearty laugh that rolled through the room.

"Likkle girl, yuh are fire. Too spicy. Yuh will fit right in, in Jamaica." He shook his head, still grinning. "Nuh, mi nuh expect yuh tuh fuck mi...as yuh suh eloquently put it. Mi jus' wan privacy, tuh get tuh kno yuh a likkle betta. Yuh men are right outside, suh relax. Mi told yuh already, mi nuh here tuh harm yuh. But mi duh wan yuh honesty. Tell mi, Shai... why yuh suh worried? Wah story dem people feed yuh bout mi?"

"Why do you assume I was told anything?" I shot back. "You're holding my friend hostage in return for my cooperation. You separated her from her baby and hid her God knows where. You stopped her from starting a new life alongside me. That's enough to think ill of you. And I already have trust issues when it comes to men. From my experience, they can rarely be trusted. You let your guard down, and they fuck you over. So yeah, my experience tells me my feelings are valid."

Montague leaned forward slightly, his gaze burning into me, his lips twitching into a faint smile.

"Yuh tink yuh got mi all figured out. An maybe yuh half right. Mi kno trust is rare. But mi nuh move sloppy. Mi nuh move cruel. Mi only duh wah mi muss tuh survive, an mi always tek care of who mi claim. Give mi time, an yuh will si mi nuh di monsta yuh tink. Yuh might even like wah yuh find."

His voice was low, smooth as silk, and the way he said "like wah yuh find" made my pussy jump even though I tried to shake it off.

He patted the bed beside him. "Now, are yuh a guh stand dere looking beautiful an defiant, or sit next tuh mi an talk?"

He didn't wait for me to answer, just reached out and gently tugged me down. His touch wasn't rough...it was confident, like he knew I wouldn't pull away.

"Shai, ave yuh eva been tuh Jamaica before?"

"No, but I've always wanted to go. Before I lost my job, I worked nonstop and never had time to vacation. Always chasing the bag. Then, once I lost my job, I had all the time in the world but no money. Funny how life works."

"Suh, di reason yuh moved in wid yuh aunt is because yuh ran out of money?"

I blew out a breath. "Precisely, Montague. I couldn't find work, and I'd drained my savings trying to keep my head above water. My ex decided he was done and left without warning. Walked out, left me with the bills, left me to fend for myself. Another reason why I don't trust men. Y'all are too damn fickle. Men love to say women are complex, but I disagree. Men are way more complex than we are. We don't require much. At least I don't. Love me, date me, fuck me, cherish me and I'm good."

His eyes sparkled, and a slow grin spread across his lips.

"Mi tink mi cyan cover all dem bases," he said, his tone dripping with certainty. "Eff yuh let mi."

"We'll see, Montague. I don't know about all this, but I don't have a choice but to give it a go."

He smiled wider, his gaze never leaving mine. It wasn't just a look. It was a hold, like he was peeling back layers of me with his eyes. The whole time we talked, he didn't blink, didn't flinch, just studied me with that calm, predatory patience. I wanted to know what he was thinking, plotting, planning but I was afraid to ask.

About forty-five minutes in, my eyes grew heavy. The valium and the weed hit all at once, loosening my tongue in ways that weren't like me at all.

"Montague, would you mind if I climbed up on this plush mattress and rest my eyes for a bit? You were right...this ganja wasn't shit to play with. Now I'm high as hell," I laughed.

He chuckled, his teeth flashing. "Of course, mi luv. Get yuh rest. Once wi land, everyting begins."

I climbed onto the bed, tucked the pillow behind my head, and let the sandman drag me under.

A few hours later, I felt his hand on my thigh, warm, steady, and rocking me gently awake.

"Shai, wi getting ready tuh land. Mi nuh wa yuh tuh hurt yuhself, suh cum. Let's buckle up."

Back in the cabin, Rocky and Kenzo were knocked out. Some bodyguards they were. Montague could've done anything to me, and they'd never have known. I sucked my teeth loud enough to get their attention. Kenzo cracked one eye open and winked.

We landed and exited the plane. Montague spread his arms wide, his presence commanding even in the humid Jamaican air.

"Welcome tuh mi home! Let di fun begin." He glanced at me, his eyes glinting. "Cum, Shai. Dere people mi wan yuh to meet."

Three men approached. Smiling, but their smiles didn't soften the fact that they were armed and dangerous. Guns at their sides, carried like accessories.

"Shai, dis is mi bredda, Maxim. dis striking young fella is mi nefyu, Winston. An last but nuh least, Wicked. Mi an Wicked been bredrin since wi were likkle pickneys." He grabbed Wicked by the neck, and they slapboxed playfully.

"Hi, nice to meet you all," I said shyly, realizing

Montague's accent had thickened so much on home soil that I could barely keep up.

"Wacha! Yuh need tuh listen, Shai. Mi will ave yuh by mi side most of yuh stay, but mi ave business too. Wen mi nuh available, one of dem tree will stay wid yuh. Yuh will neva be alone on dis island. Too many stepping razors round here. Mi nuh wan yuh near any of dem. Now dat is settled. Yuh muss be hungry. Let's guh feast."

Nodding, I let him take my hand again. He walked me to a blacked-out G-Wagon and opened the passenger door like a gentleman. I slid in, and he jogged around, slipping behind the wheel.

"Are yuh ready tuh ride, likkle lady?" he asked, flashing that knowing grin.

Forcing a smile, I quipped, "I'm as ready as I'll ever be."

Rocky and Kenzo climbed into the backseat. Once the luggage was loaded, Montague hit the gas, and the G-Wagon roared forward. My stomach dropped into my ass.

This was really happening. I was praying for the best but bracing myself for the worst.

Chapter Twenty

W e navigated in and out of traffic, and I tried to soak up the island views, but what I saw didn't match the glossy picture I'd always carried of Jamaica. This wasn't the sun-kissed postcard version shown on TV. We were riding through one of the most poverty-stricken areas I'd ever seen. Yet, despite the cracked streets and tin-roofed homes, the children we passed were grinning wide, their laughter echoed into the air as they chased each other barefoot.

Montague said nothing as he gripped the wheel, his attention locked on the winding roads. His expression was unreadable. He was deep in thought. My jaw clenched as we curved around a dangerous bend with nothing but empty air and a long drop below. I wanted to know what he was thinking but I didn't dare break his concentration.

Whatever thoughts I had, I kept to myself. My prayers stayed silent in my head, begging God for traveling grace and to arrive safely. Wherever the hell "safe" was.

After a tumultuous thirty minutes, relief washed over me as we turned into a sprawling resort. My breath caught, eyes widening at the sweeping ocean views and manicured grounds.

"Wi are here, mi luv," Montague muttered, killing the motor. "Dis is weh yuh, mi, an yuh men will stay fi di duration of dis trip."

"This is beautiful, Montague," I whispered, awe dripping from my voice. "Do you stay here often when you come home? Shittt... this looks like somewhere I'd never leave. Honestly, I thought we were going to your house or something."

He smirked knowingly. "Wi are. Dis is mi house. Mi own di entire resort an two more jus' like it. Look tuh yuh right." He pointed to a towering building. The glass gleamed in the sunlight. "Dat entire building is mine. Di top floor is weh wi will lie wi heads."

My mouth dropped open. "Wow. Seriously? I can't believe you call this paradise home. This is nothing like the streets we drove through to get here. This is pure luxury."

"Indeed," he said, his tone low and steady. "But dem streets wi passed... dem are mi roots. Mi breddas an mi grew up dere. Nuh long ago, wi were running dem same corners. Most of mi family still live dere. Yuh will meet dem in time."

As we pulled up, four valets rushed to open our doors. Two armed men grabbed the luggage while Montague placed a steady hand on my back, guiding me forward. Inside, the foyer gleamed. Polished marble floors, gold-trimmed columns, and a grand staircase curling upward. Three maids stood silently, hands folded, eyes dropping respectfully when Montague passed. But I felt their stares on me...sharp and assessing.

My eyes darted to the ceiling, where crystal chandeliers hung. The air smelled faintly of sea salt and lemon polish, everything was pristine. There wasn't a speck of dust in sight. The walls were filled with massive oil paintings. Some of lush Jamaican landscapes, others of men in sharp suits that looked like Montague's bloodline staring down at me with pride.

The whole place screamed money, power and control. Aunt Trucee told me Montague's operation was "small." She was misinformed. This mansion was a whole empire. He wasn't just running shit, he *was* the shit.

I wandered toward the massive bay window, the Caribbean sparkled like nothing I'd ever seen before. This was a long way from Roseville. For the first time since we'd landed, excitement swelled in my chest. Maybe paradise could be mine, even temporarily. I was already imagining the sun on my skin, sand between my toes, when Montague's voice slid into my ear, smooth and husky.

"Shai…" His hands slipped around my waist, firm but gentle. My body shuddered involuntarily. "Mi wan yuh tuh cum sit. Yuh lunch is ready. Adessa prepared ackee and saltfish, johnny cakes, callaloo, breadfruit. Eff dat nuh please yuh, mi will ave har mek something else."

Caught off guard by my own reaction to his touch, I cleared my throat. "No need. That sounds great. Please, show me the way."

We entered a lavish dining room where Montague sat close, watching me intently as I tore into the food like I hadn't eaten in days.

"It muss be good," he teased. "Yuh aven't seh a word since di plate touch di table. Mi tek it yuh satisfied?"

"More than satisfied," I mumbled around a mouthful of fish. I flashed a grateful nod towards Adessa. She smiled approvingly before slipping out.

When I glanced around for Kenzo and Rocky, I realized they were gone. "Um, Montague… where are Kenzo and Rocky? You didn't feed them to the alligators, did you?"

A sly grin slid across his lips. Flashing those pearly white teeth. "Alligators? Only crocodiles live in Jamaica. But nuh…yuh men are upstairs getting settled." He pulled out his phone and flashed a video of them unpacking clothes and placing their things in the closet.

"Okay then, Montague... what's the move? What's the plan? You said you wanted to get to know me. What exactly does that mean? Because I promise you, there's not much to know."

"Dat will cum wid time," he said easily. "For now, mi wan yuh belly full, yuh mind at peace. Relax by di ocean. Mi ave a likkle business tuh handle, suh mi muss leave yuh fi a while. Mi will return inna few. Anyting yuh need, Adessa will provide."

He rose from the table and started toward the door.

"Wait, hold up." I snapped, pushing back my chair. "I know you didn't drag me all the way here just to bounce. This was *your* idea, Montague. I could've stayed in Macon for this bullshit. You said you wanted to get to know me, to share time and space. That was you, not me. And now—"

His head whipped around, eyes wild, voice sharp as a whip. "Kibba yuh mout! Nuh backchat mi. Yuh tink mi an yuh deh pon di same level? Mi told yuh mi wud be in and out. Dis is di out. Mi seh mi will be back."

I froze at the fierceness in his voice, my heart beating on ten. "First of all, I don't know what you just said, but if you told me to shut up, then we're about to be thumping in this bitch. I'm not Umi, and you damn sure ain't Lincoln." I folded my arms, scowling.

Montague wagged a finger at me, brows tight, then turned on his heel and stormed out. The heavy slam of the door echoed through the hall.

Seconds later, Kenzo rushed in, eyes wide. "What the hell's going on? I heard you yelling from upstairs. You good, Shai?"

"Yes, I'm fine," I snapped. "That man brought me out here just to leave me. What kind of shit is that?"

Kenzo sighed, biting into an apple like he wasn't fazed. "Shai, please. I thought that it was something serious. This is his island. His resort. Of course he's got business to handle. Yo ass is uptight. This place is beautiful as hell, something I will probably never see again in my lifetime and you're complaining? You need to put on a swimsuit and come down to the beach. Rocky's already there."

I narrowed my eyes. "I'm not taking advice from either one of you. Y'all been acting brand new since we left Aunt Trucee's. You are supposed to be here to see about me. How can you protect me if you're never around? What if I said that I didn't feel like going to the beach? Would you even give a damn, or would you leave me in this mansion and say fuck me and head down to the water?"

"Whatchu mean girl? We got you forreal. I'm just

telling you to make the best of the situation. Trust me, you don't have shit to worry about. You are good."

I beg to differ Kenzo. Aunt Trucee told me that you two were the best men for the job, but I don't think that she knows you all like she thinks she does. It seems to me that you and Rocky are making shit about you. Has anyone even called her to say we landed safe? I bet you haven't. I'll do it myself."

I quickly stood up and yelled out, "Adessa!"

"Madam?" she responded.

"Will you please show me to my room? I have an important call that I need to make. I could use some privacy."

Kenzo tried to protest, but I shoulder-bumped him as I passed. Adessa led me into the elevator, and we ascended to the top floor.

"Dis is di master bedroom," she explained softly. "Montague's quarters. Di men brought up yuh luggage already. Wud yuh like mi tuh unpack an put yuh tings away?"

"Thank you, but no. I can handle it." I paused, then added, "Adessa, can I ask you something? Woman to woman."

"Of course, Shai. Wha yuh wan to kno?"

"First, you don't have to call me madam. Shai will do. I

just want to know a little about the man that I am going to be staying with for two weeks. This is only my second time meeting him. I barely know this man. Is he dangerous? Is he cruel? Does he... have a lot of women?"

Adessa's lips curved into a knowing smile. "Ah, yuh nervous, eh? Nuh need. Mi been here a long time. Mr. Montague is nuh a bad mon. Him kind, especially tuh him staff. But yuh, women luv him. Most girls wud trade places wid yuh inna heartbeat. A man of him wealth an power? Rare in dese parts. Yuh shud enjoy it."

I raised a brow. "Ladies' man, huh? I don't need drama with other women. Especially since it wasn't even my choice to come here."

Her eyes softened. "Only one woman give trouble. Lotus Hartley. Shi an Montague were a ting years ago, but shi neva let go. Every month, security drags har out. Shi jumped gates, hidden in vans. Shi mad, obsessed an will duh anyting jus tuh get a glimpse of him. Oddah dan Lotus, him keep him affairs clean. Suh, Miss Shai, mi advice is simple...be grateful. Many wud kill tuh be in yuh shoes."

I sighed. "Thank you, Adessa. That makes me feel... better, I guess. I'll unpack, then maybe head to the beach since he left me here."

Adessa gave me a playful scolding look. "Stop di

pouting an lift yuh chin, child. Montague busy, yuh. But him will mek time fi yuh. An wen him duh…" She winked. "Mi sure yuh will enjoy it."

She left me with that thought and I couldn't decide if it made me more nervous… or intrigued.

Chapter Twenty-One

I dug the international phone from the bottom of my luggage and dialed Aunt Trucee's number. The phone barely rang once before she picked up.

"Hey, Shug. I've been waiting on you. I saw you made it safely from the tracker, but I was just sitting here waiting for your call." I could hear her smiling through the phone.

"Yes, Auntie, I did. We're here and this island is beautiful. He has me staying at a luxury resort."

"Not a resort, chile. Why aren't you where he lays his head? Hell, I could've booked you at a resort if that's what it was."

"He owns this resort. A couple others too, according to him." I muttered as I ran my hand across the buttery softness of his Versace comforter set. "He's got a whole building here to himself. Aunt Trucee, it's gorgeous.

Massive. I haven't even toured the whole place yet, but from what I've seen, it's like something out of a movie."

"Shit. I didn't see anything like that when I had my men do a search. That nigga probably got half his shit in other people's names. Anyway, is he treating you right?"

"Yes, so far. He's nice, but I'm not falling for none of that, Auntie. Soon as we got here, he turned around and left, and that pissed me off. I let him know about it too, and he politely shut me down and walked out like I was a child. Who does he think he is?"

Aunt Trucee laughed. "Girl, you're in that man's territory. If he's running things, then let him run it. You don't always have to say the first thing that comes to your mind, you know. Sometimes it's okay to just shut up and let things play out, baby. Besides, you said you didn't want no 'Jamaican menace.' So why are you upset if he leaves you for a little while? You getting sweet on Mr. Montague already?"

"No, Auntie. I'm just like the men in jail, I'm here to do my time and that's it. I'll play the game as long as I need to if it means getting myself and Umi back home safe."

"Well, do that then, niece. And don't complain while you're at it. Anyway, I'm glad you're safe. I want you to enjoy yourself as much as you can. And I expect a phone call every single day. Do you hear me?"

"Yes, ma'am. I hear you."

"Good. Now chile, you'd never guess who called me today," she squeaked.

"Auntie, I'm not in the guessing mood. Just tell me."

She clicked her tongue. "Niece, you ain't no fun. Anyway, your cousin called about two hours after you left. Said she'd been trying your phone, but it kept going to voicemail. I told her you were out the country, and she acted like I was lying."

"If we're being real, Auntie, she probably did think you were lying. She knew I was broke before I left, so she's probably wondering how a bitch like me ended up out the country. Hell, I'd be wondering the same thing."

Auntie burst out laughing. "Now that you put it that way, it *is* kind of unbelievable. She really wanted to talk to you though, so I hope you don't mind me giving her the number to the phone I gave you."

"I don't mind. Did she say what she wanted?"

"No, baby. She didn't. But there was some urgency in her voice. You know she's nosey as hell, so I'm sure you won't have to wait long before she calls. Oh, and how are my boys doing?"

"Those negroes are fine. Better than me. They acting like this is a damn vacation. They ain't really studying me."

"Trust me, they are. Nothing gets past them. They just playing it cool. But if something pops off, you'll see what they're really about. Anyway, I love you, niece. Try to enjoy yourself, and we'll talk soon. Bye for now."

When the line disconnected, I sat on Montague's enormous bed and took it all in. This man was living *lavish*. His bedroom looked like a designer showroom--crown molding trimmed every edge, Italian marble sprawled across the floor, Versace wallpaper shimmered against the light, and the bedding beneath me was the softest I'd ever touched. The bathroom was as big as my old apartment, with a soaking tub, a vanity fit for a queen, and a shower with four heads. I just knew his ass was clean. Everything about him and this place radiated money, taste, and power.

From the first time I laid eyes on him, I knew he was fly. But this? I didn't know he was rolling in dough like this.

Adessa's words about his stalker came back to me, and I couldn't shake them. Women don't chase unless there's something worth chasing. Knowing there was a woman out there risking arrest just to sneak onto this property just to *see him,* made me curious. Dangerously curious.

Kenzo was right. I was in paradise and until Montague stepped to me the wrong way, I needed to relax and do my best to enjoy myself.

Chapter Twenty-
Two

I shoved thoughts of Umi to the back of my mind as I slipped into my bikini and checked myself in the mirror. Now listen. I wasn't the baddest bitch alive, but I sure as hell wasn't a slouch either. Thick, curvy, and holding 224 pounds like a trophy belt. Aunt Trucee always said, "Only dogs want bones. Real men want meat on the plate." Well, this plate was full and ready to be served.

I threw on my lace cover-up, grabbed my straw hat, phone, and Bluetooth speaker, then sashayed toward the elevator like I was on "America's Next Top Model: Plus sized Caribbean Edition." That's when Montague's best friend, Wicked, popped up outta nowhere like he'd been hiding in the wallpaper.

"Weh yuh goin', gyal?" he barked.

"Lawd! You scared the hell outta me." My hand flew to

my chest. "Where the hell did you come from...out the damn shadows? And who you calling girl? I'm a grown-ass woman. I'm going to the beach. Is that okay with you, security?"

He smirked like he wanted to laugh but couldn't. "Montague seh yuh spicy like curried goat. Him nuh lie. Listen, him told mi tuh watch yuh an nuh let yuh or yuh men out mi sight. So dat's wha mi gunna duh. Now are yuh ready? 'Cause mi ready."

Before I could answer, Kenzo popped up too, like this was a damn magic trick.

"Oh, hell nah. Where are all y'all coming from? Y'all crawling out the vents?" I groaned.

Kenzo grinned. "What, you thought you was going to the beach alone? Nah, cousin. We on bodyguard duty. Plus..." His eyes trailed over me. "You look nice, by the way."

Wicked's eyes cut sharp at him, finger twitching on the elevator button like he was pressing it for stress relief.

From down the hall, I heard a muffled laugh and turned. Adessa was peeking around the corner, folding laundry like this was the funniest soap opera she'd ever seen.

"I see you, Adessa. What's so damn funny?"

She smirked. "Well, Miss Shai... yuh want to be looked afta. Dem lookin'."

I rolled my eyes and stepped on the elevator. Wicked was sizing Kenzo up like he wanted to fight, while Kenzo puffed his chest like he was auditioning for "Love & Hip Hop."

"Umm, Wicked?"

"Ya mon."

"I see you sizing up my cousin, but calm down. He's family."

"Yuh sure?" he quipped, eyebrow raised.

Kenzo cut in before I could answer. "Man, I don't need her speaking for me. I can handle mine."

I groaned. "Oh my God. Will y'all please put your dicks up and stop it with the dumb shit? We're going to the beach, not a dick-measuring contest. We are going to enjoy ourselves right?"

"If yuh seh suh," Wicked muttered, staring at his feet, suddenly fascinated by his shoes.

Kenzo grinned wide. "Hell yeah, twin. You know how we do. We about to go dumb out dis bitch!"

"Kenzo, please," I hissed. "Can you leave the country slang at home? They already think we slow. They probably can't understand half the shit we say with these country-ass accents of ours."

"Whatchu mean?" He laughed. "I can't understand half the shit they say either, but you don't see me complaining. Besides, I ain't changing me for nobody. They can take me or leave me, baby."

The elevator dinged, and boom, Montague was standing right there like he'd been waiting for me his whole life. He grabbed my hand, eyes roaming me top to bottom like I was the prize at the fair.

"Well, damn, Shai. Yuh lookin' betta dan eva. Fine as hell."

I smirked. "Thank you, sir. I'm heading down to the water for some fun in the sun. You coming with me? 'Cause I'll need somebody to rub me down with sunscreen. Gotta protect all this fine-ass melanin."

"Say less." He spun me around slow, eyes glued to every curve. "Tanks fi lookin' out, Wicked, but mi got it from here."

Wicked didn't even argue. He dipped. "Mi headed ova to da resort. Catch yuh lata."

Montague leaned close, voice dropping low. "Shai, yuh wan beach...or rooftop pool? Mi ave a full-sized pool upstairs, private. Nuh one else but mi an yuh."

I grinned. "Tempting, but I need the sand between my toes, the sun on my face. Vitamin D, baby."

His smile widened, sly. "Mi got plenty vitamin D fi yuh." He kissed my cheek and nodded at Kenzo. "Tek har down. Mi be right dere."

I walked off swaying my hips on purpose. I knew he

was staring, and I wanted him to. For once, I felt like the star player in somebody else's game.

The beach was private, with soft white sand and turquoise water glittering like diamonds. A tiki hut stood to the side, smoke curling from its grill. Rocky was already posted up under a tree, looking like a ghetto vacation ad. Gun on his chest, coconut drink in one hand and blunt in the other.

I shook my head. "This fool..."

Ten chairs lined the shore, and I claimed the one on the end. I needed space from the peanut gallery.

But first, a drink. I strolled up to the tiki hut where the bartender was so fine he looked like he'd been sculpted. I turned the charm on. Just a quick smile and a wink and boom, triple shot without me even asking.

I giggled, thanked him, and headed back to my beach chair. The sun was in my eyes but I could see Montague stretched out in it like he owned the sand too.

And Lord have mercy... shirtless. Tattoos crawling over chocolate skin, diamonds flashing in his ears, hair in a wrap, tied up like a crown. Fine as hell and the most attractive thing about him? He acted like he wasn't.

Before I could even sip, Montague called out: "Shai! Get mi a coconut spritzer wid a sprinkle of ginger please!"

I squinted. "What in the hell is that?"

Back at the bar, the bartender was already making it like he'd read Montague's mind.

"Ooooh, yuh here wid Mr. Montague," he whispered, eyes darting. "Lemme hurry."

"And why you rushing?" I asked, raising a brow.

He leaned close, dead serious. "Duh yuh nuh kno who him is? Man owns dis whole place. Him cud ave mi wiped from da earth in seconds. Di last guy who chatted up one of him women too long, missing. Mi nuh tryna be next. Suh please, ma'am, tek dis drink an walk away. Mi doing mi best ventriloquist impression right now. Nuh wan him tuh si mi mout moving."

I snatched the drink, laughing the whole way back to Montague. "Boy, you got these people scared as hell out here."

"Who mi? Nuh need fi dem tuh be scared. Mi nuh a bear. As long as dem duh wah dem supposed tuh be doing, dem ave nuh issues out of mi. Anyhow, Shai, mi hope yuh enjoying yuhself. Eff yuh nuh, dat will change lata dis evening. Mi sure yuh gunna wan a nap at sum point, den wen yuh wake, wi freshen up an ave sum fun."

"What's your idea of fun, Montague?"

"Well, mi nuh wander out inna di city too much. Everyting mi need is right here pon di resort. An whatever mi nuh ave, mi cyan get. Mi family will cum by tonight. Dere a go bi good food, good drink, an plenty of vibes. Mi wan yuh tuh wear di sexiest dress yuh brought."

I plopped down in the beach chair and gave him the side-eye. "Ohhh, so that's what this is? You dragged me all the way here just to show me off to your 'breddas'? Like I'm some kind of damn show pony?"

He leaned in, eyes steady. "Has it eva occurred tuh yuh dat maybe mi wan tuh show yuh off because mi genuinely like yuh, Shai? Mi kno wi nuh kno each oddah well yet, but mi bin alive long enough to kno wah mi wan... an mi also know wah gud fi me."

"Please. I bet you do this all the time."

"Duh wah?" he asked, brows raised.

"Bring women here, wine and dine them, then ship their asses back home. You probably got a woman on every corner. You too damn fine. You just scream... man-whore." I said it straight-faced, like I was reading a fact off Google.

His whole energy shifted. "Ha. Yuh kno, Shai, mi neva, an mi duh mean neva, will be okay wid a uhman calling mi out mi name. Mi nuh who yuh used tuh dealing wid. Nuh yuh eva disrespect mi again. Yuh undastan mi? Mi nuh disrespected yuh or called yuh out yuh name. Suh, gimme dat same respect. Dis cyan be easy, or dis cyan be hard. Choice is fi yuh."

The sting of guilt hit instantly. He was right. He'd shown me nothing but respect since the beginning, and here I was running my slick-ass mouth. I thought of Umi's words and apologized.

"You're right. I'm sorry. I shouldn't have said that. I don't know enough about you to judge. Forgive me. I know I've got a mouth on me, but I'm working on it." I put on my best sexy pout, grabbed the sunscreen, and held it up like a peace offering. "I don't want to burn out here. Would you... rub this on my back?"

"Mi pleasure." He smiled, and I exhaled in relief.

I handed him the sunscreen and slid onto his chair, straddling it backwards. "I'm ready when you are."

Montague squeezed out way too much lotion, his hands dripping with it. "Uh, Montague... you do realize I'm not a Thanksgiving turkey, right? You don't have to baste me."

He smirked. "Mi jus' making sure every inch cova. Mi tek mi wuk serious."

The first touch of his palms on my back made me shiver, so I tried to play it off. "Ohhh, okay, strong hands. I see you got a side hustle as a masseuse."

"Only fi mi special clients," he murmured, rubbing slow and deep.

His fingers worked down my spine. My eyes fluttered shut. I rocked forward, biting my lip as he spread the lotion across my lower back, then back up. "Mmhmm... just don't get too close to my wig line. If this lace front lifts in the Jamaican heat, I'll never forgive you."

Montague chuckled low, his breath warm on my shoulder. "Shai, mi nuh even notice yuh wig. All mi si is beauty."

"Boy, please," I shot back, though my voice came out a little too breathy.

As his hands slid down to the side of my thigh, I could feel my pussy growing slick. I gasped and sat straight up. "Hold up now! This is sunscreen...not rub, Netflix and chill!"

He leaned back laughing, palms slick with lotion. "Mi only following ordas. Yuh seh back. Yuh nuh specify weh it stop."

I snatched the bottle from him before he could go further. "Thanks, sir. I'll handle the rest before you get carried away and I end up needing confession."

He licked his lips and muttered, "Mi nuh tink confession cud save yuh eff mi touch yuh how mi wan."

I turned toward the ocean, cheeks burning, and blasted Bob Marley from my Bluetooth speaker to cover the tension.

"Sun is shining..." floated through the air as my hips swayed.

Montague leaned back, staring like I was the whole damn show. "Yuh bad gyal. Wah yuh kno bout dat tune?"

"Everything," I said with a grin. "And this is the perfect soundtrack. The sun is shining, the breeze feels good, I got sand in my toes, and somebody just gave me a free rubdown. Life's good."

. . .

"MI DUH AGREE WID DAT, Shai. Plenty people smile pon di outside but hurt deep pon di inside. Used tuh be mi too. Mi did build dis empire...cars, money, women. Mi had it all. Life was gud, but still, mi cud nuh find mi laugh. Wicked told mi dat mi needed help, suh mi si a head doctor. Shi told mi... mi manic depressive. Nuh even kno wah dat meant at first, but once shi explained... it mek sense. Now ya days, dem call it someting else. Same ting though."

"What's it called now?"

"Bipolar disorder," he said, casually sipping his spritzer.

"You... are bipolar?"

His brow furrowed. "Yah mon. Why yuh seh it like dat?"

"No, no, I didn't mean it like that. I just...honestly, you don't seem like it. From my experience, bipolar people are hot and cold. Up one minute, crashing the next. Truthfully, I thought I was bipolar at one point but then I realized people just piss me off and deserve to get cursed out." I smirked.

He chuckled. "Mi mellow now, but it nuh always bin dis way. Mi tek medicine every day tuh keep miself steady. Mi hate putting chemicals inna mi bady, but widout it... tings get wicked. Truss mi, yuh nuh wan si mi like dat. Mi nuh even wan si mi like dat. It's nuh pretty."

I laughed lightly, trying to ease the weight of the moment. "Well, I'll take your word for it. Just promise me one thing...don't miss a pill while I'm here."

He laughed, eyes twinkling. "Mi cyan promise dat, Shai."

"**Y**our laugh is so refreshing, Montague. Umi told me she'd never seen you smile in all the time she's known you, but all I've seen you do is grin and laugh. What's the deal with that?"

"Have yuh eva tink dat maybe yuh fren full of shit?"

"Who, Umi? No. Why would you say that?"

"Mi ave a feeling yuh nuh kno har like yuh tink yuh duh. Mi nuh like dat gyal. Too sneaky fi mi. Dat gyal wicked. But yuh will kno dat in time."

"Ok, whatever you just said." I rolled my eyes. "So... tell me, Montague, who all will be coming by tonight? Anybody I should be warned about?"

"Warn? No, Shai. Mi family is gud wid whoeva mi gud wid. Jus' be yuhself. But kno dis, dat slick mout of yuh may meet its match."

"Great," I sighed. "Personally, I don't do well around strangers. I'm private. I'll be polite, but don't expect me to be the life of the party. My go-to is finding a corner and staying in it."

"If dat wah yuh wan, dats fine wid mi. Mi will ave a gud time regardless."

"I swear your patois is getting stronger every hour. Can you say that in plain English? My head hurts trying to decipher you." I cut my eyes at him.

"Mi suh sorry, Shai. My homeland does dat to mi. Mi will try tuh speak betta English fi yuh. Mi wan yuh tuh undastan mi."

Laughing, I blurted out, "That was no better, Montague, but points for effort."

He grabbed me by the waist and pulled me close. Before I could react, he lowered his head, brushing his nose across my belly button before kissing just below it. My first thought was to punch him dead in his skull, but I reminded myself: *Two weeks, Shai. You just gotta survive two weeks.*

I let my guard down and just stood there. The peppermint, mango, and lime smell from his hair was intoxicating. Without thinking, my fingers slid through his hair, massaging his scalp. His head rested heavy on my stomach, and then he whispered, low and sure, "Yuh need sum likkle pickneys in dere. None of wi are gettin younga,

Shai."

I snapped my head down to look at him. "Pickneys?! As in kids? No thank you. Maybe someday, but not now. I haven't lived enough, seen enough, made enough money for that kind of commitment."

"Yuh duh kno yuh will neva be fully prepared tuh be a mada. It's someting yuh muss duh. Di nurturing will cum naturally."

"If you say so. Do you have any children?"

His head lifted from my stomach, and his whole vibe shifted. He laid back on his chair, staring at the sky. "Mi had one son. Him dead wen him did tree months old. Worst pain of mi life. It nuh natural tuh haffi bury a pickney."

My chest caved. I jumped from my chair and grabbed his hand, forcing him to sit up so I could cup his face. "I'm so sorry, babe. Really. Forgive me for asking. I stay putting my big foot in my mouth. Gotta stop doing that shit."

"Mi gud, Shai. Really. Mi dealt wid it."

Did I just call him babe? What the hell is wrong with me? This is a mission, Shai. Treat it like one. Don't get attached to this man.

Before I could check myself further, the Bluetooth speaker cut off and my phone rang. Not recognizing the number, I just answered.

"Hello?"

"There your ass is! Shai, Mama told me you were on vacation, and I'm still trying to figure out how somebody who couldn't pay their rent suddenly found money to go on vacation. Explain that to me, because I thought I was smart...but I must be dumb as hell."

Laughing uncontrollably, I muttered, "Yes, bitch, you are dumb as hell, but not for the reason you think."

"If you're talking about Calloway, you were right, cousin. He ain't shit. I met with him last night and ended up calling the police on him."

"Actually, I wasn't even thinking of him, but the police? What in the hell did he do, Cassie?"

"For starters, he tried to pin me down and force himself on me. I had to fight him like a grown man. If my homegirl hadn't been staying with me in the guest room, I don't know what would've happened. He was acting crazy. I think he was on something. I should've known better. Anyway, I had him arrested. He's in jail."

"Wow..." was all I managed.

"Is that all you have to say?"

"Well, give me a second to process! What kind of response did you expect?"

"I'm not sure but something other than wow. I just told you your ex tried to rape me, and you say wow. That's fucked up!"

"No, the fucked-up part is you calling him my ex, as to

insinuate I'm in some kind of way responsible for what happened to you. I didn't do it nor did I have anything to do with it. I'm gonna tell you what your bougie ass always tells me: choose better," I grinned into the phone.

There was a pause then she spoke.

"Shai...I know muthafu—."

Cutting her off mid sentence, I quipped, "I was just fucking with you. Seriously though cousin, all jokes aside, I'm glad that you are ok but what you had going on with him was flaw from the beginning. Knowing that bastard, he tried to get with you just to piss me off. Joke was on him though because I don't give a damn. All I want to know is did he hurt you in any kind of way?"

Sighing into the phone, she quipped, "Yeah, I've got a bruised thigh, arm and my face is a little swollen from him pressing is elbow into it but nothing major to speak of. I'll live."

"Once again, I'm truly sorry that happened to you cousin. His ass is where he needs to be because if he were still out on the streets, he would be touched. I don't know what could have gotten into him, so it had to be drugs. There was absolutely no reason for him to force himself on you or anyone else. If he'd just been a little patient, I'm almost positive that you would have given him the pussy. You done gave it to everyone else," I laughed. Montague eyeing me closely.

"See Shai, normally, a statement like that would have pissed me off, but you're right." She giggled. "I was gonna give him a little taste that night, but he got weird and ruined it. Enough about his tired ass. Where are you?"

"In Jamaica," I said, chipper.

"Jamaica?! And I didn't get an invite? Who did you go with?"

"No one you know. And I think I've been on this phone long enough. I'm being a rude guest, and he's staring a hole through my head. I'll call you later."

"Ok then. I love you, be safe in Jamaica."

"No, cousin, you be safe. I've got bodyguards all around me. I'm good. Bye."

"Wait...bodygu—"

I hung up before she could finish her sentence.

Chapter Twenty-
Five

"Trouble back home?" he asked, raising an eyebrow.

"Not for me, but for my cousin. She decided to mess with my ex, and he tried to take her cookies without permission. His ass is sitting in jail now."

He tilted his head. "Cookies? Mi sorry, mi nuh follow."

I smirked. "He tried to rape her. She put him in jail."

"Ooohhh." He nodded slowly, then his mouth curved. "Cookies as in pum pum."

"Yes, pum pum." I laughed.

"Well, dat nuh gud. Eff a uhman nuh give it freely, mi nuh wan it." His gaze shifted to the waves rolling against the shore, suddenly serious.

"That's good to know, Montague." I leaned back on

my chair. "But let me ask you something. Why are you single? A fine-ass, rich man like yourself? You've got this mansion, all this land, you're clearly successful. You obviously work hard and, I'm guessing, play harder. From what I can see, your family, friends, even your staff respect and love you. Other than the whole kidnapping thing, you seem like a really nice guy. So... why are you alone?"

He chuckled low in his throat. "Mi nuh alone, mi single. Dere is a difference. Mi wud ratha be alone dan be wid sumone dat nuh gud fi mi. Mi need loyalty. Honesty. Dats rare nowadays. Wen di right one cum along, mi will snatch har up an mek har mi wife. Mi wan family more dan anything. But mi nuh settle. She haffi be special."

I turned over on the chair, locking eyes with him. "That's real talk. Eventually, I want a family too, but just like you, I've gotta find the right one. There are too many frogs out here and not enough princes. Is that what this is about? Bringing me here to see how I fit into your world?"

"Mi told yuh mi wan tuh get tuh kno yuh, an dats wah wi doing. Yuh agree?"

I studied him, then gave a small nod. "I guess you're right." His words were spinning wheels in his head, and I didn't want him overthinking. I stretched and grinned. "Alright, I think I've had enough sun for today. I don't want to burn. Let's go inside. I've got two whole weeks to soak up all the vitamin D I can handle."

He opened his mouth to speak, but I pressed a finger to his lips. "Shhh. Don't even say it. I already know what you're thinking."

"Shai, mi dead wid laugh. Yuh a trip. Mi like dis. Yuh are getting tuh kno mi."

"Yes, I am." Smiling, I stood and tugged his hand. "Come on, old man. Let's go inside, eat some fruit, hydrate, and let me take a nap before tonight."

"Oh, so yuh excited tuh meet mi family, eh?"

"I am. I want to see what kind of stock you come from."

He smirked knowingly. "Yuh kno Lincoln's mada gaan be here. Yuh still excited?" His eyes searched mine.

"You wouldn't dare tell her. Please don't do that. I didn't come all the way here to fight for my life. And I'll never back down from a fight, but today, I'm tired and I'd be an easy win."

He laughed as we stepped through the back door. "Shai, mi luv yuh sense of humor. Mi jus' kidding. Mi wud neva duh dat tuh yuh."

"I hope not. But tell me this. Lincoln's mama, is she as mean as him?"

"Nuh at all. Mi sista sweet as pie. Lincoln got dat mean streak from him fada. Him dead now, but wen him alive, him known tuh be tuff as nails."

"If he was anything like Lincoln, I know he was hell."

Montague held the door open. "Shai, wud yuh like tuh relax in di entertainment room? Mi will ave Adessa bring wi fruit and drinks."

"That sounds perfect."

He guided me inside, but when we entered the entertainment room, two men were sprawled out, passing a blunt.

"Sorry, Shai. Mi nuh kno dem were in here." He clapped his hands. "Ayyy! Yuh two, get up and find someweh else tuh guh. Mi an mi lady friend need privacy."

"Sure, Unk," they chimed together, hopping up and disappearing quickly.

"Now who were those two?" I asked, settling onto the couch. "I didn't see them outside. Were they hiding in this house all day?"

"Dem di twins, Tyson and Tarik. Mi oldest sista pickneys. Dem luv dem uncle. Any time mi in town, family flocks here. Mi nuh mind. Mi luv family."

I nodded. "That's sweet. Honestly, I don't blame them. This place is gorgeous. I'd move in too if I could. I still haven't even toured the whole mansion, and I've been here all day."

He grinned. "Yea. Mi always kno mi wan a big family, suh mi built a house big enough tuh fit dem all. Mi seh, if yuh stay ready, yuh nuh haffi get ready."

"That's smart thinking." I chirped, spearing a pineapple chunk from the tray Adessa brought in.

Montague slid closer, eyes on my fruit. "Feed mi, gyal. It's been a long time since mi had di pleasure of a beautiful uhman feeding mi fruit."

I wanted to roll my eyes and tell him he'd starve waiting on me. But there was something magnetic about him. Something in his confidence, that smooth royal aura, the way he carried himself. He was wise, funny, and unshakably sure of who he was. That "je ne sais quoi."

And the more I sat with him, the more I started to understand why Lotus risked it all just to jump that fence.

Chapter Twenty-Six

Montague was tossing a massive monkey wrench in my plans. I came into this thing ready to hate him and everything he stood for, but I was struggling. Hard. I really tried not to let his charm, his words, or the way he carried himself get under my skin. But I was failing and worse, I was falling. These two weeks were about to feel like two years. Especially with the alcohol and weed. The two things guaranteed to make me wanna suck the skin clean off a nigga's bones.

My plan was simple: keep my pussy to myself. My reality? This was about to be harder than I thought.

Dragging myself out of my thoughts, I whined, "I'm getting tired, Montague. I need to get this sand off me and shower. Then I'm taking a nap. Adessa showed me the master quarters earlier and said that's where I'll be sleeping. You're really okay with that?"

"Yah, Shai. Believe it or nuh, mi ave di utmost respect fi women. Mi nah touch yuh eff dat's nuh wah yuh wan. Truthfully, mi wan tuh sleep beside yuh, but eff yuh nuh comfortable, mi respect dat. Dis house ave thirteen bedrooms. Mi cyan sleep anyweh. But yuh...yuh special. Yuh mi guest of honor. As long as yuh here, mi treat yuh like a queen."

His voice was smooth, but I wasn't letting my guard down. "I appreciate your hospitality and I don't want to offend you in your house, but yes, I would feel better if you slept elsewhere. At least for now. I *am* a lady, and you promised to treat me like one."

"And mi always keep mi promise. Guh bathe, rest yuhself. Eff yuh need mi and cyaan find mi, ave Adessa call mi."

"Why don't you just give me your number so I can call you myself?"

He shook his head with a sly grin. "Nuh. Jus' ave Adessa phone mi. Mi will cum straightaway. Ok, mi luv?"

Rolling my eyes, I muttered, "Your wish is my command," and dragged myself into the master bathroom.

I hadn't even pulled my bottoms all the way off before...*knock knock knock.*

"Umm, may I help you?" I called out, already irritated.

A voice floated through the door. "Mi sorry tuh badda yuh, ma'am, but Mr. Montague sent mi up here tuh help yuh bathe.

"Excuse me? And who the hell are you? You don't sound like Adessa. Your accent's thicker."

"Dat's because mi nuh Ms. Adessa, and mi from anotha Parish. Wi all ave different way wi talk. Oh, an mi name is Kiyana. Mi here tuh tek care of yuh. Anyting yuh need?"

I swung the door open, standing there half naked and fully annoyed. "Yeah. I need to be left *alone*. Back where I'm from, the bathroom is a private space. Nobody comes in but me. So, you can go right back and tell him I'm not interested."

She fidgeted, stuttering. "Ummm... ma'am... mi sorry, but mi cyaan duh dat. Nuhbody tells Mr. Montague nuh. Eff yuh nuh let mi in, mi will haffi guh get reinforcements. Please, nuh mek mi duh dat. Mi swear, mi nah badda yuh. Mi jus' wanna help."

My jaw dropped. *Reinforcements? For a bath?*

"Ok, Kiyana. Y'all real persistent around here." I folded my arms. "Fine. Get me a towel and run the water. Then you're leaving. I'll even give you a glowing review. I'll tell Montague you were the best helper I've ever had. Hell, I'll even throw in that you washed my back. Whatever it takes to get you gone."

She nodded quickly. "Yea, ma'am." She scurried to the linen closet, handed me a towel, and filled the tub while staring awkwardly like she was waiting for me to sprout wings.

When the tub was finally full, she whispered, "Ok, ma'am. Mi will leave yuh tuh yuh privacy... but mi will wait outside tuh help yuh out wen yuh dun."

"Wait a damn minute. I don't need help getting *out* of the tub either. I've been getting out of tubs my whole life. What kind of weird shit yall got going on around here?"

"Mi sorry if it displeases yuh, ma'am. But dis is customary. Yuh are our guest, an wi ave explicit orders tuh treat yuh like royalty. Mr. Montague is a nice man until sumone nah duh wah him seh. Den tings get... wicked. Wi nuh like wicked around here. Suh please, let mi duh mi job."

He did tell me he could get wicked. Evidently, he wasn't joking earlier.

I sighed, defeated. "Alright then. I don't want anyone getting in trouble over little old me. I'll play along. No more arguing."

Slipping into the warm bath, I let the water soothe me. But as I sank lower, reality sank in deeper. For the next two weeks, I was Montague's property. His people treated me like a queen, yes, but one under lock and key. I made a deal, and I had to keep my end.

Sure, I had my own protection squad lurking around, but their job wasn't to interfere. Only to keep me breathing. And here, in Montague's territory, we were outnumbered a hundred to one. By the time Aunt Trucee would get to us, we'd already be seasoned, skewered, and grilled like jerk chicken.

Montague ran this island, no doubt about it. His people obeyed him with a fear and loyalty that was absolute. And me? Secretly terrified, yet equally thrilled. Either way...I was here now and I wasn't about to test him.

Two weeks, Shai. Just two weeks.

Chapter Twenty-
Seven

The sun had drained me, and the bath relaxed me. I was out cold the second my head hit the pillow.

I woke to the sounds of reggae blasting through every room like The Wailers had set up camp in the living room. Springing from the cozy bed, I spotted a clothing rack full of dresses. They weren't there before, so I assumed these things were for me. Designer everything: Chanel, Prada, Dior. None of it my style. I sighed and sauntered into the closet and set off to find something I actually liked.

In the bathroom, I curled my tresses and applied makeup, still trying to figure out what all of this was about. He said family was coming, but I had never felt the need to get all dressed up for family. Still, I promised to be compliant, so I picked the sexiest dress I owned and slid it on. Then came the zipper.

Peeking out, I saw Rocky lurking.

"Pssssss, Rocky," I hissed.

"Yes, Madam," he snickered.

"Don't be funny. Stop it with the madam shit and come help me zip this dress and strap these shoes, please."

"That's not in my job description. I'm not your fairy flunky," he protested.

"Boy, get your ass over here! Slide a zipper and wrap some shoes around my leg. That's it. Not rocket science."

"Ok, damn," he muttered as he stepped in. Turning my back to him, he zipped me up while I plopped into the nearest chair and extended my leg for the shoes.

The door flew open, and Montague cleared his throat.

"Wah da fuck yuh doing in here?" he growled.

"I... needed help with my dress, and he—"

Cutting me off, he barked, "Mi nuh talking tuh yuh, Shai. Mi talking tuh Rocky."

I huffed and sucked my teeth. "But I'm not done talking yet. As I was saying before I was rudely interrupted, he was standing guard outside the door. He's just helping. Is that a problem?"

"Hell yea. Nuh oddah man allowed in mi bedroom. Yuh need help, yuh call one of da females."

I rolled my eyes. "Music was loud, I didn't think

anyone would hear me. Or I could have called you... if I had your number. But since I don't, I asked him. He's family and I trust him. You should too. He won't hurt me."

Montague threw up his hands. "Like mi told yuh on di plane, mi nuh really truss nuhbody."

Rocky eased the tension. "My bad, man. Just helping my cuz get fly. I'll leave... but I'll be right outside, Shai." He winked and backed away.

I turned to Montague. "You didn't have to do all that. I'm fully dressed. Why are you tripping?"

"Yuh dressed, but are yuh gunna wear any of di dresses mi picked?"

"No. None of them are me. I went into my own closet and found something I like. Montague, I'm not a Barbie doll. You can't just pick things out and make me wear it. We're getting to know each other. And you can't trip every time things don't go your way."

"Mi nuh trippin." His hands running across the back of his neck. "Mi tink mi handled dat well."

I laughed as my hands fell to my hips. "Handled? You may as well have bit his head off."

He stopped himself from talking. Frustration clearly etched across his face. "Mi want tuh..."

"Want to... what...nut up? Relax, he's family. It's okay for family to help each other."

"Yea, but mi nuh like seeing an oddah man touching yuh. Made mi skin crawl."

"Montague, seriously?"

"Yea, seriously. Mi cyah help yuh get dressed? Tell mi wah tuh duh."

I instructed him on the shoes. He followed perfectly. Then we waltzed out hand in hand. Rocky shook his head in the corner. I wanted to laugh so badly once I saw his face, but I ate the laugh because Montague was watching. I didn't want him to feel as if he were being made fun of.

In the elevator, he was quiet...too quiet.

Before we opened the door that let out to the main area, I turned to him. "Montague, what's wrong? This is supposed to be a fun night. Your family's here, and from the sound of it, they're having a good time. I'm looking fine, Versace has you looking handsome as fuck. Why is your face scrunched up? There is nothing to be angry about."

"Mi sorry, Shai. Mi cyaan control it sometimes. Wen mi saw Rocky touching yuh leg. Mi wan tuh throw him out di window."

I cracked a smile. "Well I'm glad you didn't. That for sure would have ruined the evening."

"Yea... Mi duh too much sometimes. Mi trying tuh duh betta. Maybe mi need tuh tek two pills tonight," he chuckled. "Before wi get out, mi ave tuh tell yuh...mi luv how yuh checked mi back dere. Mi was rude, cut yuh off. Gentleman nuh act like dat. Sumtimes even gentlemen need correction, and yuh give mi dat." He laughed while he gently stroked my face. "Mi sorry. Dat look dat yuh give mi mek mi kno tuh neva duh dat again. "We both laughed hysterically, his teeth gleaming and his eyes sparkling as he stared into my eyes.

"Yeah, that triggered me instantly. I hate being interrupted. Growing up, my mama never let me talk. Like never. I told myself when I became grown, I'd never let anyone shut me up again. If I had to say something, I would say it, and I wouldn't give a fuck who didn't like it. I promised to never let anyone silence me again and I still stand on that."

"Mi luv dat. Dat spiciness...dat's wah set mi soul on fire in di parking lot. Neva loose dat fire an tenacity, Shai. Moving di way yuh move, yuh cyan ave di world. Oh, an yuh look absolutely stunning."

Gently kissing my cheek, he pushed the elevator open revealing a packed house. People were everywhere. Moving about without stepping on someone's dress or shoes was a daunting task. Montague waved us through a crowd of people, never letting my hand go. Never losing his grip and in that second, I realized he was becoming my safety net, my protector.

I knew no one here, yet I knew I couldn't be touched.

Kenzo's eyes was locked on me from the third floor. Rocky hovered nearby and was watching my every move. It was at that moment, I knew I couldn't be fucked with. Not tonight... A bitch couldn't even fuck with a picture of me.

WE CONTINUED WADING through the crowd of attendees until we stepped into an open, semi-empty space. There were only five round tables sectioned off, each beautifully draped with white and gold linen and adorned with a striking centerpiece. The way these tables stood out, I knew they were reserved for his closest family members.

It wasn't until I sat down that I realized we weren't on the first floor...we were on the second, in a ballroom. This man had a ballroom in his house. This kind of wealth was on a different level.

As I got comfortable, a young woman around my age leaned over to me and said, "Yuh dress is beautiful, and suh are yuh. Montague did well wid yuh. Mi nuh si nuh snake on yuh. Yuh carry a clean heart and spirit. Mi like dat. Dats wah him needs."

The shit freaked me out, so I just smiled and said thank you. So much for hiding in a corner. I was in the thick of it now with nowhere to run.

Still holding my hand, Montague lifted our arms in the air and announced, "Welcum everyone. Mi wan yuh tuh meet mi lady friend, Shai. An unfortunate event brought har an mi togetha, an now wi doing wi best tuh get tuh kno one anotha. Now dat is out of di way, wi cyaan all eat an be merry."

Everyone stood and introduced themselves, explaining how they were related to Montague. He was right about Lincoln's mother; she was one of the kindest people I'd ever met. Lincoln was still on my shit list, but his mother was good with me. It was hard to believe such a vile person could come from an angel like her. His brothers and sisters were kind too, except one. Her name was Drexa, and she didn't have much to say. Which was fine by me. I wasn't here for them anyway.

The night was a success. Everyone was merry. No arguments, no fights, no drama. Just good music, dancing, and food. Jamaicans sure do know how to party. By the time the night ended, I was completely worn out. Between the champagne and the ganja, I was blown and needed the nearest bed.

Montague was still sitting at the table with his family, and I didn't want him to leave them on my account. Leaning in, I whispered in his ear, "I'm tired and a little tipsy. I need to lie down. Stay here and enjoy your family. I'll have Rocky escort me upstairs." I kissed him on the cheek, waved goodnight to everyone, and trekked barefoot across the ballroom with my shoes in hand. Rocky was waiting for me at the door.

"So, Madam, did you enjoy yourself tonight?" he teased.

"Stop it with the Madam shit before I kick your ass. But yes, Rocky...I did. The vibes were right, the food was great, the music too. That was one hell of a party."

"Yes, it was. And that man is really sweet on you, Shai."

"What makes you say that?"

"Shidd, he invited the whole damn town just to meet you. Everybody's eyes were glued to you the whole time. I been watching how they move. I've been watching him too. That man couldn't wait to show you off. Now, I don't know how far you want this thing to go, but I can tell he's serious about you."

"Rocky, you know the only reason I came here was to save my friend. I'm being as cool as I can because I'm just trying to make the best of the situation. Don't get me wrong, he's likable and sweet to me, but I didn't come here for a love connection. I came here because I had to. Let's not forget...he kidnapped my best friend."

"I didn't forget anything, Shai. I'm just telling you what I see. This ain't a game to him. He really is trying to get to know you."

"Listen, Rocky, my head hurts. I'm high and drunk. I need a bed, so please just help me get there," I slurred.

After everyone started to dispersed, the staff went into full swing, restoring the place to pristine condition. The sharp mix of Clorox and Pine-Sol filled the air, so strong it made me queasy. By the time Rocky ushered me to the top floor, I was done. Sick to my stomach and too drunk and high to function.

In the bedroom, I clumsily tried to get out of my dress but gave up. With no energy left, I climbed under the sheets in my ballgown and passed out cold.

When morning crept in and the sun invaded my personal space, I woke up, not in my gown, but in a pajama set and bonnet. Mortified, I sat up. I had no idea who dressed me. Truthfully, there wasn't a soul on this island I'd be comfortable enough with to let them undress me. Day two, and already somebody had to get their ass handed to them. I was starting with the man of the house. That was as soon as I found him.

I rolled out of bed and cracked the door, finding Wicked asleep in a chair.

"Heyyyy!" I yelled, startling him awake.

"Shai! Wah gwaan? Yuh fraid di shit outta mi!"

"I'm sorry, Wicked. I didn't mean to scare you, but don't you have to be awake to protect someone?"

Chuckling, he muttered, "Gyal, mi had a gud time laas

night. Maybe too gud. Mi tired as hell. Kenzo and Rocky gaan downstairs tuh breakfast. As soon as dem cum back, mi gwaan home tuh sleep."

"So if you haven't been here all night, then who was?" I pressed.

"Mi nuh kno, Shai. Mi nuh here. Mi had a time elseweh afta di party ova. Yuh haffi ask Adessa or Kiyana, or maybe even yuh fellas. Mi nuh kno though."

"No, I don't want to bother the ladies. They've got enough to handle without me. Where's Montague? I need to see him immediately."

"Him down in di entertainment room wid him nefyus. Mi will call him fi yuh an send him up."

"Please and thank you." I shut the door and waited for Montague to show his face.

Eight

I sat there seething. Ten minutes passed before Montague appeared at the door, smiling and cheerful.

"Shai... gud morning, mi luv. How are yuh feeling? Yuh bad off last night."

"I know. I don't remember anything after the last act performed. I got too high, and trust me, I will never do that again. Listen, I went to sleep with my dress on because I couldn't get out of it. But when I woke up this morning, I was in pajamas. Would you happen to know who's responsible for that?"

"Of course mi duh. Duh yuh really tink dat mi wud let jus' anyone handle yuh in such a state? Nuh ,mi wud nah, suh mi dressed yuh an put yuh tuh bed. Mi guh through yuh tings an find di likkle cap tuh put on yuh head an everyting. Mi made sure yuh were gud. It was a likkle more tuh it but mi will explain dat lata. Mi ave sum business tuh tend tuh downstairs. While yuh were sleep last night, mi had a batty boy try mi. Dat's di shit mi nuh play bout. Yuh nuh worry. Mi and yuh gunna solve dis problem togetha. Okay?"

Looking bewildered, I answered, "Okay. Whatever I can do to help, I will."

"Dat's wah mi like tuh hear. Mi gunna send Adessa up here, but mi ave tuh guh fi now. Get dressed. Help yuh stomach and tell Adessa wah yuh fancy tuh eat dis morning tuh calm dat belly growl. Once yuh dun eatin', yuh will help mi solve di problem. It won't be too much fi yuh, it's light wuk."

As he headed toward the door, he stopped, turned around, and kissed me on the lips. "Mi kno mi muss like yuh, cuz mi kiss yuh before yuh even brush yuh teeth," he chuckled, then exited the room.

He left, but his scent lingered for a while. I found myself smiling and taking it in. This man was seriously growing on me, and I couldn't process it. While I pondered the whys, my phone rang.

"Hello."

"Hello, Niece. How are you on this good morning?"

"I'm good, Auntie. Just a little hungover, but I'll be okay."

"Hungover, huh? You must've had a hell of a night."

"I did, Auntie. It was nice. He invited his family over to meet me...turned out the whole damn island was here. He must be related to everyone. The drinks and ganja were flowing, and I think I may have overindulged."

"Shai," she gritted. "That's exactly what you don't need to do. I told you to keep your head on a swivel. Don't get too damn comfortable, girl. We still don't really know this man or what he's capable of."

"I know, Auntie, but he puts me in such a soft-girl space. I don't have to worry about shit when he's around. At the party last night, I felt like nothing could touch me. Between Kenzo, Rocky, Wicked, the twins, and Maxim, I knew no one could get to me. He told me when we first got here that there were bad men all over the island and because of that, I would never be alone. He was absolutely right. Since we've touched down, there's always been somebody watching over me."

"Well, Shai, I trust you know how to handle yourself. Just don't get so caught up in this man. I know how that can go."

"I'm doing my best not to get attached to him, but ... it's so hard. He's kind, thoughtful, and so damn sexy to me. He loves his family, and above all, he makes sure I'm good before he makes any moves. Oh, and he smells like heaven. Oooooh and the way he looks at me makes me melt...I swear I could drink his damn sweat."

"Ohhh shit, niece. Sounds like you're already gone. Tell me something...Have you fucked him yet?"

"No, I haven't, thank you very much." I snickered as I turned on the shower.

"Well, from the sound of it, it won't be long before you do. I was young once, so I know how it is. That man is powerful. Powerful men will always have a bitch ready to slide those draws to the side."

"Auntie, stop!" Chuckling, I asked, "Do you have to be so nasty?"

"Girl, please, stop your shit. You're grown and you are clearly not a little baby anymore. Besides, I'm not the nasty one. I heard your little nasty tail fucking Bakari early that morning. I came to your wing to check on you, to make sure you were settling in well, and I heard Bakari beating the brakes off your ass. You sounded like you were getting your whole life," she giggled, and I gasped.

"Auntie, don't say that! Oh my God, I'm so ashamed. I gotta go. I'll call you back tomorrow."

She laughed until she started coughing and whispered, "Bye, freak nasty," and hung up.

I was mortified, but I was also tickled. Before I could walk back into the room to lay my phone down, Adessa was knocking at my door.

"Good morning, Ms. Shai. Mr. Montague tell mi dat yuh were up an getting yuh day started. Was dere anyting dat yuh want tuh eat in particular?"

"Good morning to you too, Adessa. Yes, I loved that ackee and saltwater fish you made. It was delicious. May I have that?"

"Yea, mi dear, an it is called ackee an saltfish. Did yuh wan di Johnnycakes and plantain too?" She asked as she headed toward the door.

"Yes, and as soon as I'm done in the shower, I'll be down to eat."

"Okay. It will be ready by di time yuh dun up here. Si yuh downstairs." She waved her hand and sauntered out of the room.

"Thank you, Adessa."

Kiyana came in behind her. Standing around looking crazy.

Before she could utter a word, I started with, "Listen, just sit on the bed and wait until you hear the water stop. Then you can go back out there. I promise you I've had this pussy long enough to handle it all by myself. I won't protest you being here but I have to draw the line somewhere."

"Mi undastan, Madam. Me will jus' sit here and let you wash yuh own pum pum."

"Good, I laughed as I stepped into the shower.

Chapter Twenty-Nine

"Adessa," I yelled, as I ate the last bite of my food. "You did it again. This breakfast had me biting my fingers. It's so good. Before I leave, you are going to have to teach me how to make this."

"Of course, Madam. "Now," she said as she gently slid my plate to the side. Her face tightening. "Mr. Montague has requested yuh presence in him studio."

"Studio? Shit, Adessa. I wasn't aware that he made music. I can't sing for shit, so I don't know why he wants me in there."

Covering my hands with hers, she quipped, "Shai, its nuh dat kind of studio. Dat is weh him often handles business. It's soundproof. Nuh bady kno wah happens inna dere. It's nuh our business. Jus' kno dat him already spoken tuh Kenzo and Rocky an dem are all in dere waiting fi yuh. Are yuh ready tuh guh?'

"Adessa, you are scaring me. Hell no I'm not ready but I'm not no punk either. Take me to him."

She whistled loudly and Maxim walked into the room. "Ms. Shai. Please cum wit mi."

Getting up from the table, I looked back at Adessa. Flashing a kind smile my way, she nodded then turned her head. Maxim led the way to the elevator, where we descended to the basement. Another area of the house that I didn't know existed. *I swear, as soon as we are done in this "studio," someone will give me a proper tour of this big ass place. This is just too much.*

Maxim stopped and slid a card key. The door unlatched and Maxim gestured me to walk in first.

"Yuh nice and full mi luv?" Montague questioned as I entered the room.

"I am, now what is all this about?"

"Well, let mi set di scene fi yuh. Mi family leave, mi home is clean and now it's time fi mi tuh turn inna bed. Mi cum upstairs tuh check on yuh an mi find dis mudda-fucka in yuh room standing ova yuh wid him meat hanging out. Touching himself an rubbing on yuh legs. Yuh were dead tuh di world."

"Are you fucking serious Montague? Where in the fuck was Rocky and Kenzo?"

"We are sorry Shai," Kenzo spoke. I slipped away for two minutes to go drain the main vein and I came right back. Those two minutes were enough for him to sneak his ass in your room without anyone seeing him. I didn't know that he was in there until Montague yelled out."

"Well, where is this fucking pervert. Show him to me," I demanded.

"Mi thought dat yuh wud neva ask." A devilish smile appeared across his face as he knocked on the wall two times. The wall wasn't in fact a wall but a secret concealed door that led into another room.

"Him right inna here." he pointed in the direction of a chair with a bare-naked man strapped to it. His hands, legs and feet were all bound. There I stood frozen, breathless but most of all furious. Walking around to face him, I ordered Montague to take the gag out of his mouth.

"So tell me you sick muthafucka. What were you going to do to me? You had your dick hanging out and shit! Were you going to fuck me? Were you going to run your dick across my drunk and high lips? Let me guess, you were going to violate me, then walk home and eat a beef patty like nothing happened, huh? See, this is the shit that I can't stand. What the fuck be wrong with men like you? There are tons of loose ass women willing to fuck any and everything out here and you wanted the pussy that wouldn't have even known that you were in it. What kind of fucking psycho wants lifeless pussy," I barked. Slapping him across the face. "Answer me!!!"

"Umm, umm, umm, mi sorry ma'am. Mi wasn't gunna duh anyting tuh yuh. Yuh are jus' suh beautiful. Mi jus' wan tuh luk at yuh. Mi promise dat mi neva a guh touch yuh. Mi swear on mi mada grave."

"Shut up you lying piece of shit. If Montague hadn't come in when he did, there is no telling what you would have done to me. Somebody hand me something to beat his ass with. I see that he needs what a lot of men need. A good old fashion ass whooping. Ask Montague, I'm just the bitch to give it to you."

"Here yuh guh mi luv. Yuh preferred weapon of choice. A nice brand new axe handle."

"Please, ma'am, please. Mi promise mi nuh gunna touch yuh. Mi only wan tuh luk," his voice trembled with fear.

"Don't worry. I'm not a killer, but I *do* enjoy handing out a nice ass whooping," I yelled before smashing his hands with the bat.

The sound of bone cracking echoed through the room like a sick drumbeat. Each swing fueled me...rage mixed with relief. I had the power in my hand and *I* was the one in control. I thought about every time a man ignored my no, every time I had to shrink myself just to feel safe. Now? No shrinking. No silence. Just me, an axe handle, and this sorry excuse for a man strapped to a chair.

"You sick bastard," I spat, my chest heaving. "Do you know what it feels like to wake up wondering if somebody touched you while you were out cold? To not know what happened to your own damn body? I'll tell you what it feels like!! it feels like hell!! And lucky for you, I'm about to let you sample a small taste."

I swung again, harder, until his whimpers turned into muffled cries through the gag. A twisted satisfaction washed over me. Not because I enjoyed violence, but because justice was finally in my hands.

"If you ever try this shit again with another woman," I barked between swings, "you're gonna remember me. You'll remember the crazy bitch with the axe handle who made you rethink life. Every. Damn. Time. You. Move."

And still, I wasn't done. The axe handle connected with his knees, his shins, his ankles. By now, sweat rolled down my back, my arms screaming, but I didn't care. "Oh, you thought you were gonna take advantage of me? Thought I was just some drunk easy pussy waiting on your nasty ass? Well, congratulations. You just became my stress reliever. And trust me, I had plenty to get off my chest."

Finally, I raised the handle one last time, eyeing his shriveled meat stick. "Now, since you wanted to lead with *that*, let's make sure it retires early." With a swift blow, I brought the handle down. He screamed through the gag, his body jerking in the chair.

I leaned over him, panting, a wild laugh poured out of me despite the fury coursing through my veins. "Damn. Look at me. Out here swinging like Serena Williams. I bet you didn't think your night would end with me turning your dick into scrambled eggs." I dropped the stick at his feet, shaking my head. "Men like you make me sick. But thank you for the workout. I appreciate your cooperation." I turned, walking out of the hidden room like a woman who'd taken her power back.

Montague closed the concealed door shut and followed behind me. "Clean dis shit up. Nuh need tuh kill him. Him wutless now. Drop him off sumweh in di countryside. Now dat di business is handled. Mi gonna spend sum time wid mi lady."

"Shai, are yuh ok mi luv?"

I let out a sharp laugh, the kind that comes out when you're either about to cry or about to break something else. "No. No, I'm not okay. I'm so angry I could bite the marble out of your floor. Hell, I'm two seconds away from ripping the chandeliers down just to burn some of this adrenaline off."

I pressed my hands against my thighs, still trembling from the weight of the axe handle. I was out of breath as if I'd just ran a marathon. "You know what, Montague? That shit was therapy. Better than any therapist could ever give me. Swinging that axe handle? That was for every man that thought they could take something that didn't belong to them. For every woman that felt that at some point, her body wasn't hers. I swear, if I could bottle this feeling up, I'd sell this shit as 'Closure in a Can.'"

Montague stepped closer, his eyes searching mine, but I kept talking. Too full of adrenaline to stop. "And don't get me wrong, I don't glorify violence. But damn if it doesn't feel good to remind somebody that I'm not the one. He thought I was a sitting duck. His ass learned today that I was the wrong bitch to hunt."

Finally, I chuckled, the corner of my lips tugging upward. "Honestly, I think I got a little carried away. Poor stick didn't even ask to be part of this fight, and I damn near retired it on the first day."

"Yuh sure did mi baby. Yuh put dat stick tuh work," he chuckled.

"Tell Adessa she's gonna have to make me a plate of rice and peas later, because I burned every calorie swinging on that fool."

He smirked, but I caught the flicker of seriousness in his eyes.

"You know Montague, I do appreciate you letting me be the one to handle that. You could've done it your-self...quietly, swiftly and clean, like it never happened. But you gave me the chance to face him. To take my power back. That means more than you know."

I sighed, the fire in me settling into a steady glow. "So yeah, I'm not okay. But I will be. And now? I feel lighter. I don't care what they say about you, you're alright with me," I chuckled again, softer this time.

"Jus' alright? Mi hoped dat made mi more dan alright."

"It did. Trust me," I said, as our bodies grazed one another as we entered the elevator heading back up to the master suite. Gazing into his eyes, I cupped his chin in my hand and softly kissed his lips. "Thank you for protecting me, Montague. Thank you."

"A uhman like yuh needs tuh be protected at all cost. Eff yuh were mine, yuh wud neva, an mi duh mean neva ave tuh worry bout anyone fucking wid yuh eva again. Although mi si dat yuh are fully capable of seeing bout yuhself, jus' kno dat I'll die behind mine. Ask mi family. Dem kno how mi cum behind wah mi luv."

"I'm the same way. That's why I take it so hard when someone fucks over me. I'm solid as a rock when I'm locked in. I'll ride with you to the end of the earth especially if I know that you will do the same for me but if you cross me, then it's curtains for you. I will forgive because that is what my God requires me to do but I could never forget or let go of betrayal."

"Is dat suh? Well tell mi how yuh really feel," he chirped.

"I'm serious Montague. I need you to keep that in mind if you are even thinking of being mine because if you are with me, it's me alone. I love hard and it's pure. Loyalty means everything to me. Hell, loyalty is why I'm here."

"Eff dats suh true, den why yuh deal wid Umi. Umi looks out fi haarself. Nuh one else. Dat gyal nuh kno wah loyalty means. Mi telling yuh, sumting nuh right wit dat one. Eff di roles were reversed, mi wud bet dat har wud nuh duh di same fi yuh."

"Why do you dislike her so much? What did she do to you? She had to have done something for you to feel the way that you do about her."

"Truthfully Shai, sumone nuh ave tuh duh anyting tuh me fi mi tuh kno dat dey nuh shit. Mi cyan smell it on har. Di dishonesty, di sneakiness. It's a nuh fi mi. Watch wah mi tell yuh. Yuh will si in time. Jah will reveal tuh yuh wen di time is right."

Chapter Thirty

O ver the next week and a half, Montague and I carved out real time for just us. No interruptions, no chaos. Just me stepping deeper into his world. We finally ventured off the resort grounds and walked through some of his old stomping grounds. He showed me where he grew up, the corners he used to post up on, even a cracked basketball court where he swore he used to "run di place." I soaked it all in, wide-eyed like a kid, realizing there was so much to him I hadn't even scratched the surface of.

I learned the history of his family and how he amassed his fortune. I had assumed drugs, of course...because what else could explain the kind of wealth he flaunted? But I was wrong. Sure, he dabbled here and there in purchasing marijuana, but it was for his own personal use, not some drug kingpin empire.

Surprisingly, most of his wealth came from investing. My jaw nearly hit the ground when he pulled out files and showed me his stock portfolio. Who knew this man, with his heavy patois and bad-boy aura, could rattle off stock trends like he was ringing the opening bell on Wall Street? He only moved to the States to expand his portfolio, gain knowledge on the companies he was investing in, and position himself closer to other investors.

That's how he ended up in real estate development too. Land, houses, buildings...you name it, he had it in the bag. He owned spots not just in Jamaica, but Alabama, Texas, Connecticut, Cali and even a brownstone in New York. The man had keys everywhere.

He was smart, witty, and wise beyond his years. And after the night he snatched that pervert out of my room, his attentiveness hit code red. I couldn't sneeze without him reaching out to make sure I was okay. If I left a room, he left with me. If I looked lost in thought, he'd nudge me, "yuh alright, mi luv?" He needed to physically reach out and touch me, as if reassurance lived in his hands. And I can't lie. It felt so good.

With Montague, I didn't feel lucky. I felt blessed. His generosity was unmatched. He splurged and spoiled me without blinking. Shopping trips, yacht rides, excursions, even hopping on a private jet just because he "felt like lunch in another island." Me? I was lowkey exhausted. I'd never been so tired from being treated like royalty. Half the time I was thinking, *Lord, let me get a nap in before this man books another damn boat.*

But I loved every moment, because it was with him. When we were together, the world faded. Nothing else mattered. I'd never had that kind of devotion before. Where I didn't have to beg for attention, where I wasn't competing with other people or other priorities.

Rocky and Kenzo trailed right behind us, and I swear those boys were living their best lives. Before Jamaica, they had never been out of the South, so watching them eat lobster on a yacht and try to say "bougie" in a Jamaican accent had me hollering. I wanted them to enjoy it, too. So, I gave them half the money Aunt Trucee had slipped me before I left. They deserved to splurge as much as I did.

As promised, I talked to Aunt Trucee every day. And every day she asked the same nosy-ass question: had I slept with Montague yet? My answer stayed the same: "No, Auntie. Not yet." But she refused to believe me.

Cassy called, too, her voice dripping with that fake sweetness only she could pull off. She wanted to know when I was coming back. I played it cool, never giving her a straight answer. She hated that, and Lord knows, I loved that for me.

But beneath all the joy, there was this quiet dread building in me. The days were slipping away fast, and soon I'd have to leave the island. I wasn't ready. Jamaica had become a bubble of peace I didn't want to pop. Still, Umi sat heavy on my mind. Montague didn't like her, and it made it awkward to even say her name, but he promised she was fine. He promised I could talk to her before I left. I needed that conversation.

But my chest tightened every time I thought about it. What would she say when she found out I was falling for the very man who had her locked away? Would she understand that the heart doesn't take orders. It just... feels? Or would she look at me like a traitor? Maybe she'd be too grateful for freedom to care. Maybe she'd freak out. I didn't know. And the not knowing gnawed at me.

One evening, I sat quiet, my mind running wild, when Montague's voice snapped me out of it.

"Wah yuh tinking bout, gyal? Yuh luk spaced out ova dere."

"Do you want the truth or a lie?" I asked, half-joking.

"Di truth of course. Mi neva wanna hear nuh lie."

"I was thinking about Umi and her baby. I was also thinking about how I'm not ready to leave this beautiful place you call home. But most of all..." I smirked, leaning closer, "I was thinking about that handmade dress you bought me at that little shop. And how it made my ass look so good."

His laughter was warm, rumbling from deep in his chest. "Shai, baby, yuh ass luk gud in anyting yuh put on. Gyal, don't yuh kno yuh flawless in mi eyes?"

"That's sweet of you to say," I teased. "But I could stand to lose about forty pounds. I was already plush when I arrived, and Adessa's cooking is about to have me huge."

He frowned, shaking his head. "Yuh nuh need tuh lose nuttin. Nuh one pound. Yuh hear mi?"

I laughed softly. "I do." But in my heart, I wondered if I really believed it.

"Montague, can I ask you something?"

"Anyting," he said, his voice low and steady.

"When it comes time for you to let Umi go... does she have to worry about you coming for her again?"

"Shi nuh ave tuh worry bout mi," he answered without hesitation. "Mi nah badda her. But Lincoln probably will. Him stubborn, jus' like him fada was. Mi cyan try an tell him tuh leave har alone, but dat nuh mean him listen. Him fada was di same way. Him use tuh put him hands on mi sista all di time. Den one day, him went missing."

Montague's eyes shifted, as though he was replaying old memories. "Mi sista did hurt at first, but den shi started tuh find har laugh again, har smile. Mi knew den dat mi did di right thing." He glanced at me, waiting for my reaction, like he was bracing for judgment.

I let the silence hang for a moment, letting his words sink deep. "Sounds to me like you saw a problem, and you fixed it," I finally said. "That's the same reason I did what I did. I thought I was fixing things for Umi. I begged her to leave Lincoln and each time she said no. He had some kind of control over her. Funny thing is, she would still be with him had she not gone through his phone and saw all the women he was dealing with. I think the cheating, on top of the abuse was her breaking point.

To see someone you love be hurt over and over... does something to you.

So... Just like you with you sister.. I didn't want her to live like that either. To me, that's the same kind of love."

His eyes softened, something unspoken flickering there. "Truthfully, Shai, mi knew why yuh did wah yuh did. Mi felt it. Yuh heart, yuh strength, yuh honor. Dats wah pulled mi tuh yuh. Mi been waiting mi whole life tuh find sumone like yuh. Mi swear, God place yuh here fi mi. Yuh are mine, Shai an nuhbody cyan tell mi different."

My stomach did a little flip, the kind that made me want to smile and cry at the same time. But I wasn't letting him off that easy. "So why not just ask me out, Montague? Why take my best friend away from me first?"

He leaned forward, gaze locked on mine. "Because mi

needed yuh tuh si mi heart. Yuh wud neva dealt wid mi otherwise. Yuh wudda looked at mi an only si Lincoln an assume mi was like him. But mi and him? Nuttin alike. Now yuh si mi, fi real."

I blew out a shaky laugh. "You're right. I probably wouldn't have given you a second look. But guess what? I see you now. All of you. And honestly? These two weeks have been some of the best of my life. You're not who I thought you were. You told me you weren't a monster, and that you only 'touch people that need to be touched.' I believe that now. I can get behind that kind of justice. I'm laidback as hell, but if you mess with someone I love? Oh baby, I sit up real fast."

Montague threw his head back, laughing so hard he grabbed his side. "Shai, mi swear, yuh cud be a comedian. Yuh naturally funny widout even trying."

"Good," I smirked. "If I can't find a job when I get back, at least I've got a backup career in comedy."

He shook his head, still grinning. "It's been a long day, Shai. Wah yuh seh wi turn in fi di night?"

"I say yes to that," I replied, biting my lip. Then I took a breath and let it out slow. "But Montague... I want you to sleep in the master with me tonight. If that's okay with you."

His whole face lit up, like I'd just given him a winning lottery ticket.

"Gyal!" he hollered, throwing both hands in the air. "Yuh damn right it's ok wid mi. Mi bin wan tuh lay next tuh yuh soft, warm body. Mi cyaan wait."

I rolled my eyes, laughing. "You make it seem like you've been sleeping on a bed of nails."

He leaned in closer, voice dropping into that deep, dangerous softness that made my knees weak. "Gyal... wen mi bed nuh ave yuh in it, it feel exactly like dat."

Heat rushed up my neck, and I turned my face away so he wouldn't see the goofy smile I couldn't hold back.

"Mi jus' ave tuh run ova tuh di resort tuh sign some papers," he said, kissing my hand before pulling away. "But den, mi all fi yuh. Go on upstairs an get comfortable, mi queen. Mi soon cum."

"Hopefully, mi soon cum too," I teased. "Don't keep me waiting too long," I commanded, though my chest was thumping like a rabbit.

He smirked, brushing his lips against my cheek. "Truss mi... mi nuh keep mi queen waiting."

Chapter Thirty-One

As soon as I heard Montague leave the property, I pulled Rocky and Kenzo to the side.

"You two, come here please. I need to ask you for a favor."

Rocky narrowed his eyes. "What is it now, Shai?"

"Awww, cuz," I giggled, tugging at his arm. "Don't be like that. Listen, Montague will be staying in the master with me tonight, and I want you two to... get gone. We need some privacy."

Kenzo shook his head no instantly. "You know we can't do that. Our orders were not to leave you. Chartreuse would kill us if she found out."

"Rocky, Kenzo...come on. I'm not going to tell her and you're not leaving me. I just need a little privacy, if you know what I mean. Hell, I don't want y'all hearing us getting it on. I can get pretty loud. I want to be able to holler and scream like a rooster if I want. I can't do that if you guys are by the door." I smirked. "It's Friday, we leave Sunday. Go over to the resort. Spend some of that money I gave you, drink, dance, get some of that good Jamaican pum pum. I don't care what you do...just go. I promise to check in first thing in the morning. Please. please, please."

They exchanged a long silent look before Rocky sighed.

"Okay, Shai. But if you don't text us when you're done, we're kicking that door down. Don't make us regret this."

I hugged them both like the cousins I adored, thanking them a hundred times, before sprinting for the master suite, my heart thudding with excitement.

As soon as I closed the door, I heard a shift behind me, heels scraping the marble. My pulse jumped.

Assuming it was Kiyana, I called, "Nothing to see here, Kiyana. Just getting my things prepared. About to hop in the shower, relax, and enjoy my night. In a mocking fashion, I muttered, "And nuh, mi nuh need nuh help with me twenty seven year old pum pum." I giggled at myself.

A cold, sharp voice cut through the air.

"Suh, yuh are da new bitch him running around wid. Mi knew mi wud catch dem slipping one day. Suh wah yuh name, gyal?"

I froze. That wasn't Kiyana.

Slowly turning, I found myself staring at a brickhouse. She was tall and beautiful but nothing behind her eyes but sadness. Her hands balled into fists at her sides. Her stiletto nails looked sharp enough to slice. Staring at me, she looked ready to lunge.

My throat went dry, but I refused to flinch. "My name is none of your fucking business. But let me guess, you're Lotus."

She smirked. "Lotus, yeah. Him muss ave told yuh bout mi. Mi di luv of him life."

A sharp laugh escaped me before I could stop it. "Love of his life? Girl please. He called you the bane of his existence. Psycho ass...jumping fences, climbing walls. Girl, what the hell is wrong with you? Don't you see he doesn't want you? Seven years is a long-ass time to hold onto someone who clearly is no longer interested."

Her nostrils flared as she took a step closer. I held my ground, though my heart was beating out of my chest. She was beautiful, yes, but her beauty was mixed with danger.

"Mi nuh wan nuh one else. Mi wan him," she said, her voice low and guttural, as if she could chew through brick.

"But '*him*' all mine now and I'm the love of his life, Lotus. So please, just leave us alone." I lifted my chin as sweat broke across my back. "He'll be back any second. Do you really want him to drag you out again? Aren't you tired of being thrown out on your ass? "

Her lips quivered. For a second, I thought she might swing at me. Then her voice cracked.

"Did him tell yuh bout di baby? Dat was mi baby. Wen dat pure soul left di earth, suh did Montague's feelings fi mi. Him blamed mi fi Jr. dying. Mi luv mi baby. Mi did nuttin'."

The fury drained out of her words and left behind nothing but grief.

And just like that, my fear disappeared and was replaced with grief for her.

"I'm sorry, Lotus," I whispered, my tone softening. "He told me about him. I don't think he truly blamed you. I think he was mad at God for taking his baby. And when we hurt, we lash out at the people closest to us. He doesn't hate you. He hates the pain. Give yourself some grace."

Tears spilled, heavy and non-stop. Her shoulders trembled.

This woman wasn't crazy. She was broken.

"Lotus, come here," I said gently, opening my arms.

For a minute I wasn't sure if she'd hit me or fall into me. But then she fell forward, clinging to me like her life depended on it. She sobbed against my shoulder, shaking so hard I thought she was convulsing. She held me so tight that my back cracked.

We stood in the bathroom, hugging and crying like two women who'd known the pain of losing someone you loved. I was now her human tissue, but I didn't mind. We were still holding each other, two strangers bound by pain, when the door flew open.

Montague stormed inside, his eyes wild, his chest heaving like he'd sprinted from the resort. The moment his eyes landed on Lotus wrapped around me, his whole face twisted into something feral.

"Wah...wah di fuck is dis? Lotus!" His voice roared, filling every corner of the room. "Get off her! Shai, did shi hurt yuh?" He was already reaching for the gun at his waist.

Lotus jumped like a child caught red-handed, stepping back with her hands up. Her tear-streaked face filled with fear and sorrow.

"Montague, no!" I shouted, stepping between them with my hands up. My heart raced so fast it felt like it would burst. "It's not what you think. Put the damn gun down."

"She trick yuh, Shai. Step away from har. Har nuh mean yuh nuh gud!" His voice cracked, filled with rage, spit flying. "Shi nuh belong in mi house! Mi told security tuh keep har off dis property. How shi get in?"

"Because it's easy for broken people to find cracks, Montague." I continued. "Listen, she didn't hurt me. She just needed to be heard. She needed to say what she's been carrying. That's all."

He cut his eyes at Lotus, disgust tightening his jaw. "Mi nuh wan hear nuh more of har madness. Mi tired."

"Then don't hear it from her, hear it from me," I snapped, surprising myself. "Lotus said when Jr. died, she lost you too. She feels like you blamed her for everything. And all she wanted back then was your arms around her. You weren't the only one who lost a child, Montague. She was grieving too."

For a moment, silence fell, thick and haunting. Montague's gun dropped to his side, though his hand stayed tightly wrapped around it. He glanced at Lotus with sadness behind his eyes.

"Shi right," he said finally, his voice low, almost ashamed. "Mi was gaan too far in mi head tuh comfort anyone. Mi sorry. Mi sorry dat mi nuh dere fi yuh wen yuh needed mi, Lotus. Mi sorry dat mi let grief turn mi cold. Mi really did luv yuh, but dat time gone. Mi cyaan go back."

Lotus's lips trembled as more tears fell. For the first time, she looked... lighter. "Dat's all mi needed, Montague. Jus' tuh hear yuh seh it. Mi promise, mi jumping fence days ova. Mi a guh. Jus' kno, yuh ave a real gem in Shai. Treat har right."

Before either of us could speak, she turned and slipped past him, her body swaying like a ghost.

Montague rushed to the cameras, his fingers flying. "Security!" he barked into the intercom. "How dis woman end up in mi house?"

Seconds later, his men stormed in. "Boss, we swear, we never saw her come in. We only jus' now saw har walking out. She nuh seh a word."

Montague rubbed his temple, exhaling like the weight of ten years sat on his chest. "Guh back tuh yuh post. Pray shi neva cum back."

The door shut behind them, and the silence that followed was thick enough to cut.

I placed a hand on Montague's chest. His heart was pounding as hard as mine.

"She didn't come here to hurt me, Montague," I whispered. "She came here to finally let go."

His eyes softened, but anger still coursed through his veins. It was all over his face. "Shai... yuh nuh undastan. Eff Lotus cyan slip in here, anyone cyan. Tonight mi tink mi almost lost yuh."

I held his face in my hands. "No. You didn't. I'm right here."

Chapter Thirty-Two

After all was said and done, the room felt almost impossibly quiet again. Montague's chest rose and fell against mine, his hands gripping my arms like he was afraid I might vanish.

"You're still shaking, Montague." I smiled softly, teasing just enough to make him look at me.

"Mi... mi tink shi had hurt yuh, Shai," he said, his voice low, but filled with emotion. "Mi... cyaan even... tink bout dat."

I cupped his face, pressing my lips to his forehead then sliding down to his mouth, hovering over his lips. "I keep telling you, I'm fine," I whispered. "I'm good and I'm not going anywhere."

"Mi suh sorry dat yuh had tuh deal wid dat, but mi

tank yuh fi showing har compassion an empathy. Mi had nuh idea dat shi carrying all dis pain from wah happened wid us, an da baby. Yuh are really sumting special, gyal."

"No need to thank me. It needed to be done," I chimed.

Seconds later, his hands wrapped around my waist, lifting me slightly as he pressed his mouth to mine in a kiss that was part relief, part hunger, part need. It was messy, breathless, and desperate, like we were trying to convince each other we were still alive after surviving a storm.

I clung to him, letting all the fear and adrenaline dissolve, as he pressed his body against mine. His arms felt like home. His chest, warm and strong, he was a shield I never wanted to leave.

Montague smirked against my lips, "Mi gunna keep yuh safe. Always."

I whispered, "Tonight has been a lot for both of us. We could use a nightcap or something, or we could use each other," I smiled. Let's just be us. Forget what just happened and let's not think about anything but us... Just... us, okay?"

His grin was sweet. "Us it is, gyal. Mi nuh lettin' guh."

Suddenly, a smile spread across his face.

"What are you smiling about, Montague?

"Yuh. Mi smiling at yuh. Mi lucky dat yuh are here wid me. Mi feel suh blessed tuh ave yuh near."

As if a lightbulb went off in his head, he trekked to the door and peeked into the hallway, "Ummm, weh is Rocky and Kenzo?"

"I sent them over to the resort so that we could be alone," I quipped, my fingers brushing his beard as I flashed a devilish smile.

"Yuh wicked gyal. Muss ave sum ting on yuh mind?"

"And I do," I murmured, my pussy already thumping at the thought. "Yes, I do have something on my mind, and I plan on getting it, and other things off, tonight."

Grabbing my hand, he led me to the shower, his eyes fierce and needy. We began undressing each other, slow and deliberate, savoring the anticipation. I couldn't help but admire the masterpiece that stood before me, and he did the same.

The moment we stepped under the four cascading showerheads, I grabbed the bodywash, lathered my sponge, and handed it to him. He began washing me tenderly, every stroke from neck to feet filled with care and intimacy. Once done, he lathered his sponge, and I returned the favor, watching the water wash away every worry and tension.

Then his finger lifted my chin, guiding me to his mouth. Our tongues met, a new dance of passion, exploring what had been forbidden until now. His fingers trailed down my body, finding my pleasure button, and I bit his lip softly as he teased and circled my clit. He slipped two fingers into my snatch, finding my G-spot and motioned "come here," until I did. Trembling and shaking, I came all over his fingers and watched the water wash the evidence of my pleasure down the drain.

Before I could catch my breath, he pressed me back against the wall, his length sliding deep inside me. I gasped, almost cumming again from the sheer pressure and depth alone.

"Ooooh Shit, Montague. You feel so good," I moaned.

"Yeaaa, Shai. Tell mi, tell mi how good mi feel," he groaned, rocking with precise, passionate intent. Each thrust, each subtle flick of his hips, had me clinging to him as if I'd never let go. He touched my cervix with ease and the pressure was as painful as it was pleasureful.

Montague's length and girth was intimidating but enticing as well. With each stroke, I could feel my walls stretching, quaking and contracting. Nothing like I've ever experienced. He didn't even have to move. I could cum from the size and penetration alone. He swayed his hips, pumping fiercely. He fucked me like he owned me. In that moment, I was utterly and completely his.

"Shai, Fuccckkkkk. Yuh pussy is suh good. It's suh tight. Damn gyal. Yuh are gripping mi suh hard, yuh bout tuh push mi out." he whispered as he continued rocking me into ecstasy.

I'd never been with an older man before. He was nine-teen years my senior, but he was fucking me like a YN. His stamina was crazy. It made me wonder if he'd stopped and gotten one of those gas station pills from somewhere. There was no way this forty-six year old man was about to make me tap out.

Without warning, he yanked me by the hair and spun me around. Sliding in from the back he began to fuck me so hard, a single tear rolled from my eye. Reaching around from behind, he grabbed my neck with the perfect amount of pressure. He pumped nut after nut from me without ceasing. Each time I attempted to catch my breath and recover, there was another one.

The gentle fucking was over. He was in that mode and his strokes were relentless. My body was giving away as the water splashing around us sounded like a private symphony. Montague's lips and hands were everywhere... licking my neck, kissing, and grinding while cuffing my ass. There was no part of my body he left untouched. The direct eye contact, the intimate pressure, sent me into multiple orgasms. Leaving me gasping and trembling for more. He was a bad man in the best way possible.

Afterwards, completely exhausted, I wanted nothing more than coconut water, a puff of good ganja, and a bed. I had found my champion lover, and I hated myself for waiting until the last hour to experience him fully.

We ran to the kitchen like two teenagers for snacks before collapsing into the bed. Later, I sent a quick text to Rocky and Kenzo letting them know they could return.

That night, wrapped in his arms, I felt a peace I hadn't known before. Two weeks had woven us close, and the thought of leaving this paradise, and him, was bittersweet. I prayed he was genuine, that his words weren't just promises whispered in the heat of the moment. I couldn't take deception again; I'd probably end up jumping fences like Lotus, but I would be jumping them to fuck someone up. Not to gain closure.

The next morning, I woke to Adessa smiling by the bedside.

"Good morning, Madam. Mr. Montague is downstairs in him office but ask mi tuh cum upstairs tuh si wah yuh wan fi breakfast."

"Damn, Adessa. What time does he get up? It still feels early as hell."

"Mr. Montague day starts 'round 5:30 A.M. Him very much indeed a mawnin person. It's 8:00 now. Yuh wan saltfish and ackee?"

"You know it, Adessa. I don't have much time left to enjoy your cooking. Everything here is so fresh. I'm gonna miss it for sure."

She laughed. "Nuh talk like dat, Ms. Shai. Mi ave a

feeling yuh will be back sooner dan later. Mr. Montague nuh stop wen him like sumbody."

"I don't want him to stop. That man has me hook line and sinker. I don't know what I'm going to do without him. I've gotten so use to his presence," I admitted.

"Him told mi dat yuh two nuh live dat far from each oddah. Truss, him will mek it wuk. Him really likes yuh. Him may even luv yuh."

"You really think so, Adessa? I've been thinking about this whole thing, and I hope that we aren't moving too fast. I'm crazy about him too. It feels like love to me as well, but I just don't know. Can you really fall in love with someone in two weeks? We are still getting to know each other. We still have a lot to learn about how one another moves, but after being here with him, I can't see myself with anyone else. He makes my heart do back flips."

"Si child, yuh may still be confused but Mr. Montague is nuh. Him is middle aged an kno wah him wan. Mi sure dat him will give yuh time eff dats wah ya need."

"No Adessa, I don't need any time."

"Oh, suh yuh sure now, ehh? Must ave been all dat activity dat mi heard lass night. Mi heard yuh clean through di oddah side of di house. Dat sealed di deal, ehh." She chuckled.

"What are you trying to say Adessa, you think that I'm

dickmatized? I can't lie, that certainly was a factor but not the main factor. I started to feel this way about him before he blessed me with that good sturdy meat."

She laughed uncontrollably, wagging her finger. "Get yuh robe on an cum eat. Breakfast waiting fi yuh. Mi kno wah yuh wan before mi ask."

Chapter Thirty-Three

I brushed my teeth, slipped on my robe, and went downstairs to find breakfast waiting. Montague joined me, and we couldn't stop smiling at each other, completely smitten.

"So, mi luv, dis is di last day wi ave tuh spend together until mi get back tuh di states. Mi ave a few business meetings coming up shortly suh unfortunately, mi nah be on di plane wid yuh while yuh return tuh Georgia. Is dat ok wid yuh."

"Well, I really wish that you were coming back with me, but you are a businessman. That means that you have to do what businessmen do and I will never step in the way of your livelihood. I'll miss you being with me, but I can handle a flight. Smiling, I muttered, "All I need if a few puffs of that good shit that you've got and I'll be ok.

Without you beside me, I'll probably sleep the whole flight anyhow."

"Well mi lady, everyday ave bin all bout yuh. Todeh is nuh different. Wah duh yuh wan tuh get into?"

"Honestly, I just want to stay in, lay under you, maybe watch TV. Just really enjoy these last moments before I leave."

Sadness washed over me at the thought of leaving him. He knew it the moment he looked into my face.

"Wah wrong, sweetface? Why dat look all of a sudden."

"You know why." I pouted.

"Mi will be back in di states sooner den lata. Mi will cum straight tuh yuh. Plus, mi cum tuh Jamaica twice a month. Yuh cyan always cum wid mi. Mi actually wud luv dat."

"I don't want to stress about that now and spoil the day. I'm sure that we will figure it out. Now, about Umi... when will she be free?"

"Shi already back wid Lincoln and shi already ave har phone. Yuh may call har weneva yuh like."

I laughed in relief. "Seriously? Baby Lincoln too?"

"Of course, mi not gunna bring di mada back widout da pickney."

"I'm so happy to hear that. Thank you for keeping your word. I'm going to finish eating and then call her."

"Mi happy dat yuh happy. While yuh guh chat wid

Umi, Mi gunna ave dem set di entertainment room up suh dat wi cyan lay out an relax."

He kissed me before leaving the table then trekked off to find someone to set up the projector for us. Once I was done eating, I went outside in the garden. Finding the nearest bench, I placed a call to Umi's phone.

"Hello."

"Umiiiii, how are you doing?" I asked cheerfully.

"Shaiiiiiii, it's so good to hear your voice girl."

"Same here. How's everything going? Are you good?"

"Well with all things considered, I'm doing fine. Lincoln is a little fucked up, but he will be ok. They did have to amputate his hand but he's in good spirits. He's still talking about killing you, but not just you, Montague as well."

"Whaaaaat? Why does he want to kill Montague? I'm the one that whooped his ass."

"Because he took me away from him for two weeks. He was mad as hell when I showed back up at the hospital and told him where I'd been. I tried to tell him that I was in a house, safe and sound but he didn't want to hear anything that I had to say. He went on and on about how he couldn't trust anybody, and he questioned why his own blood would want to spend time with the very person that ruined him."

"Umi, if Montague hadn't taken you, you were going

to leave him anyhow. You must have failed to mention that little tidbit to him?"

She sighed deeply and paused before she spoke again.

"Umm, yeah, I kind of did. I didn't want to kick him while he was already down."

"Whatever Umi. Fuck Lincoln!! I think we both know he is barking up the wrong tree when it comes to Montague. I've been with this man for two weeks. I see how he moves. Listen, if you've decided to stay with that lying, cheating piece of shit....that's on you. But if you want what's left of his ass, you should advise *your man* to back down. Montague isn't what he wants. Trust me. Everyone around him is locked and loaded and ready for that action including him. Being that Lincoln is his nephew; you would think he would know better."

Popping her lips, Umi muttered, "Now you know nobody can tell him shit. He feels how he feels, and nothing is going to change that. He is mad at the world right now. He has one hand, and the other has just a little function. So yes, he's ready to kill the world but in time, he should be alright."

I snapped, "Anyhow Umi, I asked how you were doing, not Lincoln. I could give a fuck less about him, his condition or his delusion. Please let's not talk about his ass."

"Shai," she chuckled, "This shit didn't change you one

bit. You are still as mean as a rattlesnake. Anyway, I'm doing alright. They brought me right back to town and I told them to take me to the hospital. He apologized for everything that he'd done to me. He looked so pitiful laying up there in that bed and --."

Umi, I barked, cutting her off mid-sentence. "I could have sworn I said not another word about Lincoln. Did you hear me say that? Because I heard me say that."

"Ok, Ok, Nothing else about Lincoln. You know, before I say anything else, I want to tell you thank you for doing what you did for me. You really took one for the team because I know spending two weeks with Montague must have been miserable."

Laughing, I muttered, "Girl, you have no idea."

"I can only imagine, Shai. That man is something serious. No one fucks with him because he is mean as hell. They are all scared of him. He is crazy. For goodness sake, that nigga had me kidnapped. Who the fuck does something like that?"

I stood silent. Holding the phone to my ear, almost ashamed to say another word. *She hates him and he hates her. This should go very well.*

Clearing my voice, I belted out, "I'm aware of what people may say but trust me, once you get to know him, he isn't half bad at all."

"Wait, so are you telling me that you enjoyed your time with him?"

"Umi, I can't lie. Enjoy doesn't even begin to describe how much I loved being here and with him. I don't know what Montague you met but I can assure you that it isn't the same one that I'm getting to know. This one is sweet as ever."

"Bitch, I know that you've got to be fucking with me. So are y'all together now?"

"I don't know what this is Umi, but Montague and I are definitely feeling each other. In other words, we are working on it. I wasn't going to tell you at first, but I figured you would find out anyway. I may as well get it out. He has been nothing short of amazing to me. We've done so much together in such a short time. I'm actually dreading coming back home but wheels go up tomorrow at 8:00 A.M. Umi, it's still not too late for you to come stay with me at aunt Trucee's house. The offer still stands."

With anger in her voice, she snapped. "Nawl, I'm good. Imma just stay here with my handicapped man. That muthafucka took me from my baby, held me captive for damn near two weeks and you are over there in Jamaica laid up with him."

"Umi, I only came over here for you. I didn't know I would start feeling this way about him."

"Whatever...I can't believe you Shai. I hope you and

Montague have a nice life." she said before hanging up in my face. I knew there was a possibility that she would react like that, so I wasn't going to use it against her. I would simply wait a little while before reaching out again.

I then called Aunt Trucee.

"Hey Niece. Are you ready to come home?"

"Auntieeeeeee. I'm as ready as I'll ever be."

She laughed. "What does that mean, Shug?"

"It means if I could climb inside this man's skin, I would. He is everything."

She giggled. "Well, did you fu—"

"Yesss, Auntie! We finally made love. It was amazing. That man gave me the best loving of my life. It was our first time, and I have to tell you. If I could make love to him every day for the rest of my life, I would."

"Well damn, Shai. Does he have any brothers or uncles? His ass ain't too far in age from me," she teased.

I laughed. "His best friend, Wicked. You'd like him. He's loyal, fine, and about business. He does have an older brother, but he's taken."

"Well, if you're feeling him like that, I need to meet him. Pronto."

"You will. We're about to have a relaxing movie day so I gotta run. I'll call in the morning before the wheels go up."

"Ok, baby. Talk to you then. Love you."

"I love you too, Aunt Trucee."

I left the garden and sauntered into the entertainment room. Montague was laid out on the plush sofa staring at the ceiling. I started to tell him what Umi said about Lincoln, but he looked like he had some shit on his mind so I abandoned that idea. I'd mention it to him later. Instead, I laid across his chest and asked, "What's wrong baby? Why are you looking so serious?"

"Same ting dats wrong wid yuh," he chuckled. "Mi dreading watching yuh leave mi. Mi nuh kno wah mi gunna duh widout yuh."

"Don't worry, I muttered. We will figure it out. For now, lets just keep the energy positive and enjoy each other for as long as we can."

We watched a little tv while cuddling, kissing and hugging. His arms felt so good wrapped around me. This was a feeling that I knew I would crave and miss long after I was gone.

After cuddle time, we made our way to the kitchen to make lunch together. Adessa provided gentle guidance while Montague and I flirted over chopping boards and sizzling pans. I accidentally spilled jerk seasoning on his chest, and he clicked water at me in retaliation. We were soaked, laughing and completely lost in our little bubble.

By late afternoon, we found ourselves frolicking a quiet stretch of beach. Montague pulled a small blanket from his bag, and we sat in silence, letting the waves crash around our feet. I leaned against him, breathing in his scent, savoring the warmth of his body and memorizing the curves of his shoulder.

"These two weeks went by so fast, Montague. I wish we had more time," I whispered, my fingers tracing his strong jawline.

"Time is a fickle friend, Shai," he murmured. "But remember dis, distance cyaan compete wid wah real. Yuh mine, Shai. Nuh matter wah *distance* say."

I smiled, stomach full of butterflies but also feeling the ache of knowing that a piece of my heart would be gone tomorrow. That night, we made love again, over and over. Each kiss, each touch, each moan was a soft reminder that what started as a call to duty, had turned into a world wind romance. One that I couldn't see myself doing without.

While nuzzling in my bosom, he whispered, "Stay Shai, yuh nuh haffi guh."

A single teardrop fell from my eye. I closed them while I wrapped myself with his arms.

Chapter Thirty-Four

The next morning, as light the color of fresh honey poured across the bedroom, Montague and I lay still, clinging to each other like the silence itself was breaking us apart. The air was heavy with goodbyes we refused to speak. The memory of his touch from the night before still burned across my skin, making the thought of leaving him unbearable.

Adessa had quietly packed my things while we slept. It was one less thing to worry about, but it made everything feel too final. I would miss her cooking, her laughter, her soft words of wisdom that greeted me in the mornings. But more than anything, I would miss waking up to the warmth of her kindness...and to him.

I forced myself out of bed, bathed, and dressed with trembling hands, each movement feeling like a countdown. I wasn't ready to walk away from the man I had grown so deeply attached to. Infatuation or love, I didn't know. But I knew one thing with painful certainty, no other man had ever touched my soul the way Montague had.

I gripped his hand and stroked his beard. I hung on to him like it was the last time I'd ever touch him. "Yuh ready tuh break mi heart, gyal?" His voice was low, almost broken as he carried my suitcase to the elevator.

"Montague, stop. I don't want to leave either, but I have to. I need to get back to Macon. I have to find a job, a place to stay, and get my life together. I can't do that from here."

He stepped closer, his breath warm against my cheek. "Mi kno wah yuh tink yuh haffi do. But mi cyan get yuh a place. Mi cyan give yuh money, mi cyan give yuh everyting yuh need. Yuh nuh haffi depend on nuhbody or nuttin. All yuh need tuh duh is seh yuh mine."

Sucking in a deep breath, I quipped, "After what we've shared in just two weeks, you know I'm yours. But we still need more time. We have to get to know each other better before—"

"Mi nuh need nuh more time." His grip tightened on my hand. "Mi seen all mi need tuh si. Shai, yuh one of a kind. At first mi jus' wanted tuh kno yuh. Now, mi only need tuh kno how tuh keep yuh. Mi nah guh chain yuh tuh mi life, but promise mi dis...nuh let wah wi ave guh tuh waste. Promise mi yuh call wen yuh land."

"I promise," I whispered, choking on the words.

His kiss was slow, desperate...an imprint, as if he were branding me with his memory. I melted into him, aching to pack this moment in my suitcase and carry it home with me.

Not long after, we drove to the airport. Kenzo, Rocky, and I boarded the jet, while Montague followed us up the stairs to speak with Neeko. He came to my seat, leaned over, and buckled my seatbelt like he couldn't let go of even the smallest detail of me. Then, without a word, he kissed me so deeply my toes curled, so fiercely my soul cried out.

Kenzo and Rocky groaned and expressed their displeasure of our public display of affection. We didn't give a damn. Montague and I ignored them. He dapped them up and pinched my cheek like I was something precious. Then he turned and descended the stairs, his figure shrinking with every step.

The door hadn't even closed before the tears came. My chest heaved like I was being torn in two. Kenzo just sighed, opened his arms, and let me soak his shirt, knowing I needed to let it go.

"See, Cuz?" Rocky said softly. "I told you that man was serious about you. And look at you...bawling like your heart just walked off with him. Guess it did. I gotta admit though, Montague and his crew? Solid as hell."

Kenzo nodded. "Shidd, I'm gonna miss this island. Back home don't look and feel shit like this. This felt like paradise and that man...He's living right. Taking care of his people. Doing right by folks...that's rare. He's the real deal."

I popped two valium and stared out the window. My phone buzzed, I answered with tears in my eyes.

"Safe flight, Shai. Call mi wen yuh land. Nuh duh nuttin crazy without mi."

I smiled, feeling the warmth of his words. "Always," I said. Hands trembling slightly.

As the plane lifted off, I pressed my head into Kenzo's shoulder. Leaving a piece of my heart in Jamaica. I lay there thinking about the mansion, the pool, the beach, his arms, his lips, the way he looked at me, the way he made me feel. I realized with a mixture of dread and excitement; my life was now split. Two places, two worlds, but one heart and it was completely his. I closed my eyes and woke up to the jet humming to a stop.

Silence filled the cabin like a funeral. As we descended down the stairs, the hot Georgia air hit me in the face like a ton of bricks. The warmth wasn't tropical, but it was comforting in a way that made me sigh. It was thick and heavy with exhaust instead of sea salt. A black car waited on the tarmac, the driver already holding the door open like he'd been expecting us.

Kenzo whispered, "Shidd, they can't fuck with us. We movin' like celebrities now. Aint nobody gonna believe this shit."

I wanted to laugh but couldn't. My chest hurt too much. This wasn't the island, this wasn't the beach and none of these men were Montague. This was now my home and my new beginning, and somehow, it didn't feel like mine anymore. I missed *my* man.

Within an hour of sliding into the car, we arrived back at Aunt Trucee's house. Rocky and Kenzo didn't waste any time teasing me about Montague.

"Gawwwt damn, Shai. You must have put that monkey on that man real bad. He hasn't stopped texting you since we touched down."

"Shut up Kenzo and mind your business, I said as I galloped up the steps. The door swung open, and Aunt Trucee stood there with open arms.

"Let's try this again, Shug. Welcome home baby," she laughed. Hopefully you will be here more than one day this time."

"If it were up to me Aunt Trucee, I'd hop in my car and drive my ass across the water to get back to that man."

"Baby, yo ass trying to die. Talking about driving over

water. You've got money now. Just take a flight," we both chuckled.

I spent the rest of the day unpacking and lingering over every item from Jamaica... the small carved wooden fish, the handmade dress Montague had picked out for me, to the little seashells we'd collected on our last beach walk. Every piece held a memory, and a touch of him.

Chapter Thirty-Five

Aunt Trucee called for me over the intercom and asked me to join her for breakfast in her wing. I immediately requested ackee and saltfish, plantains, and Johnny cakes for breakfast.

"Child, I don't know if chef has those ingredients, but I will surely call down to the kitchen to see. Damn, niece, grits ain't good enough anymore, huh? I bet you like porridge and shit now, don't you?"

I could feel her smile through the phone.

"Just kidding with you. Get on down here now. We need to have a serious conversation."

Her voice was still soft but with a tinge of angst.

What on earth could she want to talk about? I'd only been back a day, and I was already being hit with something else. My life was always filled with some kind of drama. I'd grown accustomed to always being involved in some shit.

I'd never experienced the kind of peace that I experienced in Jamaica. However, when I truly examined my stay, it was filled with drama as well. The difference was, I had a buffer in Montague. It was like being surrounded by stingless hornets. Of course, they are scary to look at and be around, but no matter how hard they tried, they could never hurt you. They simply didn't possess the capability. That is how being with a man like him makes you feel...untouchable.

But there was no buffer here. Every second that melted away made me painfully aware of that. From Umi leaving hateful text messages on my phone, to my mother leaving frantic messages on my voicemail, it was as if everyone was losing their fucking minds.

I pushed my frustration aside and sauntered out into the hallway where I was greeted by Bakari.

"Well, hello, Shai. It's great to have you back."

I stared into his grey eyes and had a flashback of the evening we shared before I left.

"Ummm, good morning, Bakari. Would you mind showing me where Aunt Trucee's room is? I wasn't here long enough to learn the layout, and I don't want to get lost."

"Sure thing. Just follow me."

Grabbing my hand, we walked to the elevator while he asked about my "little vacation."

"Honestly, Bakari, I'd rather not talk about that if it's ok with you. I'm still tired, and I'm trying to get my bearings back."

"Well, I think I can help you in that department. In case you forgot, I offer a hell of a massage."

He smiled as he peered down at my breasts. I closed my robe. He winked, and we hopped off the elevator to the first floor.

"Shai, go down this hallway and take a right. Her room is the one with the French doors. They are painted purple. You can't miss it."

"Thanks, Bakari."

I winked my eye and jogged to her bedroom door. I knocked twice before the door opened with Teezy standing behind it.

"You may go ahead and leave, Teezy. Shai is here, and it's time for her and I to have a heart-to-heart."

Teezy nodded his head as he swiftly exited the room.

"Aunt Trucee, why are you sounding so serious? Is there something wrong? Are you sick? Are you mad, wait... is this about Cassie? What in the hell did she do? I know her ass did something because she is about the only person that can make you sad like this."

"Cassie didn't do anything, baby. This here is all about me."

She patted a seat right beside her. I looked around. Aunt Trucee's bedroom was nothing short of a sanctuary...luxury wrapped in elegance with a touch of southern charm.

"Auntie, what is this about? Please hurry up and tell me what's wrong. I've got knots in my stomach."

I looked at her and knew that I'd set myself up for a joke.

"Are you sure those are knots, or are those Montague's kids fighting in your belly?"

Cackling, she grabbed her side, doubling over with laughter.

"That shit ain't funny, Auntie. Seriously, what's going on?" My voice was now low, but firm.

"Ok, baby. I'll be serious now, but I had to get that one out. Have you talked to my sister?"

Her head tilted to the side.

"Now you know I haven't. She left a few voicemails, but I've yet to check them. I'm sure it has something to do with her finding out that I've moved away from Roseville. She's probably pissed that I didn't say goodbye or something like that. You know my mama is petty Betty."

"Yes, my sister is petty as hell. She called me a few days ago.

She had a few choice words for me. She told me that I was a piece of shit for letting you come stay here and not telling her that you moved. I don't know who in the hell she thinks she is, but I told her you were a grown-ass woman. If you wanted her to know you were moving, she would have known. I also let her know I didn't need her permission to do a damn thing. Well, as you can guess, that pissed her off. She said that I would regret not telling her, so I am getting to you before she does."

"You know your sister is the most dramatic person on the planet. Whatever it is, I'm sure it's not as bad as she would have made it. What is it?" I asked.

As she opened her mouth to speak, Aunt Trucee's phone buzzed, alerting her of someone's presence at the gate. She picked up the receiver, placing it on speaker. A voice yelled out:

"Mama, open the gate. We need to talk."

Trucee's eyes got big as saucers.

"Ummmm, Ok, baby. Give me a minute. I'll have one of my men let you in," she spoke into the phone.

"What in the hell is she doing here? What in the hell is going on?" Confusion spread across my face.

"I promise, baby, I'm going to tell you everything, but we've got a guest. Let's see what she wants first."

Trucee phoned Teezy, telling him to let her daughter in. We both got up and sauntered to the front door. Cassie approached the steps with a scowl on her face and heat in her stride. As the door unlatched, Trucee and I stood as she walked in and walked past us. She didn't look at Trucee or me.

"Well hello to you too, Cassie. I know you have better manners than that. You don't walk past your mother and not say hello. That's just rude. You don't have to speak to me because I don't give a shit if you do or don't, but you are not about to do my auntie like that. Not in my face you are not and how in the hell did you find out where your mama lived? I know your ass didn't ask her or she wouldn't be so surprised to see you."

"Shai, did you forget that you share locations with me? That's how I found you. I purposely waited until you got back before I made this trip."

"Yes, I forgot. I don't be thinking about shit like that. Thanks for reminding me because I really need to turn my location off. This shit is getting ridiculous. Anyway, I don't care about all that. Use your damn manners and speak to my auntie like you've got some sense before I knock fire out your ass." I demanded.

"I'm here to clear some shit up," she huffed. "I talked to Aunt Lenora a couple of days ago. She told me some shit I couldn't believe so I'm here to get the truth from my mama."

"Cassie, what in the hell is wrong with you? Don't come over here with some bullshit my mama told you. Y'all are always trying to start some mess. Damn, do you enjoy being a bitter-ass bitch?" I barked.

"I'm not bitter, Shai," she retorted. "I just want this no-good, poor-ass excuse of a mama to tell me the truth."

I braced myself because I just knew Aunt Trucee was about to touch every wall in this room with Cassie, but she didn't. She stood there frozen and motionless. I'd never seen her let anyone talk to her like that without popping off.

Seeing the look on Trucee's face pissed me off even more. I turned towards Cassie and barked, "Who in the fuck are you calling no-good? If anything, your ass is the one that's no good. Driving all the way up here to start some shit. Hell, I just got back. Aunt Trucee and I were just about to have a sit-down and enjoy a nice breakfast, and here you go with your hateful ass. Rolling up in here like you coming to check somebody. Why don't you take your prissy ass back to Roseville and leave us the fuck alone."

"Gladly. I'd be happy to do that as soon as my mama tells the truth. Tell me, Mama. Is it true? Don't stand there quiet now, Mama. Tell me. Is what aunt Lenora said true?"

The tension between Cassie and Aunt Trucee was unnerving. Something was happening and whatever it was, I didn't want to be privy to it. I tried to excuse myself out of the conversation but was stopped dead in my tracks.

"Maybe I should let you two have a little time for your-selves. It's obvious that y'all need to work some things out. Auntie, I'll go eat my breakfast in the kitchen. Why don't you come get me when you two are done?"

"Shai!!!" Cassie yelled. "Don't you move another fucking inch. You need to hear this because this has just as much to do with you as it does me. Now, is what Aunt Lenora said true, Mama?"

"Yes, it is true. But because of the lying bitch she is, I'm sure you were told a completely different story from what really happened. He lied. He lied to everyone. And now an innocent man is paralyzed for something that *his* ass did."

"Aunt Trucee, what are you talking about? Who is he?" I asked, my head beginning to swoon.

What was about to be told I wasn't sure, but from the looks on everyone's faces, I needed to brace myself.

"Please, come with me. There is a lot to talk about."

Chapter Thirty-Six

We walked back to her room. Cassie and I did what we were told and took a seat on the couch in front of her bed. Sitting between the both of us, she reached for our hands, holding them tightly as if she was grounding herself. She leaned back and closed her eyes, drawing a staggered breath.

"Before I start, I need you to understand... every word I'm about to tell you is the truth. If I had a Bible, I'd lay my hand on it and swear on my life that this is exactly how it happened. Cassie, being that you came in here, hot and ready to pounce, let's me know that whatever you were told was a lie. No one has ever heard this from me in detail before, not even Lenora."

Her voice wavered, and I could feel the weight of every second she held her breath before speaking again.

"I was... very young when I had Cassie. Sixteen. Too young to understand everything, too young to even be a mother. But I knew love, even at that age. I knew how to care, to protect, to nurture. And I tried... I tried to be a good mother to you, Cassie. I loved you and I wanted nothing but the best for you."

Her hands tightened over ours, and her lips trembled.

"I hid my pregnancy from everyone. Even my big sister Lenora. But when those labor pains hit, I had no choice but to tell someone. I told my mother... and she was furious. Furious! She demanded that I quit school because she said she refused to be held down by someone else's mistakes. She said, "If you are going to have this baby, you need to drop out so that you can stay at home with your own child." I did, and she put me out two weeks after giving birth to you, Cassie. And just like that. I had no home, no support, no education. Nothing."

I didn't know where this was going but suddenly, my stomach dropped into my ass. That couldn't be good.

"I had nowhere else to go," she continued, her voice breaking, "so I called Lenora. I begged her to let me stay. I knew she didn't want me there, but she agreed... reluctantly. We showed up at her house with nothing but a bag of diapers, some formula, two bottles, and five little outfits that friends had gotten together and purchased for me. I tried to lay low and provide for my own baby. Only asking

Lenora to watch Cassie when I went to work. I'd gotten myself a job at McDonalds. I wanted to be a responsible mother. One that could bring home a paycheck, even if it was pennies, but I was forced to quit after only three weeks. Lenora told me she no longer wanted to keep my 'hollering ass baby.' Lenora and her piece of shit husband, Rasheed... they made everything miserable for me. Every.S-ingle.Day, it was something."

"Wait, Auntie," I said, my throat tight. "Do we have to... do we have to talk about my dad?"

Her head nodded slowly. "I'm sorry, Shug. But yes... we do." Her voice deepened. "Within a few months, your father started sneaking into my room. First, he started with just talking to me. Slick little side conversations. Complimenting me when Lenora wasn't around. Buying Cassie little stuffed animals and whatever else he could do to get my attention. I wasn't studding his ass. I ignored him as much as humanly possible. Soon after, he was threatening to kick me and my baby out if I didn't do what he wanted. No matter how many times I said no... he kept coming at me and so did the threats."

She swallowed hard, tears forming in her eyes.

"I didn't tell Lenora. I couldn't... I didn't want to sew discord into her marriage. So, I stayed quiet. I kept my head down and took care of my baby. I survived."

She paused, sucked in a deep breath and exhaled slowly.

"One night... Mama got sick and called Lenora to come stay with her. She took her kids with her. I offered to go because I didn't want to be left alone with him, but my mother was still upset with me. She didn't want me there, so I had to stay home. I thought I'd be safe because he had friends over... dominoes, cards, music, laughter, drinks. Everyone else was having a good time. To avoid being noticed, I decided to confine myself to my room. I bathed the baby, put her to bed, locked the door... and tried to get some sleep."

Her voice dropped to a whisper. "But at three in the morning... I woke up to him standing over me, touching himself."

I felt vomit rise in my throat because I just gone through the exact same thing in Jamaica and I was floored. I couldn't hear the next words, I couldn't. My hands gripped hers, pleading. "Please, Auntie... don't tell me what I think you're going to tell me."

She shook her head, tears spilling down her face. "I'm sorry, baby... I have to. I promised you the truth. Your father... he broke into my room, gagged my mouth with Cassie's baby beanie... and raped me."

Cassie and I sat frozen...mortified. Cassie eyes widened. She looked as if she wanted to disappear into the couch. My chest ached. I felt sick. My hands shook as tears ran down my face. Trucee's voice quivered, indicative of all the pain that she'd endured. As hard as it was to hear, it carried her truth.

She continued. "I thought everyone had gone by then, but there was still one person left in the house. His name was Rudy. He had passed out on the couch but woke up searching for the bathroom. It was dark, he got confused, took a wrong turn and ended up in my room. He saw what Rasheed was doing to me. By then... Cassie had woken up. She saw it all too. Baby girl, you were only five months old. Too little to remember, thank God. But I... I remember it all."

Cassie began to sob. "Mama... no... I'm so sorry. I'm so, so sorry," she whispered.

Trucee's hands shook violently. "Rudy pulled him off me and they began to tussle. In my haze, I grabbed the knife I had hidden in my nightstand. I swung, blind with fear, with rage. I blacked out. When the lights came on... the wrong man was on the floor... bleeding. As soon as I saw what I'd done, I called the police. My young mind thought that everything would be ok because it was a mistake. I was defending myself. Surely, they would be on my side. But they weren't on my side and things were not ok."

Her face twisted with guilt. "I hurt the wrong person.

I will never forgive myself. I didn't mean to... I swear I didn't. I just wanted to protect myself, my baby. And now... he's paralyzed. It was all my fault."

My throat tightened. "Auntie... why... why did my father not go to jail? Did the police not believe you?"

"I told them, baby. I told them everything. But someone called Lenora... she got wind. She came home frantic. I tried to tell her what he'd done. And she... she wouldn't listen. She said I was always causing problems. Said I was jealous because she had a man, and I didn't. That night... I was arrested and taken into custody."

"She told the police that I was promiscuous and was known for sleeping with everyone's man. Roseville is a small town and if you know the right people, you can make anything happen. She had the police believing that I was a fast tailed little girl chasing after anything with a dick. It was a lie. A complete lie."

Tears streamed down all our faces.

"They believed her. I was newly seventeen, with a baby... and suddenly, I was a wild, un-wed teenage mother and criminal. They charged me as an adult with attempted manslaughter. When I went away, Lenora promised she would take care of you, Cassie. That she wouldn't let you go without... That was until my stomach started to swell and I found out I was pregnant again, but this time, I was in jail... carrying Rasheed's child."

"There was never any question about who the father was. I'd only ever had sex once before. Yes, I got pregnant with you, Cassie, the very first time I had sex. The second time, I was raped and conceived you, Shai. Once I gave birth to you, Lenora told me that she and *her* husband would raise you like their own."

"When I was finally released from prison, I wanted to tell you so badly. I wanted to build a real relationship with you. I wanted you to know that I was your real mother. Not just the cool auntie that would come see you and take you to get your favorite food and ice cream. Shai, I didn't know how to tell you the truth, so I lied to you. I lied for years and I am sorry. So, so sorry. That is why your mama has always been... angry towards you. Not because of who you are... but because of who your father is."

Cassie's wails echoed through the room. "That bitch lied to me. She told me that you seduced her husband and got pregnant on purpose with Shai just to spite her. Mama, I'm so sorry for treating you like that all those years. I'm sorry. Please forgive me." she pleaded.

I sat motionless, the truth cutting through me like a laser. My stomach churned, my heart ached, and I realized how fragile we all had been... how much pain had been hidden behind years of silence.

Chapter Thirty-Seven

The room was so still after her confession that I swore I could hear the blood rushing in my ears. My chest tightened, every breath jagged like glass stabbing my lungs.

Cassie's hand ripped away from mine. She clutched her stomach as if the words had gutted her. Her sobs started small, then echoed through the room. I stared at Aunt Trucee, but it felt like my eyes weren't working. My vision blurred, then sharpened, then blurred again as if my body couldn't decide whether to cry or faint. "You are my mother?" I whispered. My voice broken and unrecognizable.

Her face collapsed under the weight of my words...her own truth. "Baby, I couldn't continue to lie to you anymore. You needed to know. You deserve the truth.

Whether Lenora threatened me or not, I was going to tell you anyway. You are my baby. You are mine."

The words pricked at my skin like thorns. My body trembled.

"All this time..." I whispered, my throat raw. "All this time, she hated me because of what *he* did to you?!?!" I couldn't bring myself to say *my father*. It tasted like bitterness on my lips.

AUNT TRUCEE CUPPED my face in her hands, forcing me to meet her eyes. Her tears streaked down her cheeks, hot and steady. "It doesn't matter, Shai. You are mine. You are love. You are light and I love you more than you will ever know."

Her words were kind, comforting even but her words couldn't pierce the darkness unraveling inside me.

Beside me, Cassie slammed her fist against her own chest. "It's my fault!" she screamed. "If Mama hadn't had me so young, she wouldn't have had to move in with Lenora. None of this shit would've happened! Mama, you should have aborted me. Because I brought a demon into our lives!"

Her voice filled the room, while she dropped to her knees.

"No!" Aunt Trucee's voice cracked as she turned

towards her, reaching out. "Don't you dare blame your-self! You were the only thing that kept me alive. You were the reason I fought so hard to survive!"

But Cassie only shook harder, rocking back and forth, whispering, "I'm so sorry, Mama...All this time I hated you. I hated you for not being there, I hated you for having me. You were locked up for 10 years because of Uncle Rasheed's doing. Not yours, and the next time I see Lenora, I'm dragging that bitch," she scowled.

"I can't understand how she could sit around and let her husband do something like that to family. Her ass should be put in front of a firing squad," Cassie barked." I can't believe this shit. Mama, all this time you never said nothing, and they got away with it. That pisses me off even more! Why didn't you tell me the truth? Why didn't you tell me what they did to you?"

Hearing Cassie ask those questions to Trucee made me sick to my stomach. I couldn't take it. My body caved, and I sunk to the floor. "*I was a rape baby.*" The words tore out of me like shrapnel. "Never loved, never wanted. I'm just a reminder of a man who ruined everything?"

Aunt Trucee heard me whispering to myself and slid off the bed to the floor, wrapping her arms around me so tightly it hurt. Her chest heaved against my back as she rocked me like I was a child again. "Don't say that, Baby. Please, don't say that. It didn't matter how you were conceived. You were always loved...By me...By God. You were the one good thing to come from one of the worst moments of my life."

Her words only made the pain sharper. My entire being recoiled. I buried my face into her chest and let out a sound I didn't even know I could make. A scream that was more than a scream. Like grief, rage, and disbelief ripped from the center of me all at once.

Cassie latched onto my arm like she was drowning, like if she let go, we'd all sink forever. We held on to each other, broken pieces pressing together, but nothing fit anymore.

And in that moment, I realized the truth didn't set me free.

It chained me to a history I never asked for, never wanted. One I would be forced to carry for the rest of my life.

We all lay on the floor, silently crying. Not another word was spoken. After a while, Teezy knocked on the door. None of us moved. He cracked the door open, saw us huddled together in a puddle of tears, and quickly backed out, leaving us to our grief.

My robe buzzed beneath me. A message from Montague lit up my phone.

Montague: Mi luv. Mi miss yuh suh much. Mi rolled ova dis mawnin reaching fi yuh. Mi gunna finish mi business and get back tuh yuh as soon as mi cyan. Being widout yuh is pure agony. Mi cyaan do this.

Dragging myself up from the floor, I excused myself from the room of exploding secrets and stumbled back to my own. Texting him wasn't enough. I needed to hear his voice. I needed *him*.

I dialed, and he answered on the first ring.

"Hi, mi luv. Mi suh happy yuh called," he said, his voice warm, cheerful.

But mine cracked. "Please... please come to me. I need you. We don't have to go to Jamaica, but I can't be alone right now. Please, Montague." My words spilled out, trembling through tears.

I heard the urgency sharpen in his voice. "Wah happen? Wah wrong?"

"My auntie's not my auntie," I whispered, choking on the words. "She's my mother. I was conceived in the worst way. My whole life is a lie. My heart... my heart is broken. Please, Montague. I can't do this alone. I need you. I'll tell you everything later, but right now... I just need you to get here."

There was a pause, then his voice turned fierce, steady,

and sure. "Ok, mi luv. Mi coming. Jus' wait fi mi. Mi ago bi dere soon. Jus a few hours. Mi coming."

When the call ended, his promise hung in the air like a lifeline I could barely hold on to. I sat on the edge of the bed, staring blankly at the wallpaper. The flowers on it twisted, melted, blurred into one another until they looked like faces that mocked me and whispered lies in my ear. All I could feel was pain. And the desperate need to escape it.

My mind kept circling back to the sound of Auntie, correction....Mama, saying the words. *"I am your mother."*

It didn't feel real. It felt like my whole existence had been written in someone else's handwriting. Every memory I had, every punishment from Lenora, every sideways look, every time I wondered why I was never enough, it all snapped into view. Focused and clear as day...she was cruel, conniving and evil.

I pressed my palms against my eyes, willing the tears to stop, but nothing I did or thought of helped. What hurt the most wasn't just the lie...it was the years. The childhood I lost. The love I'd been starved of, thinking it was my fault.

And Cassie... poor Cassie. She didn't deserve this either. She was just a baby when it all began, and now she carried her own wounds, thinking her Mama didn't think enough of her to stay out of trouble and get her life together. I thought of her cries, her face twisted with pain.

I was usually the strong one. I was the one that always pulled us out of whatever funk we were in. Not this time. I wasn't strong enough to help her. I wasn't strong enough to help myself.

I flopped into bed, knees pulled tight to my chest. I rocked, like maybe if I kept moving, I could soothe the pain. The room felt too small, the air too heavy, and time... time wasn't real anymore. It stretched. The hours just blurred together.

All I could do was wait. Wait for Montague. Wait for his arms to pull me out of this hell.

And in the silence, one question kept echoing inside me, louder than my heartbeat, louder than my sobs: *If my whole life was a lie... then who the hell am I?*

Chapter Thirty-Eight

I don't know how long I sat like that... knees pulled to my chest, body trembling, and eyes raw from crying. Minutes bled into hours. The house around me went quiet...the kind of quiet that makes you feel like you're the last person alive in the world.

Then... a knock.

Not on my door, but faint and steady from the front of the house. My heart stuttered. I stumbled to my feet, wiping my face with the sleeve of my robe. Before I could even make it down the hall, I heard his voice...low, commanding.

"Mi luv? Shai? Yuh in dere? "

Montague.

I broke. My knees nearly gave out beneath me as I rushed to the front of the house. By the time I reached the door, Teezy had already opened it, and Montague stormed inside like he'd been holding his breath the entire drive. His eyes locked on mine instantly, and in three strides, I was swallowed in his arms.

"Shhh, mi baby. Mi got yuh," he murmured into my hair, rocking me as if I were something fragile he could piece back together.

"I can't breathe, Montague," I gasped against him. "It hurts too much."

"Mi kno, mi kno," he whispered, kissing the side of my head like a prayer. "But yuh nuh alone. Nuh again. Nuh ever. Mi wid yuh."

The weight of the day hovered in my mind, but in his arms, I finally felt like I could let some of it go. Like maybe the pieces of me could be held together until I found some strength to process my truth. For the first time since the truth unraveled me, I let myself believe that I wasn't alone.

When I lifted my head, Cassie stood in the hallway watching us, her face puffy, her expression full of pain. For a second, she looked almost... relieved. Like she knew I couldn't hold it together by myself, but now someone else had stepped in to help carry what she knew I couldn't.

She whispered to Montague, "Stay with her. Please don't let her go."

Her voice cracked on the last word, and she quickly turned away. She pressed her back against the wall as if she couldn't stand to see me break any more than I already had.

Behind her, Aunt Trucee appeared in the doorway. Her eyes were swollen, her whole-body sagging like she was drained of every ounce of energy she had. She looked at Montague holding me, and a strange kind of sorrow passed over her face. Like she knew she had broken me with the truth but was grateful I was still together.

"I'm so sorry, baby," she whispered again, her voice low and breathy. "I didn't mean to hurt you. I just... I couldn't let you live a lie any longer."

Montague glanced at her, his jaw tight but his hold on me gentle. "Yuh did wah yuh thought right," he said, his tone firm but not cruel. "But mi uhman gaan need healing now. An mi nuh leave till shi get it."

A sob broke from my chest, and I buried my face deep into his neck. Cassie slipped away down the hall, and Aunt Trucee pressed a trembling hand to her mouth, quietly weeping.

The whole house felt split in two...grief on one side, love and protection on the other. And here I was in the middle, clinging to Montague like he was gravity.

THE NEXT MORNING, I opened my eyes to the softest touch against my cheek. Montague had stayed the night, stretched out in the bed. His hand resting on me like even in sleep, he couldn't let me go. His head tilted back, chest rising and falling steady, and I wondered how he could look so calm and peaceful when my whole world was collapsing.

Carefully, I slid out of bed and wrapped my robe tighter around me. I wandered down the hall toward the kitchen.

Cassie was already there, sitting at the table with a mug of coffee cupped between both hands. Her eyes were swollen; her hair tied back in a messy bun. When she looked up at me, she tried to smile, but it was weak, broken.

"Morning," she whispered, her voice hoarse.

I nodded but couldn't force words past the lump in my throat. I sat across from her, and we just stared at each other... sisters, cousins, both and neither.

After a long silence, Cassie finally said, "I don't know how to fix this... but I need you to know I love you, Shai. None of this changes that. I know we fuss and fight, but you are my heart. Nothing and no one will ever take that away."

Tears slipped down my cheeks before I could stop them. I reached for her hand and held it tightly. Hoping that the pain each of us felt would collide and dissipate.

A faint shuffle came from behind us. Aunt Trucee

entered slowly, her body dragging, her spirit even heavier. She was tired. Defeated. No walls were left. Just guilt on her shoulders. She plopped into the chair beside Cassie, her eyes glossed over as she looked into mine.

"You hate me now," she said softly, almost like she was confessing it to herself. "And I can't even blame you. But I had to tell you the truth. I couldn't die with it in me."

Her words dug to the core of me, and all the anger I wanted to feel just... crumbled under the weight of her pain. I hated what had been done to her, to me, to all of us, but looking at her trembling hands, I couldn't hate her. None of this shit was her fault.

Montague appeared in the doorway then, his presence filling the room. He leaned against the frame, watching quietly, his eyes sharp but tender. He didn't say a word, but the message was clear...I'm here. Whatever happens, I'm here.

Just the site of him was a comfort to me. I looked at Trucee and muttered, "I don't hate you." My voice cracked. I got up and stood behind her, hugging her as tight as I could. I needed her to really feel and receive what I was saying to her. She tensed up but relaxed as I gently rubbed her back. "I could never hate you. I love you to life. Nothing can change that. It's just that my heart is hurt. I feel like your life was stolen from you... from me, from

Cassie. I'm pissed...but not at you. At Lenora and my fath....I mean Rasheed."

"I don't want you to feel any worse than you already do. You've apologized to me but now let me say something to you. I harbor no ill feelings towards you, Auntie... Mama. I'm disappointed, yes, but none of this was your doing. I don't even know if you realize it, but you are a victim too."

"To know that lady could take me in and treat me like shit all these years because of something her trifling-ass husband did? That's shit is diabolical. I never felt like I belonged there. I always felt more comfortable with you and if I don't understand anything else, at least now, I understand why that is."

"Cassie, you've always been the sister I never had. We always called each other sister-cousins. Now we can drop the cousin part. You are my sister." I smiled warmly at her, needing her to know that we were going to be okay.

"Anyhow. I prayed all last night for God to give me the peace that passes all understanding. I want to focus on being better...whatever that looks like for me. I know now that we are going to be alright."

I saw Montague nodding from the corner of my eye.

"And since we're all in one room under the same roof, let me give my man a proper introduction." I waved Montague into the room.

"Montague, this is my auntie Trucee. Well... this is my...my—"

"It's okay, Baby," she muttered. "You can call me Auntie if you want. Or you can call me Mama, whichever you're comfortable with."

"Montague, this is my biological mother whom I thought was my aunt all this time. This is the famous Chartreuse. What she's famous for, I still don't know, and honestly, I'm not sure I want to find out right now. I can't take any more excitement for today, so we'll leave it at that. And that beautiful, puffy-faced lady sitting next to her," I chuckled through the hurt, "is the pain-in-the-ass cousin I always talked about when I was in Jamaica. Her name is Cassie. I'd like to introduce you both to my love, Montague."

"Ow yuh duh. As shi told yuh, mi Montague. Mi nuh kno wah yuh bin told bout mi, but mi hope it was good."

"Honestly, baby," Trucee said, her voice softer now, "she didn't have to tell us anything. The way you got here so fast tells me all I need to know. It's clear you don't play games when it comes to our Shai. You're alright with me, Mr. Montague. You're welcome to stay as long as you like."

Montague's expression softened. He moved closer to her, lowering himself to her level so she wouldn't have to turn her neck. "Mi tank yuh, Mama Trucee," he said, the word deliberate, and full of respect. "An mi wan yuh tuh kno, yuh nuh alone in dis eitha. Mi nah jus' stand wid Shai. Mi stand wid di whole family. Yuh bin carryin pain too long. Now mi here, an mi nuh turn mi back pon family."

The words shifted something in her. Her eyes glinted again, but this time it wasn't with guilt, it was relief. She nodded, pressing her lips together as if she couldn't trust the words that may escape her mouth.

Then Montague turned toward Cassie. She'd been quiet, sipping her coffee, trying to keep her emotions under wraps. He studied her for a moment, then said gently, "An yuh... mi si how yuh luv mi uhman. Yuh a real sister tuh har. Nuh tink mi nuh notice dat. From now on, shi nah carry dis burden by haarself, an neitha will yuh. Mi protect har... an by extension, mi protect yuh too. Yuh both safe wid mi."

Cassie blinked at him, her eyelashes moving so fast, I thought she would fly away. Her mouth opened like she wanted to say something but couldn't. Instead, she let out a laugh. "Damn. You just show up like Super Save a Hoe and say all the right shit, huh?" She wiped her face quickly. "Alright, I'll give it to you. You're good for her. You're good for us."

Flashing them both a warm smile, he wrapped his arms around my waist and held me closely. Shame and sorrow still polluted the air, but Montague's presence softened it.

Like his certainty created a space where we could all finally breathe without breaking.

After speaking to Montague, Trucee's energy seemed lighter. I was glad to see the corners of her mouth turn upward for the first time in what felt like forever. One thing was clear, Montague's arms may have been wrapped around me, but he was holding all of us.

Chapter Thirty-Nine

The next couple of days were hard for everyone. The way my mother painted a picture of my father taking her cookies made me gag every time I thought of it. So, I tried not to think about it but that was virtually impossible. My mother was just a child when she got pregnant with both of her children. She didn't deserve to be deserted and discarded.

To have everyone that she knew and loved to turn their back on her must have been one of the worst feelings ever. Then to go to jail when all she was trying to do was protect herself and her baby is crazy. I hate Roseville PD for that. I'm so glad I moved from that little ass town. Knowing what I know now, I'd probably never go back and if I do, they better watch out."

Montague's deep baritone voice pulled me from my reverie.

"Shai, mi luv. Yuh neva tell me wah yuh wan duh. Mi left mi property manager in charge back at di resorts. Mi nuh haffi be back fi a few days. Are yuh coming back wid mi?" He gently stroked my cheek while staring in my eyes.

It's so hard to say no to this man. He's so damn fine.

"I want to come back with you for sure, but I need to make sure that my mother is good. Whewww, that sounds crazy coming out of my mouth. *My Mother.* Anyhow, I need to make sure she and Cassie are good. We are all hurting right now. Everything inside of me wants to run away and ignore it all as if it never happened but I know I will never heal if I do that."

"Well, wah yuh need tuh heal? Mi asking suh mi cyan help yuh."

"I have to face it head on. I need to sit down and have a talk with my so-called mother and father. He may have escaped jail time but he's going to wish he was in jail when I get through with him."

"Suh, yuh plan is tuh confront dem."

"Yes, at some point, but maybe after the swelling goes down. If I do it now, everybody over in 8205 Gordon Drive is dying. Trust me, baby, it's better that I stay away for now."

"Mi hate dat yuh nuh wan guh tuh Roseville. Mi a goh

todeh. Mi need tuh si bout mi people. Mi wan yuh tuh cum wid. Yuh tink yuh cyan behave yuhself?" He shot a small chuckle as he wagged his finger at me.

"Of course I can, as long as you are around. You keep me calm. I know I don't have to burst a grape as long as you and your men are near. Oh wait, are you going to see Lincoln?"

"Yuh, mi may ride through dere? Why yuh ask?"

His gaze was heavy upon me as he awaited an answer.

"Umm, because I don't think that we are him and Umi's favorite people these days. She's been leaving threatening text messages on my phone."

His stance shifted from calm and relaxed to *jump and pounce*. I wasn't sure if I should tell him the rest, but I didn't want to start off with lies and half truths.

"I didn't tell you when I was in Jamaica, but when I called her and told her that you and I were working on seeing where this goes...She got pissed and hung up on me. Before she did, she advised me of Lincoln wanting to hurt us. The both of us. Lincoln was basically on a rampage, spewing all kinds of hateful shit about you and me. He's mad at me for fucking him up and he's mad at you about your dealings with me. He told her that he felt like he couldn't trust anyone, and you betrayed him because you were with the very person that ruined his life."

Montague's entire body went stiff, his hand fell from

my cheek, and his jaw clenched tight enough to crack a Brazilian nut in half.

"Mi Beg a pardon? Yuh jus' seh dat mi nefyu bin threatening tuh duh yuh an mi harm, an yuh neva tell mi?"

"Baby, I didn't want to ruin the last moments we had in Jamaica. That's why I never said anything. I'm not really worried about Lincoln or Umi. I've got enough shit on my plate. I just wanted to tell you what was said before you and I take a trip to Roseville. It's very possible that we could run into them and I don't want any trouble."

"Mi nefyu is a hot head, but mi tink him kno dat mi nuh di one tuh be fucked wid. Efff him nuh kno, him will find out. Put on sum clothes an meet mi downstairs. Inna few, mi driva waiting. Wi ave a few cornas to bend.

He left the room, descended downstairs. I called Trucee to let her know that I would be stepping out with Montague for a few but that I would be back shortly.

With concern in her voice, she pleaded, "Shai, please don't take your ass to Roseville and do anything that will get you hurt or locked up. I don't need you getting in trouble. Should I send Rocky and Kenzo with you two?"

"No auntie. There is no need. Montague travels with his own security. Look outside, I'm sure you'll see a couple SUV's waiting on him. Nobody is going to mess with us. Besides, I'm just tagging alone. I have no plans on seeing any of my relatives when I get there. I've got nothing for them and what I do have, they better duck from."

Trucee let out a big hearty laugh. "I know that's right, baby, but we have a lot of healing to do. I know from personal experiences that when we are hurting, we don't think correctly. I don't want that to happen to you, so I wanted to make sure that you are leaving this house with a level head...and heart."

"Please don't worry about me. I'm fine. I know that I can be a firecracker at times and pop off, but what would it solve. Nothing. With that in mind, I'm simply taking a quick ride with my man."

"Speaking of your man...I really like him Shai. He seems so level-headed and good for you. If you never believe anything else I say, believe me when I say, that man loves you. Men don't move the way he moved for women they don't love. Everything about him screams your safe space, your protector, your calm. Girl, I know it was only a couple of weeks, but those weeks had to be hot and heavy. That man's sheer aura is passionate. That's the type of man you never want to lose. Shit, while we are talking about men, where is this Wicked, that you spoke of? Is he in the States with Montague? If he is, I need to meet him."

Laughing, I muttered," I don't know. I'll ask him while we are out. Well, I've got to make myself presentable and meet him downstairs in a few. I love you and I will see you when I get back."

"I love you too, baby. Please be safe out there."

By the time I made it downstairs, Montague was already outside, slowly pacing back and forth like a lion on the hunt. The SUV idled in the driveway waiting with the engine running. Two more SUVs sat idled as well. One behind and one in front, both with windows tinted and men inside like shadows. His world never moved without protection.

Montague's eyes found me the second I stepped out the door. He opened the car door, his hands guiding me in, and slid in behind me. The moment he shut the door; the air inside grew thick with fury."

"Mi called mi sista, Toni. Toni is di one dats closest tuh Lincoln. Yuh did right. Lincoln ave bin running around telling everyone wid ears dat wen him si yuh or mi...wi dead. Mi sista seh him act like him lose him mind since him leave di hospital. All him talk bout is teking a life. Mi asked mi sista did him kno yuh and mi were togetha. Shi seh him kno an him nuh give a fuck. Suh, yuh kno wah dat mean right?"

A chill ran through me because although I hadn't known Montague that long, I knew what that fire in his eyes meant.

I swallowed hard, unsure if I should reassure him or

let him cook. "Babe, I told you that I'm not worried about him, so you shouldn't be worried either. He talks like he's big shit but Lincoln's not going to do anything."

Montague cut his eyes towards me, sharp enough to slice. "Nuh eva seh dat. Nuh eva undarestimate a desperate man. Him wish death pon yuh, pon mi. Dat nuh idle talk. Dat is promise."

The car fell silent again, the hum of the engine making the only sound. My chest tightened. I wanted to believe we had nothing to worry about and we would be protected no matter what, but the way his fist was balled up, told me he wasn't taking any chances. He was already planning Lincoln's punishment.

As we rolled through the city, Roseville came into view. Familiar streets felt like haints dragging me back to the shitty reality I'd escaped from. My stomach twisted harder with each mile.

Montague reached over, his hands covering mine. "Mi kno dis place hold pain fi yuh, but remember, yuh nuh walk back in alone. Mi promise, Shai...nuhbody put fear in yuh heart again. Not while mi breathing."

The driver's voice came in low and steady from the front. "Boss, wi reach di corner. Yuh wan mi pull up or circle round first?"

Montague's hand slipped from mine, he leaned

forward, eyes narrowing through the tinted glass. I followed his gaze and swallowed a hard lump in my throat.

Across the street, leaning against a car with two men on each side of him, stood Lincoln. His smile was crooked, his eyes locked on our SUV like he'd been waiting.

"Drive slow," Montague ordered, his voice a growl. "But nuh stop. Mi need tuh si wah dis fool up tuh."

The car rolled forward. Lincoln lifted his gauzed wrapped hand and raised two fingers in a mock salute, his smug grin spreading wider and wider.

Montague didn't blink. He sat back slowly, his jaw clenching while his fist landed on his knee.

"Mi nefyu jus' sign him death warrant," he scowled.

And in that moment, I knew that the streets of Roseville were about to bleed.

Chapter Forty

Montague's eyes stayed locked on Lincoln as our SUV rolled past. His whole body was rigid, every muscle ready to pounce, but he didn't move. He didn't utter a word. The only sound was his knuckles popping as his fist flexed against his thigh.

Lincoln's grin widened, his flunkies laughing like they were in on some kind of inside joke. He raised his chin at Montague, daring him to step out.

I sat with bated breath, waiting for Montague to give his men a go. One word from him and the streets would have been a war zone. Instead, he leaned back in his seat.

"Keep drivin," he muttered. His voice low and serious. "Dis nuh di place, nuh di time."

We glided forward, putting distance between us and

Lincoln. I could still feel his stare burning holes in the back of my head.

I turned to Montague, scanning his face before kissing him softly. Hoping to disarm him and put him at ease. I knew if I didn't, he was sure to grind his teeth to the gums.

"You did the right thing baby. Trust me, he isn't worth it."

"Mi only did dat 'cause yuh inna di car. Mi nuh putting yuh inna harms way fi nuhbody. Yuh too precious tuh mi and mi sista and har pickneys inside. Him lucky, him get to breathe a likkle while longer, but mi kno, mi gonna ave tuh put him down jus' like mi did him fada. Him nuh kno wen tuh stop, suh mi ave tuh put a stop tuh him."

He took out his phone and placed a call to his sister Toni again.

"Mi a guh tap by another day. Lincoln up tuh nuh gud. Mi nuh trying tuh put yuh inna harms way, suh mi roll passed. But please tell yuh nefyu dat fi him own safety, him need tuh be easy. Dis nah end well fi him. Dis is him only warning.

He hung up the phone. His face was set like stone. He was calm on the outside, but I knew better. Inside, he was already planning Lincolns funeral.

Before we would make it around the corner, my phone

rang. The car still silent and tense. Montague looked over and saw Umi's face illuminate the screen.

"Should I answer it?" I question while staring at the phone.

"Fi wah? Shi duh nothing but talk shit. Dat jus' piss mi off, so please, nuh badda wid dem foolishness. Si mi kno mi nefyu. Him kno how mi roll. Him expecting violence, him expecting war. Mi nuh gunna give him eitha. Mi gunna give him silence. Him nuh kno wah tuh duh wid dat.

"That sounds like a good idea" I agreed. "Who would have thought that teaching him a lesson would have turned into all this. I mean, he deserved what he got, but he can't handle that a woman gave it to him. And Umi, tsk tsk tsk, you tried to tell me to watch her. I didn't understand then, but I do now. It sucks because I only did what I did to help her. No other reason. I hate ungrateful bitches."

Montague's frown turned into a smile. He peered over at me and burst out laughing. Shaking his head. He leaned over and kissed me on the lips.

"Si, dats wah mi need. Dat natural comic relief. Now, yuh see, mi need yuh jus' as much as yuh need me. Let's put di bullshit tuh di side. Yuh hungry?"

"Surprisingly, I am. Usually when I'm going through

something I don't eat. My appetite is intact so yes, let's find us a nice spot and get some breakfast."

"Mi kno jus' di place. He leaned towards the front and whispered something in the driver's ear. We got on the freeway, headed to the outskirts of Roseville. We arrived at a quaint little restaurant. One I'd never seen before. The driver opened the door. Montague's men in the SUVs got out first and surrounded our car. Montague exited next, then reached for my hand.

We sauntered inside where two little girls ran up to Montague, grabbing him by the leg and pulling him down. Both girls beamed with excitement as he squatted to meet them at their level. They grabbed him by the neck, each giving him a penguin kiss. My ovaries exploded.

"Wait, wait. One at a time please. Wah yuh need from mi dis time." He smiled.

"We want what you always give us. We want some monies," they said as they giggled and ran circles around him. He reached in his pocket and gave them each a crisp fifty-dollar bill.

"Dat should be enuff tuh last yuh two anotha week."

"Thank you Uncle Monty," they said before taking off around the corner. A tall modelesque beauty glided from the back and greeted us both.

"Shai, mi wan yuh tuh meet mi niece, Amoy. Dis mi

oldest bredda's pickney an dem two little girls are har pickneys."

Flashing a smile, she eagerly reached her hand out to shake mine.

"Hello Miss Shai. It's nice to meet you."

Stuttering, I retort. "It...It's nice to meet you too but how did you know my name."

Chuckling, she walked us to a private booth, seated us and placed menus on the table. She then turned to me. "The dinner party that my uncle had..., my father was there, and my father can't hold water."

Looking at Montague, then at the menu, I quipped. "I see. Well, I hope that what you heard about me was positive."

"It was, now what will you have. I heard that you have a favorite meal."

"Well damn, did they report everything I did while I was in Jamaica." I snapped.

Montague interrupted, "Nuh, mi luv. Mi plan tuh bring yuh here afta leaving Toni's. Mi called ahead. Mi hope yuh nuh mind."

I quickly softened, "Now you know I don't mind at all. In that case, yes please. Bring me that saltfish and ackee please ma'am. Along with the plantains and the johnny-cakes. I gots to have it. Oh, and please don't forget the cucumber water."

"Coming right up and Unk, I will bring you oat porridge, fresh fruit and plantain."

"Tank yuh, Amoy."

She flashed a quick grin and trekked to the back.

"So, is this your restaurant?" I asked while looking around at the way the place was decorated. The place screamed I'm from Jamaica and I'm damn proud of it.

"Yea, dis mi latest business venture. Mi niece a star pon di grill an di stove. Adessa teach har everyting shi kno. Shi wan tuh be a chef an run a restaurant, suh mi an mi bredda mek it happen."

"That is so sweet of you. You really do love your family something fierce. It's wonderful to see a man put his family first. I can't relate because my father...ummm, my mother's attacker was never there for me or made sure that I was ok. Which is sad because I was in the same damn house with him. When I have children, they will never know what it's like to lack in any department. Love, support, wisdom. I will be there to give them as much as they need and I won't make them feel like shit when they ask."

"Mi kno dat all dis is new tuh yuh an dat yuh are still hurt, but mi nuh wan yuh tuh carry it around. Mi wan yuh tuh really si bout yuhself an get di proper help. Mi get a gud head doctor dat cyan help yuh."

"Well, in America, a head doctor is someone that's

excellent in eating pussy or sucking dick. That is the only head doctor that I'm interested in seeing right now." I said, biting my bottom lip and fucking him with my eyes.

"Yuh nasty gyal an mi luv it. Only if yuh nasty fi mi cause mi definitely nasty fi yuh. Yuh got mi nose wide open, Shai. Neeko cyan land mi plane right through it, " he chuckled. "Mi will duh anyting yuh ask. Including suck dat sweet pussy fi yuh. Follow mi.

Grabbing my hand, he took me to the back office where the little girls were playing.

"Wah gwaan mi babies, why nuh yuh two guh out dere an help yuh mada. Mi and Miss Shai, need tuh ave a moment alone. Duh yuh mind?"

"No, Uncle Monty," they say in unison before hitting each other and running out the office.

Montague closed the door and wasted no time slipping down my panties. He turned me around, bending me over the desk before hiking my leg up and placing it on the desk as well.

"Mi luv yuh pum pum, Shai. It's suh good. Suhhh tight. Mi gunna suck all di pain out yuh body.

He kneeled down to his knees and spread my pussy lips with his fingers. Before I could catch my breath, his mouth claimed me like I was the only source of air he'd ever need. My body thrust forward involuntarily. Surprised at the urgency, the hunger. A sharp gasp tore from my lips as his tongue moved with a rhythm that sent shivers down my spine. Every lick felt like he was healing and feeding my soul.

I reached back, tangling my fingers into his hair, pulling, needing something to grab onto as waves of pleasures crashed against my body. Every flick, every kiss made me lose a little more of myself to him. My legs trembled, but his grip tightened. Steadying me, grounding me while pushing me higher at the same time.

"Montague..." my voice breathless but filled with aching.

He looked up at me with eyes blazing, his mouth still wet with my essence. A growl sat low in his throat. In one fluid moment, he sprung to his feet, scooped me up like I weighed nothing, and flipped me over. His mouth found mine, stealing whatever breath I had left. The world around us blurred as the pressure of his manhood slipped slowly and deeply into my yoni.

Covering my mouth, I winced from the pain... the pleasure. His dick was like medicine. It healed me. His hands roamed like he couldn't decide where he needed me most. He was gripping, exploring and claiming. I wrapped my arms around him, desperate for this feeling, pulling him closer and closer until it felt as if we were one. I steadied myself with his shoulders, nails digging into his back. "OOOh baby, shit. What are you trying to do to me," I purred through each thrust.

As he pushed into me, it was a force that stole the very air in my throat. I whispered his name like a vow. Every thrust felt like he was giving me a piece of him that he'd never given to anyone else. I took it gladly, moaning in his ear while I fucked back.

When the final pleasure wave broke over us, we clung to each other, trembling, gasping and neither willing to let go. His forehead rested against mine. His chest heaving as he whispered, "Mi luv yuh, Shai. More dan mi cyan seh."

I had always heard that island men fall in love faster than anyone else. Before Montague came along, that thought was hilarious to me, but I couldn't laugh too hard because I felt the exact same about him. In less than a month, I was head over heels in love with him and would go to the end of the world if he asked me. I also knew that within a shadow of a doubt, he'd do the same.

Once I love you rolled off his lips, I knew whatever came next, whatever dangers or truths we had to face, we'd face them together.

Chapter Forty-One

With shame plastered across my face, we emerged from the office to find our food covered and waiting. Sitting down, we ate, laughed and talked before saying our goodbyes and trekking back outside to our SUV.

"Well, that was fun," I muttered, while walking bowlegged to the SUV as I stroked his thick arms.

"Yea, it was mi baby. Anytime dat wi spend togetha feels like freedom. Mi wan yuh tuh keep dat in mind because mi neva wan yuh yuh lose dat feeling wid mi. Now, since mi cyaan guh visit mi family jus' yet, weh yuh wanna guh now?"

Excitement rose in me. "There is a little mom and pop shop that I used to frequent. They have all the penny candies and snacks from my childhood. I would like to go

there so that I can buy some to take back to Macon
with me.

"Let's duh it," he said before leaning forward, advising
the driver of our next location. As we cruised, we sat back
in our seats, enjoying each other.

We were still on a high from earlier when suddenly, a
shot rang out. Montague pushed my head down as he
looked around, trying to see where it came from when he
noticed that the SUV behind him had a hole through the
windshield. The sound of the gunshot still rang in my ears.
My heart was beating so fast, I thought I would pass out.
Montague shoved me down against the floorboard,
shielding me with his body while his eyes scanned every
angle outside the tinted glass.

"Shai, baby, keep yuh head down!" he ordered, his
voice sharp but steady.

I trembled; my palms dripping sweat. Through the
crack of the seat, I caught a glimpse of the SUV behind us.
The windshield was shattered, a gaping hole right where
the driver's face had been. The trailing SUV jerked to a
stop in the middle of the road.

"Drive," Montague barked at the driver.

The tires screeched, and we peeled away. "Nuh luk
back, Shai. "Mi nuh wan yuh tuh si dat image in yuh
mind."

It was too late. My curiosity got the best of me, and I

was able to see the drivers blood shattered against the glass. My stomach churned, fear and anxiety gnawed at my chest. My hands wouldn't stop shaking. Montague noticed. Without looking away from the windows, he reached over and covered my fingers with his hand. "Steady yuh heart, mi luv. Everyting is gunna be alright. Truss."

Montague leaned forward, giving the driver a new order." Tek wi tuh di house. Now!!"

The driver nodded, no questions asked. The candy shop was forgotten, so was the laughter and love making from earlier. My heart grew heavy realizing that the outside world wouldn't be safe for us, not even for a moment until Lincoln or whoever responsible, was dead.

Minutes passed in silence. The only thing I could hear was the sound of my heart beating in my chest. Just when I started to calm down, Montague's phone buzzed.

He glanced at the screen, his brow furrowing. An unknown number was calling and he answered without hesitation.

"Chat," he ordered.

I watched his face tighten as he listened. His silence was so loud. His eyes narrowed until they were nothing but slits. Then he hung up. For a moment he didn't move, he didn't breathe. Finally, he turned to me.

"Dat bullet was meant fi yuh," His voice was merely a whisper; however, I heard it loud and clear.

Finally, the SUV slowed. We turned down a narrow, tree-lined dirt road with potholes big enough to snap an axel in two. At the end of the road, a tall iron gate creaked open, controlled by someone I couldn't see. Our SUVs rolled inside, pulling up to a sprawling house tucked back from the road. Hidden by shadows and thick greenery.

A safe house.

As soon as we stopped, the men that were in the SUV in front of us surrounded our SUV. Montague slid out first, scanning the perimeter with sharp eyes before opening my door. "Come."

I slid out, legs unsteady like a baby deer. Adrenaline still coursing through my veins. He kept a firm hand on my back as he guided me inside the house. The interior was dim, stripped of any personality. Nothing like the mansion in Jamaica. This kind of place was meant to keep people alive, not comfortable.

I sank onto the dusty couch, my breath uneven. Silence was too heavy, yet too loud. Something had to be said.

"I can't believe that muthafucka shot at us. I know he had to have help because there is no way he could have aimed and pulled the trigger himself. The bastard only has one hand, and the other one is barely working. Plus his knees are fucked up so there is no way that he's steady enough to hold a gun." I said, stating the obvious.

"Yuh right, Shai. Had tuh be one of di men dat was standing beside him in Toni's yaad. Nuh matta which one. Dem all dead. All tree, four or five of dem."

My mind instantly went to Trucee. I knew she would be expecting us shortly. I called her to let her know I would not be returning directly. That Montague and I decided to stay in Roseville for a couple of days. If I'd told her what really happened, she would have exploded. We'd both had enough excitement these last few days. She deserved a break. I was young and virile, I would be ok, but I wasn't sure how much more her heart could take.

His phone rang again.

He stood, retrieving it from his pocket. Another unknown number flashed across the screen. A pause.

"Undastan. Get here." He ended the call without another word.

"Dat was di head of mi security. Lincoln kno weh wi are an dem tink him coming here. Which is fine. Perfect actually. Wi wait fi him tuh run up. Wi dead him den move pon wid wi life.

Montague placed the phone back into his pocket. His shoulders bowed out as if the phone call strengthened him. His voice was calm, almost too calm when he spoke again.

"Lincoln waan test mi. Him tink mi soft cause mi blood run through him veins. But family nuh excuse wah him did. Eff him set foot pon dis property...mi end dat Pussyclaat!!"

I leaned forward, searching his expressions. "Montague...that's your nephew, Can you really---,"

He cut me off with a look so fierce, the words dried up on my lips.

"Love cyaan save man wen him already sell him soul." He said. His accent was thicker now. "Him choose him path di minute dat bullet left dat gun. An mi choose mine. Yuh tink mi enjoy dis? Mi nuh, but tuh protect yuh, mi ave tuh bury him."

My chest tightened and grief covered me like a blanket. Although, Lincoln has taken it somewhere that he could never come back from, I can't help but to think that my actions caused this. Lincoln deserved every lick I gave him, but I didn't have to make it my responsibility to be the one to hand them out. Now I had two family members feuding over some shit I did. Montague shouldn't have to bear this weight on his shoulders. It wasn't his weight at all but mine.

The house fell silent again. Only the tick of an old clock on the wall filled the space. I couldn't escape the truth settling over me. This wouldn't end with words. Lincoln was coming, and Montague would be waiting to end him.

Twenty minutes went by before he moved to open the

door. Two men stepped in, both tall and husky, dressed in all black and moved with urgency. One carried a black duffle bag, the contents weren't a mystery. I could clearly hear the steel clicking as the bag dropped to the floor.

Montague exchanged quick words in patois with them, words that were too fast for me to catch. I watched as they unzipped the bag and laid out its contents on the wobbly dining room table. This safe house was now doubling as an arsenal and they were now locked, loaded and ready for any threat.

Plopping back down on the couch, Montague pulled me gently into his arms. His lips pressed against my temple. Breath warm against my skin.

"It's ok, mi queen," he murmured, voice softer now but still filled with intent. "By tomorrow, wi free."

I couldn't rest though. As I closed my eyes against his chest, I knew freedom wouldn't come without a price. And by dawn, that price would be paid in blood.

The house grew quiet again. Too still. I remained on the couch. My thoughts were literally suffocating me. Montague was moving around the house with his men, his voice low and firm, issuing orders I couldn't quite hear or understand.

Every now and again, the creak of a door, the snap of a magazine being locked into place and the slip of steel against leather.

Preparations.

For War.

I wanted to be strong and believe that we'd be free after this, but I know I would carry the weight and guilt long after this was over. That didn't feel like freedom to me. My heart was telling me otherwise. Every shiver that crawled up my spine made me believe that I was about to lose the man that I'd waited all my life to find. And if it were to happen, it would be all because of me.

The lights in the house were dimmed. Curtains pulled tight. This was the calm before the storm. We tried to eat dinner normally but my nerves wouldn't allow it.

Hours passed. Then... the low growl of engines approached. My blood ran cold.

I sprung from the couch, but Montague's man stopped me and ordered me to the back of the house.

"Stay back, Shai," he said firmly. His eyes flicked toward the door, jaw clenched. "Dis nuh fi yuh eyes."

The sound of gunfire shattered the night. I covered my ears as glass rattled in the windows. The floor seemed to vibrate beneath my feet.

"Montague," I whispered to myself, voice cracking.

Outside, short, sharp burst of gunfire rang out. Shouts in voices I didn't recognize. Tires screeching. Then silence. Then another shot, louder, closer. My stomach grew nauseous. I could only imagine him out there, moving through the chaos, his heart steady while mine was frantic.

Minutes felt like hours. My lungs burned from holding my breath. Every sound made me flinch. Then------Nothing.

The silence seemed worse than the noise. I couldn't bear it anymore. I rushed towards the door, but his man blocked me again, shaking his head, no. His lips moved, saying something to me, but I couldn't hear it over the roar in my ears.

Then finally...footsteps.

Slow, but heavy and certain.

The door creaked open, and Montague stepped inside. His shirt was tattered, sweat clung to his skin, his eyes were fierce, but alive. He was alive.

I gasped, running towards him before I even realized I was moving. He caught me in his arms, holding me so tight I thought my ribs might crack.

"It done," he whispered in my ear. His voice was raw and deep. "It finish now."

I clung to him, trembling, the scent of gunpowder clinging to his clothes, the weight of everything pressing down on both of us.

It was over. But as I buried my face against his chest, I knew we would never be the same.

Chapter Forty-Two

The silence between us felt louder than the gunfire. Even in Montague's arms, my body trembled, refusing to believe we had made it through. My mind replayed the chaos outside the safe-house...the flashes of light, the screams, the smell of smoke burned into my memory. Through it all, we were still here. But Lincoln and four others weren't.

MONTAGUE DIDN'T SLEEP. His eyes remained wide open, scanning every shadow as though danger might slip through the walls at any moment. His body was tense, his breathing shallow. I pressed my hand against him, trying to calm him, but it was like trying to calm a storm.

"You're okay," I whispered more than once, my voice low, soothing. "Nothing's going to get to you here."

But my reassurance seemed to have no effect on him. After his men cleared the scene, we left the safehouse and returned to Trucee's house. Even there, behind thick walls, I could see the sadness inside him.

"Shai," he said finally, his voice breaking the heavy silence. "Mi nuh worried 'bout nuh batty boys. Mi nuh scared of anyting." His eyes shifted away, hard and distant. "Wah mek mi heart hurt is mi sista. Mi dread calling har tuh tell har dat her first born is gaan and mi da reason. Mi kno har heart gunna be broken."

His words gutted me. I'd never heard him sound so vulnerable, so torn. The man who had stared down bullets without flinching was suddenly afraid...afraid of the grief his sister would carry.

I cupped his chin, turning him toward me. "Montague... you didn't take Lincoln's life. His choices did. He set this shit in action the moment that first bullet left the gun. You only did what you had to do."

He searched my eyes, pain swirling in his own. "But mi hands still da one covered in mi nefyu blood. Yuh nuh undastan, Shai. Family different. Blood run deep, even wen it poison."

I leaned my forehead against his chest, my own heart

twisting. "Then let me carry some of that weight with you. Don't take it all on yourself."

His arms wrapped around me, tighter this time, as though my words managed to reach some place inside him that even bullets couldn't touch.

I realized survival wasn't the hardest part. It was living with the aftermath, the grief, the guilt, the way love could be both salvation and torment.

We lay there in the quiet, his body stiff but his grip was unforgiving, and I knew sleep wouldn't come easy for either of us. It was almost dawn. I knew today would bring new wounds, new consequences, new hurt. All I could do was hold on to the man who had fought the world for me and pray that love would be enough to keep him from breaking.

Montague's phone rung and buzzed all night and all through the morning. Leaving him with over 72 missed calls and 44 text messages. He took the deepest sigh as his eyes fixed on his screen.

"Shai, mi need someweh mi cyan guh dats private. Mi need tuh speak tuh mi sista. Dis nuh gaan be easy fi mi, but mi ave tuh dweet. Mi owe har dat."

"Sure baby," I said, trying not to let on how hurt I was for him. "You should go outside in the garden. It's so peaceful and beautiful out there. It would be the perfect place.

I walked him outside, kissed him on his cheek and told him that I would be right inside if he needed me. My soul ripping a little with each step I took. The past few days had been pure hell for me but paled in comparison to what Montague was dealing with. Experiencing all this strife in such a small time frame had me more anxious than ever.

I almost jumped out my skin the moment the door opened, with Bakari and Cassie entering the room.

"Hey Shai, I was wondering what happened to you yesterday. Mama told me that you and Montague were going out for a drive. What time did you get back this morning?"

"Before sunrise. I called Trucee in advance to let her know that we were on the way. The gate was already opened when we pulled up."

"Oh, she quipped. I was dead to the world. Bakari had given me the best massage of my life." She smiled at him. I cracked my neck and shook my head as I shot him a glance.

"Oh yes Cassie I know. He's a beast with those hands. The first night I was here, he gave me a great massage as well. Had me feeling like new money. Ummm, what kind of massage did you opt for? I got the Swedish one with a side of dick. Did you get the same?"

She looked over at Bakari with eyes that could kill.

Nervously, he looked around before sauntering towards the door. "Well ladies, I'm going to excuse myself and head to the kitchen to see what the chef has prepared for breakfast. Please don't hesitate to reach out if either of you two need anything."

"We wont," we said in unison.

"Damn Shai, you fucked him too."

"And did and I'm not ashamed of it. He ate my pussy too, but we aren't gonna talk about that. Anyhow, he's all yours girl. I've found my champion lover and as good as Bakari's dick was, Montague cannot be beat."

"Whatever Shai, that wasn't the reason I came in here to find you. I wanted to know if you spoke to Lenora yet? She called me again yesterday and I was going to cuss her ass out, but I wanted us to do it together," she laughed. "I mean it's only right. She fucked up both of our lives so we both should give her the business."

"I agree with you sis but not right now. I'm dealing with some other things, but we will get to it in time."

"Shai, please tell me what the fuck you've got going on that's more important than this. This lady stole both of our lives away from us. She lied to us for twenty plus years and didn't say shit. My mama missed a huge chunk of my life and all of yours because of her," she griped.

"Cassie," I yelled. "Please pipe down. I know what they did, and they will get theirs but I'm learning that sometimes you need to let God handle folks. It seems like when I handle shit on my own...things get all fucked up."

Cassie's face turned serious. "What's wrong, Shai. What are you not saying to me?"

"I want to tell you, Cassie. I really do but it's not my story to tell. You will probably hear about it the second you step back into Roseville. You know muthafuckas around there can't hold water."

"I don't want to hear it from the streets. You're sitting right here in my face. Why can't you just tell me if something happened?"

"Because I'm not ready to talk about it Cassie. Now, please drop it." I yelled.

Montague came in the door as Cassie was getting ready to bite back..

"Ayyy, Ayyy, Ayyy. Are yuh two ok? Shai, baby, wah wrong. Why dat look pon yuh face?

"It's nothing baby. Let's go back out to the garden. They should be bringing breakfast soon, but I need to speak to you before they do."

We trekked back out to the garden and walked the grounds. I looked in his face trying to gauge his mood but couldn't. He grabbed my hand and pulled me close to him.

"Shi devastated but shi undastan. Mi told har wah Lincoln had planned fi wi before wi left Jamaica. Shi already kno bout him aving it out fi mi and yuh. Mi sista, Toni, had called har an asked har tuh ave a chat wid

Lincoln because him was running rampant. Shi seh shi told him tuh leave well enuff alone, but him nuh listen. Shi hurt, but shi ave only one request...bring har pickney home suh dat shi may give him a propa burial."

"Mi told har dat mi wud duh dat. Mi tell har mi sorry many times. Shi seh shi luv mi an forgive mi. Shi kno har son was stubborn an had devilish ways. Shi seh shi always kno shi wud get a call bout Lincoln, but shi neva tink it wud be from mi. Mi neva tink it wud be mi eitha. Mi heart still hurt Shai. Mi suh sorry but mi ave tuh leave and mek dis right wid mi family. Mi sista needs mi, an suh duh all di pickneys. Mi hate tuh leave yuh like dis, but mi gotta go clean up mi mess."

My throat tightened. "Leave? Montague, after everything we've been through, after everything I've seen, you're just... going?"

His hand cupped my cheek, thumb tracing lightly against my skin. His eyes were full of grief but also that unshakable resolve. "Shai, mi cyaan run from dis. Lincoln blood is pon mi hands. Mi owe mi sista. Mi owe mi family. Eff mi nuh face dis, mi heart will neva rest."

I swallowed hard, fighting tears back. "And what about me? What about us? You think my heart will rest while you're gone? You think I can just sit here and wait, not knowing if you'll come back?"

His jaw flexed. He pulled me close until our foreheads

touched. "Mi promise yuh, Shai... dis nuh goodbye. Mi cyaan promise it will be easy, but mi will cum back tuh yuh. Mi nuh leave yuh fi good. Mi jus'... mi haffi fix dis first."

Tears slipped free without my permission. His lips pressed to mine. My hands clung to his shirt, refusing to let go, even as his arms tightened then loosened around me.

We walked back into the house and up to the bedroom where he started gathering his things. I stood still, chest pounding and palms sweating, watching as he meticulously folded each item and stuffed it into the bag.

"Mi kno breakfast bout tuh be served, suh please guh eat, Shai. Please nuh sit here sad. Yuh need tuh keep yuh strength up an yuh cyaan duh dat eff yuh nuh eat. Mi will call yuh lata once mi get everyting straightened out."

I didn't mutter a word. I couldn't. My chest felt like it was caving in. A sound from outside the room...footsteps, voices, pulled us back into reality. The world wasn't pausing for our heartbreak.

We walked hand in hand to the front of the house and said our tearful goodbyes. A piece of my heart was walking away from me, and there was nothing I could do about it. Montague kissed my forehead, then stepped back, his voice rough. "Mi be ok. Mi luv yuh, and mi cum back fi yuh. Truss mi."

And just like that, he turned to leave me with my heart hurting. The door shut behind Montague, and the little bit of air I had left in my lungs vanished. I stood there in silence, staring at the spot where he'd stood, trying to hold myself together.

I RAN BACK to my bedroom. Sank onto the bed and wrapped my arms around myself. For the first time since all this began, I realized I wasn't afraid of the gunfire or the enemies outside. I was afraid of losing the one man who had somehow become my everything.

Chapter Forty-
Three

Cassie burst through the door, voice cutting through the stillness. "Shai... is he gone?"

"Yes, for a little while," I cried.

"Well, you can't just sit here and drown in this. Whatever business that man needs to go handle, let him handle. Bring your ass to this dining room and eat," she commanded. She came to where I was laying and grabbed my hand. "Come on, get up girl and pick up your feet. Hell, that man loves you and he will be back. You act like somebody died or something."

I wanted to shout it to the world...*Somebody did die...* but I didn't. I walked into the dining room where Trucee, Cassie, and I were served breakfast.

"Now, I know I'm your big sister, but you always took

on that role. It's time for shit to change around here because that man has made you soft."

I wanted to cuss and laugh at the same time because, damn it, she was speaking the truth. Instead, I sat down at the table, picked up my fork and began eating my eggs.

She continued, "I say that because we've got some shit to handle too. We need to face the real demons that walk this earth, and you know damn well one of them is named Lenora."

"Cassie, not now," I groaned, rubbing my temples.

"No...yes, now," she snapped. "I'm sick of that bitch hiding like she ain't responsible for what she did to us. For lying. For stealing our damn lives. She gets to walk around free while we're sitting here picking up the pieces? Nah. I won't rest until I give her all the smoke."

I opened my mouth to argue, but the sound of Trucee's phone buzzing froze me.

"Yes, she's a guest. Let her in, please," Trucee said to the person on the other end.

Cassie looked at me, wide-eyed. "You don't think..."

The knock on the door confirmed it. "Well, speak of the devil. Lenora arrived just in time," Trucee muttered.

In disbelief, I asked, "Trucee, did you call her here?"

"I sure as fuck did. We all need to talk," Trucee said, picking up a piece of sausage and gently biting into it.

My heart kicked into my throat. Cassie's face lit with a

vicious grin. "Perfect. God just delivered her ass gift-wrapped."

"Calm down babies. She's coming. Teezy will bring her to the dining room shortly. I invited her to breakfast."

A few minutes later the door swung open, and there Lenora stood. Dressed too sharp for the occasion, nose in the air like she was the one owed an apology.

"Hello, girls," she said smoothly, as if nothing had happened. "We need to talk."

Cassie pushed past me before I could even move. "Oh, we're gonna talk, alright. And this time, you're gonna listen."

Lenora's smug smile faded the moment Cassie stepped in front of me, hands on her tiny hips. "You really thought you were going to get away with telling me all those bull-shit-ass lies like I wouldn't fact-check?" Cassie snapped, voice sharp as a whip. "Do you have any idea what you took from us? From me? From Shai? My mother served time in a fucking prison because you couldn't stand up to your piece-of-shit husband. You lied daily about everything. Shai's whole entire life was ruined because of what you and your husband did to our mother. Because of you, so many bad things happened to me. Worst of all, you happened to Shai. You never loved her."

Lenora's eyes narrowed, but there was a flicker of fear in them.

"Hold on, girls. I didn't come here for this. I came to set the record straight."

"Fuck your record. We know whatever comes out your mouth will be bullshit, so we don't really need you to talk. Just listen." Cassie barked.

"Cassie, Shai...please listen," I did the best I could. None of the decisions I made were easy. There were so many things to consider. You girls have to understand, when my sister came to stay with me, I was twenty-three years old with three children already. I didn't have a job or education. I only had my husband and kids. I honestly thought that Chartreuse was lying when she said what he'd done to her. When I pressed her about it, she shut down on me. I seriously thought she was in those streets being fast because that's what my mother told me. I took you in Shai because it was the right thing to do. I didn't have to do that. I could have let you go into the system, but I took you in and treated you like my own. I can't believe this is the thanks I get." She folded her arms and looked at Trucee. Trucee head was down, and she didn't say one word. She kept eating as if she were at the table alone.

Cassie jumped up and got in Lenora's face. "You must have forgotten that I'm a psychiatrist. I can see right through that bullshit you are talking. I deal with narcissistic muthafuckas like you on the daily. Nothing is ever your fault. People like you don't even know how to spell accountability so you can miss me with that bullshit Lenora. Talking about you took her in," she scoffed.

"You took her in and treated her like trash. You don't get a fucking gold star for that. Then, you told my mama that you would take care of me and make sure I was good, but you let me go into the system. Please tell me how in the hell are you the victim?"

"Cassie," calm down for a minute. Let me speak to Lenora," I said in a calm voice. "Lenora, you put me through hell. You gave me a roof over my head but made me feel like shit for being there. You treated me like the red headed stepchild. You abused me, made me go hungry some days, no love, no affection. Nothing but insults and criticism. Worst of all, you took my mother away from me. Those are years of our lives that we could never get back. Do you know how bad that hurts?"

Lenora's lips trembled, but her stare held mine. "I was young, I was scared, and yes, I was bitter. But I kept a roof over your head, didn't I? Food in your mouth, clothes on your back—."

"And bruises on my spirit!" I snapped, my voice rising before I could stop it. "You think a full stomach cancels out being treated like trash? You think a bed makes up for being told over and over that I wasn't worth a shit?"

I inhaled sharply, "You didn't raise me, Lenora. You raised your bitterness. You took it out on me because you couldn't take it out on the man who raped your baby sister and got her pregnant."

Tears slipped down Lenora's face. Her lips parted, like she wanted to argue, to beg, but I didn't give her the chance.

"I'm done," I said, voice low and steady. "I've said all I need to say. Aunt Trucee, can you please have someone escort your sister out? I think she has overstayed her welcome. Oh, and Lenora, please know you will never see me again. You or your rotten-ass husband. May he rest in shit."

She got up from the table and stomped out of the dining hall. Trucee sat silently, only lifting her eyes once Lenora was gone.

"Mama," Cassie chirped. "I can't believe you didn't say anything to her. You mean to tell me you had nothing to get off your chest?"

"No, baby. I don't. I had ten years to think about all the things I would do to her when I got out and if I wanted to do something to her, I'd have done it by now. You see how I live, my means, my security. I could have offed her ass years ago, but you know what I've learned? Living the best life I can is all the revenge I need. Look at me," she said, raising her hands to the heavens. "I'm living good, I'm eating good, my health is great, and I have my two favorite people in the world at my dinner table. Eating *my* food paid for by *my* money. I'm much wealthier than her and her husband and I'm not talking about money. Right now, I'm the richest woman in the world. I have both my babies here with me."

With a mouth full of food, Cassie asked, "Speaking of money, Mama...how are you able to afford all this?"

"You really want to know?" she grinned.

"Yes, we wanna know," Cassie and I said in unison.

"You two aren't going to believe me, but here goes. About two years before I was released from prison, I got a new cellmate. A little tiny frail white lady who looked like she baked apple pies on any given Sunday and would feed the homeless in her downtime. I mean, she was as sweet as they come. Her name was Ethel Day. For the first couple of days, she wouldn't say much, but as time went on, she began to open up to me, and I did the same. She was convicted and serving a life sentence for shooting and killing her husband and his mistress. They'd been married for forty-five years. She'd just retired as a banker and was excited to bring her husband lunch to work for the first time in ages. She loaded the car with all the goodies she'd made for him and headed to the courthouse. She walked right into his chambers and found him with his mistress."

"Well, she was originally from Texas, and you know they don't go anywhere without their guns. Catching them in the act, she dropped the plate of pot roast, mashed potatoes, and cornbread muffins on the floor, pulled out her thirty-eight special, and fired every bullet she had until they were both dead. She said she stood there until the police arrived and took her off to jail."

"Okay, Mama," Cassie said. "That still—"

"If you let me finish, I'm going to get to it." She continued. "We became fast friends. In fact, she was still my cellmate when I finished my bid. We wrote each other every week after I was released and sent to the halfway house. One day, I got a letter from a lawyer telling me I needed to come see him. I went one day on my lunch break. That's when he told me Ethel had passed away in prison, and she'd named me the sole beneficiary in her will. She left me everything, including this house and every penny she and her husband saved. I'm talking biiiiig money. I didn't make any of this money, babies. It was gifted to me. She'd written me a final letter advising me of her wishes."

"She told me she had no children or living relatives. All her old friends had either turned on her or passed away. She said my story touched her heart and she wanted me to know I mattered, and I was loved. She told me to live my best life and never let someone have so much power over me that I end up like her...losing everything over someone who wasn't worth it. Her only wishes were to be cremated when she passed, and to spread her ashes in the rose bush in the garden. I've done that and I've been humbly living here ever since. I have invested and made quite a huge return on some of my investments, so now I have old money and new money. Now do you see why I said living good is enough revenge? Ethel told me to keep my ass out of trouble and that's what I've done and what I'm doing. When you do good to people, it comes back tenfold. But make no mistakes, the same goes for doing wrong to people. You will always reap what you sow."

My mama's story made me think of Lincoln. What you put out into this world, you get back. He just so happen to get his back in the worst way. As much as her words gave me peace, they didn't erase the ache in my chest. Montague was still gone and for all the closure I thought I'd found with Lenora, there was still so much left unsettled. The house was quiet again, but this time it wasn't comforting. It sat heavy in my chest, and I couldn't shake the feeling. It was like I was waiting for the next blow to strike.

Four

That night, I sat on the balcony overlooking the beautiful flower garden. My eyes focused on the rose bush, and I couldn't help but to think of Ms. Ethel. She'd dedicated her whole life to a man just to find out he was a lying cheating dog. I sat praying that wouldn't be my fate.

Crashing out was something I did well. I knew that was imminent if Montague were to ever play me like that.

My phone buzzed on my nightstand. I ran over to it thinking it may be Montague, but I was wrong. Umi's face lit up the screen and for the longest moment, I just stared at it, debating whether to let it ring or answer. Against my better judgement, I swiped.

"Hello?"

The sound that I encountered wasn't her usual sharp tone, but broken sobs.

"Shai...it's me. I...I just needed to hear your voice. I really need to talk to you."

I swallowed hard. "What do you want, Umi?"

"I know I don't deserve a second of your time, but I can't stop crying. Lincoln's gone and I can't...I just can't believe it.

"Why are you calling me about him. I didn't care about Lincoln when he was breathing, and I don't care about him now. Plus, I don't know why you can't believe it. He was running around here acting like a rabid dog. What in the hell did you think would happen?"

"I don't know, Shai but not this. Losing him has made me realize that life is too short to be beefing with people over dumb shit. You are my sister, my friend. The only friend that I have. We used to be everything to each other. Please tell me we can try again. Can we please fix this? I would do anything."

I pressed my forehead against the cold glass in the window. Her cries were tugging at my heartstrings. Her words touched the part of me that remembered the good old days, before everything went sideways. Montague's face popped in my mind and snapped me right out of it.

"Umi, you don't just get to cry and call me trying to erase all the shit you talked.

"I know, I know...I regret every second of defending Lincoln's stupidity. I shouldn't have been leaving you those text messages and voicemails, but I was just mad. Mad that you were getting something that I'd never been offered."

"And what exactly was that, Umi?"

"Genuine love and attention from a real man."

I bit down on my lip, silence stretching heavy between us. Part of me wanted to hang up. The other part that remembered what our sisterhood once felt like, hesitated. Her sobs bled through the phone.

"I don't expect you to forgive me right off bat. I just want you to think about it. I know you hated Lincoln, but I just lost the only thing I had here besides you. Just please don't hate me forever."

Tears burned in my eyes because I knew that I was the catalyst for her hurt, her pain. "I don't hate you, Umi." The words tasted bitter as they left my mouth. "I hate what you allowed yourself to become when you were with Lincoln. Believe it or not. I forgive you but I don't know if I could ever fuck with you the long way again."

"You knew what this maniac was planning, and you did nothing to try to stop him or warn us. I now know what I did to Lincoln was fucked up and I could have handled it differently, but shooting at us, at his own blood...that's crazy. I know that he was a grown man and was stubborn, but you could have called someone close to him to try and stop him. You didn't call his mother, his aunt or hell, even Montague. You knew he would be gunning for us and you sat back and let it happen. I don't think I could ever trust you again, so sadly it seems that this is where this friendship ends.

There was a long pause and then she spoke.

"But wait Shai, there is something that I need to tell you."

"Girl, what is it now and make it quick. I'm tired. It's been a long ass week and I'm dealing with some shit that you couldn't even imagine."

She sucked in a deep staggered breath. "I need to tell you the truth about Lincoln Jr. and Montague."

Shifting my stance, my eyes bucked. "What truth?"

Sighing deeply, she confessed. "A couple of years ago, after one of the parties Montague threw for the family at his house...He got drunk, and I put something in his drink. Just enough to make him groggy, and slow. After he passed out and everyone went to bed, I went up to his room and took what I wanted."

I froze, vomit climbing my throat. "You did what you crazy bitch? What the fuck you mean you took what you wanted?"

"You heard me, I took what I wanted. I wanted to see why the women were so damn crazy about him. I needed to see. I made him mine for just one night. A few weeks later, I found out I was pregnant. I told Lincoln the baby was his, but deep down...I didn't know. Hell, I still don't know but he looks more like Montague than Lincoln.

Tears stung my eyes. I was mortified. Filled with rage and disbelief." Why, Umi? Why would you do something like that to him?"

Her answer came quickly, like she'd rehearsed it. "Because I knew about the baby that Montague lost. I knew how much he wanted a child, and I wanted to give him what life had taken away. A child that tied me to him forever. I figured if I gave him what he always wanted, he would give me what I needed."

"Bitch you are truly nuts. I would have never guessed you could be so evil, but you've been around Lincoln so long...I guess it rubbed off on your ass."

Then suddenly, a guttural laugh exited my throat."

"What the fuck are you laughing at, Shai. I just told you I fucked your man and had his baby. I understand completely why you made that man yours. His dick is fire. And I'm sure you can't find anything funny about that. So, I ask you again. What's so damn funny?" She snarled.

I could feel her angst through the phone. Her breathing was ragged and her voice heavy with envy. "Hahahaha Umi,...you know, you almost had me bitch. Almost...but I guess you are more like Lincoln than you know. You don't think much either. Umi, there is no way that you could have done that."

"Yes, I did. I took that dick and gave him a namesake. You just mad and jealous because I did something before you got the chance to."

"Like I said, you couldn't have done that. Montague doesn't drink sweetheart. Did you forget that. 'Him nuh put poison in him bady,' you dumb bitch. Now get your stupid goofy ass off my phone before I tell *my* man about the bullshit you tried to pull, and we both come find you and put you beside *your* man."

I hung up the phone and pressed BLOCKED before I knew it. That bitch almost ran my pressure up, but I had to stop and think clearly. Something she obviously is incapable of doing.

Needing a breather after the conversation with Umi, I sauntered downstairs to Trucee's room. She and Cassie were playing Tonk. A game I'd forgotten all about.

"Can I get in on this. Y'all are going to have to teach me to play again because I forgot."

"We ought to revoke your black card. How could you forget how to play Tonk?" Cassie said as she pat the seat next to her.

"It's easy to forget when you have no one to play it with. You know I don't have many friends."

"Of course I know," she chirped. "You don't have no

friends because they are scared of you. Shai, you were mean as hell." Cassie said while she adjusted her legs to sit Indian style. "They wouldn't be scared of your ass anymore. That man has you soft as cotton."

"First of all, I'm not, nor was I ever mean. I'm just honest and my honest isn't even brutal. I throw a little sugar on that shit from time to time. I get that from Mama. You know, calling you my mama comes so easy to me because I've always wished you were. I used to tell Cassie that all the time. I still can't believe it's real. I mean, I can but I can't. It's like a nightmare that turned into a good dream. Maybe I'm not explaining it right. It's just a weird feeling."

"I know baby, but nothing stays hidden forever. What's done in the dark will always come to the light," Trucee quipped. "Speaking of light, where is that fine ass man of yours. We are missing his energy in this house. That man has a good spirit on him."

"It's so funny that you say that, Mama. A lady told me that in Jamaica. She said, 'Mi nuh si nuh snake on yuh,' That shit creeped me out."

Mama let out a huge laugh. "Girl, she was just telling you that you are good people. Caribbean people are very spiritual, very knowing. I learned a lot in prison. I've got a story for every nationality walking this earth, but I won't bore you girls with that. Anyway, is Montague coming back soon and when will I get to meet this, Wicked?"

I giggled at her excitement. "I promise we will set up a meeting for you and Wicked, Mama. And yes, he's coming back soon. I haven't heard from him since he left but I know that he will call me once his business is handled."

"Would this business have anything to do with what happened yesterday in Roseville?"

Mama's eyes met mine and I could feel her searching my soul for the truth.

"Umm, well I'm not really sure. He said he had to go take care of family so that maybe it. Why, what did you hear?" I asked, shifting from one side to the next.

"Not much, I wasn't sure if he was even involved in any of it, but your posture just told me otherwise. Shai, you called me and told me that you and Montague would be staying in Roseville for a few days, then suddenly you call and told me you were on your way back home. Now, I'm never going to be the one that gets in your business, but I don't need anyone bringing strife to my house. I live a peaceful existence, and I plan on keeping it that way." She threw out another card before giving me a 'you know better' look."

"Yes, I know. I don't think you have anything to worry about. Everything is being handled now. I really wish he would call me because I'm starting to get worried."

"Shai, climb out of that man's ass crack." Cassie snorted.

We all looked at each other and cracked up laughing.

"Yall just don't understand. My life has changed so much in these last couple of weeks. Moving here and being able to be closer to Mama was a blessing, but getting to know Montague has done something to my psyche. I mean, he took his time to learn me. It's nothing like a man who knows how you feel even before you do. He checks for my heart posture. He just wants to make sure that I'm good in every way. Excuse me for blushing over my man but I've never had a love like this. Nobody ever even came close."

"Shai, baby. I believe the word you are looking for is enamored. It sounds like you've found your soulmate." Mama said as she gently pinched my cheek.

"That's sure what it feels like. When he leaves me, I feel like I can't breathe. I just want to put him in my pocket." I stared up at the ceiling visualizing his beautiful chocolate skin and gleaming smile.

"Mama, Cassie grinned. You see how this heifer is staring up at the sky?" She laughed out loud. "That nigga must have put something on my sister. I have never seen you like this. Hell, I'm with Mama, does he have any brothers, cousins, or uncles that I can holla at. At this point, I'd settle for a handsome sister if he has one." We all cackled.

My phone rang, stopping my laughter dead in it's tracks. I looked down and saw that it was him.

"That's my man calling y'all. I'll be right back. I jumped up, running out the room as I slid the phone to accept.

"Baby, baby. Montague, is that you?"

"Of course it's mi, baby. Who else wud it be?" I could hear the smile in his voice.

"You have no idea how much I've been worried about you. What are you doing? Are you ok?"

I walked out to the rose garden to sit on the bench.

"Yea, mi baby. Everyting is fine. Mi ok. Mi sista ok. Dats who mi was worried bout di most. Mi talk tuh har again. Mi told har dat mi arranged tuh ave mi nefyu flown back to Jamaica. Suh, mi muss guh home to help mek di arrangements. Shi need mi dere."

I pressed a hand over my mouth. For a moment, silence took over me. It wasn't grief I felt, not for him, but the finality of it all sent a chill down my spine. That chapter was closed forever.

"Montague...you had to deal with that all alone?" My voice trembled.

"Nuh, mi carry yuh everyweh mi guh, suh nuh, mi was nuh alone. But dis was mi duty. Family business. Mi cyaan let mi sista walk through dat pain by haarself. Especially wen it mi dat caused it. Mi loyalty demand it."

Tears stung my eyes again, but this time for him. For the way he carried burdens heavy enough to break most men, yet still made space for me, for us.

"I wish I could've been there for you," I whispered.

"Yuh right where mi need yuh, waiting pon mi. Dat luv keep mi strong an mi coming back tuh yuh soon. Wen mi done bury di dead, mi ready tuh live. Shai, mi ready to build sumting new wid yuh."

My heart was so full.

"I'll be here, Montague. Always."

THE DAY MONTAGUE returned from Jamaica... before I even knew he was on American soil...there was a shift in the atmosphere. The air felt lighter and so did my spirit. I could already feel the weight of his footsteps on the porch. When the door opened, his tall frame filled the space. His eyes were tired but carried a peace I'd never seen before.

"It dun, mi luv," he said softly, pulling me into his chest. "Mi bury Lincoln pon di land wid mi people. Him spirit rest now. An mi ready tuh live."

I wrapped my arms tightly around him, inhaling his essence, the soft spice that lay upon his skin. He smelled like home.

Within weeks, my feet were once again on Jamaican soil...not for danger, not for chaos, but for a new life. The island wrapped me in its arms; the sway of the palm trees, the chopping of fresh coconut, the hum of cicadas, the endless stretch of a turquoise blue sea.

Montague never let go of my hand as he showed me the land he had cleared for me near the coast.

"Dis fi yuh, Shai. A new start. Dis weh wi build."

I blinked at him, stunned. "For me? Montague...I don't know the first thing about business or building anything," I snickered.

He kissed my forehead. "Den mi teach yuh. Mi wan yuh strong pon yuh own two feet. Wi ago open a ting fi yuh. Maybe a café, maybe a boutique. Sumting dat show di world yuh heart, yuh spirit. Mi put in di money suh dat yuh cyan design it howeva yuh please. An yuh cyan run it."

I stood there shocked. Not being able to believe that this was my life. I was full of gratitude, and of a love so deep it rooted itself in the very core of me.

"Nobody ever wanted to see me stand tall before. It was always about what they could get out of me. But you... you pour into me. You make me shine."

As the sun seemed to fall into the sea, it painted the sky with colors I couldn't even describe. It was truly a beautiful sight. Almost life changing. In that moment, I knew that my story wasn't ending. It was just only beginning. *Loyalty* had bound me, but *Love* freed me.

THE END

Epilogue

For the first time in years, everyone was...settled. At peace.

The sea breeze swept through the veranda, carrying the scent of salt from the ocean. I leaned into Montague's chest, his arms heavy and protective around my shoulders.

It had been two years since Montague buried his nephew on Jamaican soil, years since I closed the door on my past and opened a new one here. For me, the island had been more than a home, it was my rebirth.

Life here wasn't easy, but it was full. Montague pushed me to stand tall, to build my own legacy. Together, we laid the foundation for something I could call mine. What began as a small boutique by the water...part café, part cultural hub, quickly turned into a place the whole community loved. The tourists came for the food and handmade goods; the locals came for the warmth of the space. I'd never imagined myself as a business owner, but Montague was right: I was stronger than I ever knew.

And our family? It grew.

My hand drifted to the small swell beneath my dress, My husband's palm already resting there. Our first child was still on the way, but I could already see them...little ones running barefoot through the yard, laughter vibrating my soul as they played under the mango trees.

Years later, my vision proved true: our children filled the home with chaos and love, our lives were permanently stitched into the fabric of the island.

Montague leaned back in his chair, a glass of coconut water and ginger in hand, watching the scene before him with pride.

Our firstborn, *Zion*, was nearly twelve now...tall, serious, and already carrying Montague's quiet authority. He hovered near his father, asking questions about business, about responsibility, about loyalty and what truly made a man a man.

Beside him was *Malik*, ten years old and full of restless energy. He had inherited my wit and fire, always challenging his brothers, always the first to run barefoot through the mango grove or sneak sweets from our kitchen.

Then came *Elijah*, eight years old with a smile that melted every heart. He was the peacemaker, always smoothing over his brother's arguments, often climbing into his father's lap and staying there.

And finally, the one who had stolen everyone's heart the day she arrived: *Imani*. At five, she was the sunshine of the family, a ball of energy with curls and giggles who followed her brothers everywhere and wrapped Montague around her tiny finger. He swore that no man would be good enough for his daughter and I would laugh, because I knew he meant it.

The yard beyond the veranda was alive. The boys played a rough game of football in the grass while Imani cheered from the sidelines, her little fists balled with determination as if her yelling alone could win the match.

"Monty," I called softly, sinking into the chair beside him. He immediately reached for my hand, his thumb stroking over my knuckles. My gaze lingered on our children, my voice thick with emotion. "Look what we built."

Montague kissed my temple, his eyes never leaving our pickney's. "Dis is legacy, mi queen. Strong, rooted, unshakable. Everyting mi wuk suh hard fi, everyting mi bleed fi...it worth it."

Inside the house, laughter roared, dominoes slapped the table, and music floated through the air like the heartbeat of the island.

Mama was the loudest in the room, her laugh filling the space as she leaned against Wicked's side. Wicked, usually stoned-faced, was grinning like a schoolboy who'd gotten his first taste of honey.

Adessa's voice rang out, sharp and playful. "Wicked, yuh gunna sit dere an let Chartreuse cheat yuh out of all yuh dominoes?"

Mama slapped the table and threw her head back laughing. "Child, ain't nobody cheating. Wicked just slow. That's what happens when a man been running the streets too long...His mind gets rusty."

The whole room erupted with laughter, and even Wicked's stoic resting bitch face cracked into a smile. His arm slipped around Mama's shoulders like it belonged there. And from the way she leaned into him, eyes shining like a woman twenty years younger..it was clear, he did.

I shook my head, smiling . "My mama has got you wrapped around her finger Wicked. I never thought I'd see you like this."

"Wrapped?" Wicked's deep voice rang out, smooth and unbothered. "Nah, shi got mi tied in knots, an mi nuh even mind."

That sent the room into another round of laughter.

My eyes drifted toward the deck, where Cassie sat with her legs crossed, head tilted toward the man from the tiki hut. His name was Andre, though everyone just called him

Dre. He owned the beachfront bar where Montague liked to conduct "quiet business" away from the family compound, and from the moment Dre laid eyes on Cassie, they'd been joined at the hip. Now, she was giggling at something he whispered, her hand brushing his. I made a mental note to tease her later.

Even Umi, who once threatened to shatter everything, carved out a new beginning. She returned to Ghana with her family, trading bitterness for tradition, envy for healing. Our paths rarely crossed, but from time to time, I would see a photo on social media of a smiling Umi dressed in vibrant kente cloth, surrounded by her family. It was enough to know that peace was possible, even for her.

Mama and Cassie split their time between America and Jamaica. Never missing a flight.

Our lives were perfectly stitched together, the scars of the past transformed into threads of love, loyalty, and new beginnings.

My heart swelled, a lump rising in my throat as I watched *my* family. For so long, I thought that I was destined only to survive, to fight through one storm after another. But Montague had given me more than survival, he had given me a future.

And as the sun dipped low over the horizon, I realized that our story wasn't a fairytale at all. It was real. Raw. Hard-fought. Earned and most of all...Cherished.

About the Author

L.L. Momon is a passionate storyteller who crafts emotionally rich, character-driven novels that explore healing, love, and resilience. Born and raised in Tuskegee, Alabama, and now residing in Florida, Momon brings Southern warmth and depth to every story she writes.

A nail technician by trade and an intuitive introvert at heart, she draws inspiration from the complexities of real-life relationships and personal growth. As a wife and mother and lover girl, she deeply values the strength of family, and that love radiates through the pages of her work.

With six published novels to her name, including her latest, *Loyalty Bound Me, Love Freed Me*, L.L. Momon is known for delivering raw, honest stories centered on strong, imperfect Black characters navigating trauma, passion, and redemption.

When she's not writing, you'll find her creating beauty with her hands, enjoying quiet moments with her family, cooking up soul-soothing meals, or binge-watching her favorite TV shows. Through every story, L.L. Momon reminds readers that even the most broken hearts are capable of healing and that love, when nurtured, is a force worth believing in.

instagram.com/authoressllmomon

facebook.com/authorllmomon

tiktok.com/authoressllmomon

amazon.com/author/llmomon

goodreads.com/authorllmomon

Also by
L L momon

Whittling Wood

Whittling Wood 2

A Savage and Her Wicked Ways

A Savage and His Lying Tongue

To Love the Broken & Unhealed

The Author's Website authoressllmomon.square.site

https://linktr.ee/authoressllmomon